Praise for the novels
of Joseph A. West

"I look forward to many years of entertainment from Joseph West."
—Loren D. Estleman, four-time Spur Award–winning author of *Black Powder, White Smoke*

"Original, imaginative."
—Max Evans, Spur Award–winning author of *The Rounders*

"Wildly comic and darkly compelling."
—Robert Olen Butler, Pulitzer Prize–winning author of *A Good Scent from a Strange Mountain*

"[A] rollicking big windy." —Elmer Kelton

"Take a pair of pugnacious cowboys who never saw trouble they didn't like, mix them with a fiendish villain and his diabolical filibusters, and the result is comic delight. Joseph West [has] an encyclopedic knowledge of the West. He keeps the body count sufficient to satisfy gluttons, frosts his cake with bawds, throws a few wolfers, a boxer, and a patent medicine huckster into the pot, rings in all the Western legends worth recounting, and seasons the stew with smiles. . . . Western fiction will never be the same."
—Richard S. Wheeler, Spur Award–winning author of *Sierra*

SHOOTOUT AT PICTURE ROCK

Joseph A. West

A SIGNET BOOK

SIGNET
Published by New American Library, a division of
Penguin Group (USA) Inc., 375 Hudson Street,
New York, New York 10014, USA
Penguin Group (Canada), 90 Eglinton Avenue East, Suite 700, Toronto,
Ontario M4P 2Y3, Canada (a division of Pearson Penguin Canada Inc.)
Penguin Books Ltd., 80 Strand, London WC2R 0RL, England
Penguin Ireland, 25 St. Stephen's Green, Dublin 2,
Ireland (a division of Penguin Books Ltd.)
Penguin Group (Australia), 250 Camberwell Road, Camberwell, Victoria 3124,
Australia (a division of Pearson Australia Group Pty. Ltd.)
Penguin Books India Pvt. Ltd., 11 Community Centre, Panchsheel Park,
New Delhi - 110 017, India
Penguin Group (NZ), cnr Airborne and Rosedale Roads, Albany,
Auckland 1310, New Zealand (a division of Pearson New Zealand Ltd.)
Penguin Books (South Africa) (Pty.) Ltd., 24 Sturdee Avenue,
Rosebank, Johannesburg 2196, South Africa

Penguin Books Ltd., Registered Offices:
80 Strand, London WC2R 0RL, England

First published by Signet, an imprint of New American Library,
a division of Penguin Group (USA) Inc.

First Printing, March 2006
10 9 8 7 6 5 4 3 2 1

PUBLISHER'S NOTE
This is a work of fiction. Names, characters, places, and incidents either are the
product of the author's imagination or are used fictitiously, and any resemblance
to actual persons, living or dead, business establishments, events, or locales is
entirely coincidental.
    The publisher does not have any control over and does not assume any respon-
sibility for author or third-party Web sites or their content.

For
Jane Anderson and Susan Vaughn
and your students at
Rio Rancho High School
New Mexico

Thank you for making me
a part of your lives.

1

Indian Trouble

Deputy United States Marshal John Kilcoyn urged his rawboned dun across the shallows of Deer Creek, then swung the horse due north. The rain had stopped, at least for now, but a strong wind blew through the bare cottonwoods lining the banks, heralding the first of the fall storms.

Kilcoyn was a long way from home, some twenty-five miles south of the Nebraska border, riding through flat, open country where a far-seeing man could look from horizon to horizon and take careful note of everything.

The marshal reined in his mount, stepped out of the saddle and examined the pony droppings that lay on the creek bank. They were fresh, no more than an hour old. The Cheyenne renegades could not be too far ahead of him.

The rain started again. Kilcoyn shivered and pulled the fleece collar of his canvas mackinaw closer around his ears. He glanced at the sky where towering black clouds were building to the west, rolling in from the high Rockies, jagged forks of lightning flashing among them.

There were still three hours until dark. Plenty of time to do what he had come to do. At that time in the West, the law said murder had to be punished and punished swiftly, no matter the color of the perpetrator's skin. Black, white or red, it didn't make any difference. Murder was murder, and it was Kilcoyn's job to enforce a law that held the taking of human life to be the worst of all crimes.

Two days before, near Wagon Bed Springs, a party of buffalo hunters had come across a wagon and, beside it, sprawled and undignified in death, lay a family that had journeyed a long ways on the Santa Fe Trail from somewhere back east, no one knew where. Stragglers from a wagon train, they'd been held up for some reason. Maybe it was a broken axle or sickness or just sheer bad luck. Knowing the dangers they faced alone in a hostile land, they'd nevertheless journeyed on, for weeks keeping their eyes fixed on the Kansas horizon that stretched endlessly away from them, hoping that just beyond that line of earth and sky, about when the mountains came in sight, lay the path to the Promised Land.

But, in the end, buried by strangers, all they'd found were unmarked graves in an uncaring, windswept wilderness.

The father, a bearded man in his early forties, had

2

been shot and scalped. The mother had been used and abused, then tomahawked. Three children, the oldest no more than ten, had tried to run for it, and had been shot down like prairie chickens, just for the sport of the thing.

The wagon had then been set on fire but because of the rain it had not burned well. The flames had not destroyed it, but had charred it black all over, like a hearse.

Kilcoyn had been in Dodge City when he'd gotten the buffalo hunters' report, and he'd immediately informed the Army at Fort Dodge. But stretched thin chasing other bands of hostiles, the soldiers could only promise him an infantry company, with luck maybe a cavalry troop, when one such became available.

"But how long will that be?" Kilcoyn had asked the young first lieutenant who had given him the news.

The officer shrugged. "When one comes in. Two weeks. Maybe three. But don't worry, Marshal, we'll round up those renegades in the end."

Kilcoyn nodded, recognizing an empty promise when he heard one, knowing right then that he had it to do.

Judging by the unshod pony tracks around the wagon, three warriors had been involved in the massacre, and there were Cheyenne markings on an arrow buried in the back of one of the children.

Taking what loot they could carry, the Indians had

fled north, and Kilcoyn had headed out after them. Now, judging by the sign, he was getting close.

The big marshal swung into the saddle, his careful eyes scanning the trail ahead of him. There was little to be seen. Dark clouds lay heavy on the horizon, blurring the line between the misty land and the threatening sky, and the rain that was even now driving into Kilcoyn's face drew a shifting steel mesh across the distance, further reducing visibility.

Would the Indians hole up out of the storm?

It was a possibility, Kilcoyn decided. But now he was so near, he'd ride warily for fear of an ambush, all his senses alert to the slightest sign of danger.

Kilcoyn continued north, the silent land stretching away from him on all sides, a tossing, rippling sea of grass driven by the rain, lashed by the rising wind. Lightning forked closer, close enough that sudden, bright sheens of silver flashed across the marshal's lean cheeks, blinking off and on as though he were caught in the glare of the magic lantern at a slide show.

Like any rider out on the plains, Kilcoyn worried about lightning. Riding a wet horse, straddling a wet saddle and being the tallest thing around brought little comfort to a man. But his face had settled into grim lines, his chin determined. He had a job to do, and lightning or no, he would see it through.

Kilcoyn held no personal enmity toward the Cheyenne. The massacre at the wagon had been a bloody, vicious business, but that was the Indian way of war.

Women and children were fair targets, and had been throughout hundreds of years of intertribal warfare. And, although the time of the Red Men was now short, their memories were long, and Sand Creek and the Washita, where their own women and children had been shot and sabered, were not forgotten. These were festering wounds that would never heal, and had made recent warfare between the white and red man a bloody, merciless business.

The marshal slid a .44-40 Winchester from the scabbard under his knee. His instinct told him he must be getting close and he had no idea of what was waiting for him beyond the barrier of the rain. Now was the time to ride light in the saddle, his senses tuned to the prairie around him.

The empty, rain-swept country was deceptively peaceful and could make an unwary man careless. It looked as flat as a billiard table, but here and there were hidden shallow spots that could provide cover for a rifleman.

Kilcoyn rode along a dry wash that fed rainwater to the creek. A few inches of water lay on the bottom, pooling in the grass in some places. Beyond the wash rose a low, saddle-backed knoll, too shallow to be called a hill, its crest covered in clumps of Indian grass, withered prairie dandelion and streaks of Johnny-jump-up, a few blue flowers, the last of summer, still clinging to its ragged stems.

Fifteen feet before the wash met the rise, Kilcoyn found the tracks of a horse and beside them, judging by the length of its stride, a slower, heavier animal, no doubt one of the oxen that had been taken from the traces of the wagon.

Reining in the dun, the big lawman wiped rain from his eyes with the sleeve of his mackinaw and waited, listening. Gradually his ears adjusted to the quiet and he heard a fleeting sound that came and went, carried by the gusting wind. There it was again! A low, monotonous chant that rose and fell, most of it muffled and indistinct, scattered by the blustering gale.

But, his sense of impending danger clamoring at him, the marshal recognized the chant for what it was—an Indian death song; to Kilcoyn's experienced ear unmistakably Cheyenne. And it was coming from just beyond the rise.

The dun, smelling the closeness of other horses, tossed his head and snorted, his bit jangling. Kilcoyn quietly soothed the horse and eased the Winchester back into the boot. He drew his Colt, thumbed open the loading gate and slid a cartridge into the empty cylinder under the hammer. What lay ahead would be close work and almighty sudden. He'd be less sure with the revolver but considerably faster, and that could make the difference.

Lightning split the sky, searing the land with a blinding white flash, followed immediately by a tremendous crash of thunder. Behind him Kilcoyn heard a loud crack. One of the tall cottonwoods by the creek had been split in half by the strike, a scattering of flames clinging to its shattered trunk like fluttering scarlet moths before the pelting rain quickly extinguished them.

The marshal waited. The thunder was now almost directly overhead and he'd move on the next bang.

A few moments passed; then the sky erupted again, the searing lightning flash and thunderclap happening at the same instant.

Kilcoyn set the spurs to the dun and charged up the rise. The big horse reached the summit in a couple of bounds and Kilcoyn went over the top at a fast gallop.

Ahead of him he had a brief glimpse of two Indians rising from the ground, shock and surprise in their black eyes. They'd been kneeling by a third man, who was sprawled on his back, his shadowed, dead face lifted to the driving rain.

The Cheyenne to Kilcoyn's left threw a Sharps rifle to his shoulder. The marshal fired, missed, and fired again. The Indian went down, triggering his rifle. The bullet cut the air above Kilcoyn's head, but a split second later a round fired by the other Cheyenne thudded into his saddle horn.

The warrior was working the lever of his Henry for a second shot as Kilcoyn reined in the charging dun. The big horse reared, angrily fighting the bit as the lawman leaned out of the saddle, holding his Colt straight out in front of him. He fired at the warrior and his bullet slammed into the man's chest. The Indian staggered a step or two backward, sudden blood splashing the front of his buckskin war shirt, then moved quickly to his left.

Kilcoyn wrenched the dun around, following the Cheyenne. The warrior stopped and fired, and the bullet grazed the marshal's cheek, drawing blood. Kilcoyn again triggered his Colt. Hit with a second shot, this time higher in the chest, just below his throat, the Cheyenne's rifle spun away from him as he toppled forward and sprawled on his face.

For a few moments a sullen cloud of gray smoke ghosted over the fallen men, and Kilcoyn watched as it was taken by the wind and tattered into thin, misty shreds that drifted away into the distance. After the deafening roar of the guns the following silence seemed to stretch on forever. . . . Then, slowly, the ringing subsided in Kilcoyn's ears and he again heard the hiss of the rain and the grumbling rumble of the thunder as it growled east across the prairie.

Kilcoyn sat his horse and looked around him, still on edge. He remembered some advice he'd been given years before by an old lawman who'd told him, "Boy, never trust a wolf for dead till he's been skun." But the two Cheyenne he'd shot lay unmoving. The third man had been already dead when Kilcoyn charged the camp.

A small, smoky fire burned in the scant shelter of a plum bush growing beside a low outcropping of granite rock, chunks of liver speared on sticks roasting above the coals. The butchered ox lay a distance away, its belly split open, a black tongue lolling out of its mouth.

Kilcoyn swung out of the saddle. The first man he'd killed was an old warrior, a thin, wizened man, gray showing in his thin braids. The Cheyenne who had wielded the Henry was younger, probably in his late twenties. A deep and terrible scar ran from the corner of his left eye to his chin. He wore a war shirt made from a single elk hide, a score of scalp locks bound with red trade cloth and sinew decorating the sleeves and shoulders. Among the painted symbols on the shirt was the morning star, sacred to the Cheyenne, and a dragonfly representing quickness in the fight. There was also a hand, denoting that this man had killed an enemy in battle.

Whoever this warrior was, the war shirt revealed that he'd been an important member of the tribe. The man had been carrying a deerskin bag on a rawhide string over his shoulder, and it had fallen near his body. Kilcoyn opened the bag, found a folded red cloth and recognized it as the revered sash of the Cheyenne Dog Soldier.

Acknowledging that this man had fought well and bravely, without a call for mercy, Kilcoyn laid the sash on the dead warrior's chest. It was a small mark of respect, a last honor from one fighting man to another.

The rain hammering at him, the marshal kneeled beside the dead warrior for long moments, then rose

9

wearily to his feet. He unbridled the three Indian ponies, slapped their rumps and watched them trot away into the prairie. All three were mustangs. They could tough it out and survive on the plains, even when the winter blizzards arrived.

Kilcoyn squatted by the smoking fire and, suddenly hungry, picked up a chunk of the roasted ox liver. He ate quickly, then stepped to his dun and swung into the saddle. As the rain drove against him he looked down at the dead Dog Soldier. The warrior's eyes were wide open, staring at Kilcoyn with a strange intensity, their black depths already peering into eternity and unreadable.

Suddenly the marshal shivered, and not from the cold.

He knew the Indian was dead, yet the man seemed to be watching his every move.

But after a moment he smiled and, as is the habit of men who have ridden lonely trails, he said aloud: "Kilcoyn, you're getting mighty easily spooked in your old age."

Still, as he rode away he could not lose the feeling that eyes were watching him . . . and that somewhere a goose had just flown over his grave.

2

A Dreadful Demand

In Dodge the cattle season was over. The red, white and blue bunting had long since been taken down from the saloons, and the dance halls had closed and bolted their doors.

Over by the empty cattle pens shouldered against the tracks, a train clanked and hissed, the locomotive jetting steam, but it was unloading human passengers, not cows. The windows of the Comique Theater were boarded up; a corner of a tattered poster on the door that announced the times of Eddie Foy's performances flapped forlornly in the fitful wind. Around the theater the saloons seemed dejected and shabby, huddled together against the rain. Over at the Alamo, someone, probably a bored soiled dove who had not yet migrated with the rest, hesitantly picked out the notes of "Buffalo Gals," and from somewhere inside, a man laughed once and then fell silent.

Kilcoyn left the livery stable and walked along the boardwalk toward the office he shared with county sheriff Bat Masterson, the rain driving at him, drumming with cold fingers on his hat. It was still not three, but gas lamps were already being lit in the saloons, stores and banks against the crowding dark of the day. Black clouds hung so low that they seemed to touch the rooftops, and beyond the town limits the prairie was shrouded in a thick gray mist, threaded by the quickening downpour.

Stepping quickly, his spurs ringing, the marshal walked through puddles of pale orange light cast by the lamps on the boardwalk. Front Street was a sea of thick yellow mud. A freight wagon rolled past, lumps of clotted sludge dropping off its iron-rimmed wheels, plopping back into the glistening muck with a soft sound.

The alleys along the street were angled with midnight blue shadow as the darkness came down. People bundled up in raincoats, some carrying umbrellas that looked like huge black bats, hurried past, their smiling eyes slanting to Kilcoyn in quick greeting.

The marshal reached his office and stepped inside. There was no sign of Masterson. He hung up his dripping coat and hat, draped his gunbelt over a peg and then shoved his Winchester into the rack. He lit the oil lamp above the desk and crossed the room to the stove glowing cherry red in the corner. Masterson, a coffee-drinking man, had put the pot on to boil and Kilcoyn poured himself a cup.

He sat at the desk and put his feet up, a draining tiredness in him. He tried his coffee. It was hot and bitter, the way he liked it, and he willed himself to relax. He would have to write a report for the Army, in triplicate, about what had happened with the Cheyenne. But that could wait. Right now he just wanted to get the cricks out of his back and enjoy the welcome warmth of the office.

John Kilcoyn was a tall man, standing well over six feet in his boots. His shoulders were wide, his waist and hips narrow, his angular face tanned to a deep mahogany by sun and wind. His eyes were clear blue, his thick, unruly hair black, and he sported the sweeping dragoon mustache then in fashion. All the tallow had long since been burned out of him by long and difficult trails, leaving only thick muscle and bone. He was lean and solid and looked what he was, a determined peace officer who was a hard man to kill. He was thirty-two that fall and had been a lawman for seven years. In that time he'd been in a dozen gunfights with outlaws and renegades, and had killed three men.

Kilcoyn knew that when the law pinned a tin star on his chest it did not make him any wiser. But he realized that if he did not abuse it, the star gave him the power to do right using the wisdom he had.

He did not mistreat women, children or animals, or laugh at another's misfortune. He did not hunt trouble but met it head-on when it came at him, and he had never taken a step back from any man. Kilcoyn was good with a gun, though not as fast as Bat Masterson and a few others he'd seen, but he believed that coolness and a steady nerve would always beat quickness. If a man took his time he only had to pull the trigger once.

Those who knew him well said John Kilcoyn made a loyal, trustworthy friend—but a mighty bad enemy.

Kilcoyn laid his cup on the desk, closed his eyes and allowed himself to drift into sleep. But he woke a few minutes later when Masterson slammed open the door and stepped inside, rain running off his yellow oilskin slicker. He looked at the marshal in surprise and said, "You're back, John, and all in one piece I see. Tell me what happened with them redskins."

"I will, Bat," Kilcoyn said. "But first you tell me what's been going on in Dodge since I've been gone. They pay me to keep up with stuff like that, you know."

The sheriff wriggled out of his gleaming coat, hung it on a peg, then came back to the desk. He tipped his hat back on his head and shrugged. "Nothing much, John. Mrs. Gordon over to Bluff Creek had a baby, and mother and son are doing well. Her husband told me that himself, and then he gave me a five-cent cigar. I believe they make those things out of buffalo dung." Masterson smiled at his own joke and smoothed his carefully trimmed mustache. "Let me see, now. Oh yeah, a couple of the ladies over to the Lone Star got into it over a necklace that one said the other stole. Natchez Alice—you know her, dresses out at about three hundred pounds—well, she collected a vase over the head during the scrape. Stretched her out like a felled ox. John, I swear she lay there like a dead cat for an hour before somebody revived her with a shot of brandy. Well, three or four shots of brandy."

The marshal nodded, only vaguely interested. "You arrest the assailant?"

"Sure did. Remember that pretty little blond gal with the mole on her chin that cut loose at a customer with a pepperbox one time? What's her name . . . ?"

"She calls herself Louise L'Estrange," Kilcoyn supplied. "What happened to her?"

"The usual. Judge Walker fined her two dollars and costs, thirty cents for the vase."

"Anything else?"

"No, that's it, John. The town and the whole county are as quiet as a deaf-mute's shadow and I guess it will stay that way until spring." Bat leaned across the desk and peered at Kilcoyn's cheek, his left eyebrow crawling up his forehead. "Here, John, you've been wounded."

The marshal's fingers strayed to the crusted blood across his cheekbone. "It's nothing. Just a scratch."

"Bullet came mighty close, just the same. I told you that you should have brought me along with you." Masterson's voice took on a slightly chiding tone. "After all, I am a sworn lawman." The sheriff waited, but since his remark drew no response from Kilcoyn, he asked finally, "Want to tell me about it?"

In as few words as possible, Kilcoyn described his fight with the Cheyenne. He did not mention the strange premonition he'd felt after he discovered one of the dead was a Dog Soldier. Masterson, by nature an intelligent and deep-thinking man, would understand such a thing. But Kilcoyn was proud. There were even those who did not know him well who said he was stiff-necked and unyielding. If he told Bat about his moments of foreboding he would have to admit he had also felt fear—and perhaps that was something Bat might not understand.

"Well, good riddance is what I say, John," Masterson said when Kilcoyn had stopped talking. "After what those savages did to that poor sodbuster family out on the plains, they deserved what you gave them."

"Maybe so." Kilcoyn nodded. To cut off any more talk on the subject, he felt the bullet burn across his cheek and said, "This is punishing me some. Maybe I should let Alan Wilson take a look at it."

Masterson shook his head. "That isn't going to happen. Doc Wilson isn't back yet, John." He smiled, knowing that what he was about to say would disappoint the big marshal. "And neither is his beautiful daughter."

Kilcoyn was indeed disappointed, but not alarmed. The day he had taken out after the Cheyenne, Doc

Wilson had also left Dodge, to treat a farmer and his family who were all down with some mysterious ailment that Doc suspected might be the cholera. His daughter Angela had volunteered to go along as a nurse, explaining to Kilcoyn that if she kept busy she'd worry less about him.

When his duties allowed—which meant every chance he got, few and far between though they were—Kilcoyn returned to Dodge, and he and Angela Wilson stepped out together.

They'd met two years before, when the girl's father had cut a rustler's bullet out of the marshal's shoulder. For Kilcoyn, the first time he'd set eyes on Angela, a stunningly shapely brunette with large hazel eyes and full lips that were made to be kissed, had been like a lightning bolt hitting a tree. In that single, blinding moment he had decided that there could be no other woman in his life but Angela Wilson.

Now there was an unspoken agreement between them that at some time in the future they would become much more than a courting couple—but it was a future formed of shadows that neither of them had so far been able to solidify into a time and place. One day they would become man and wife, but when that might be they could not even guess.

"Maybe caring for all those sick folks is taking longer than they expected," Kilcoyn said.

"Seems like," Masterson agreed. "I saw cholera one time, back in my buffalo-hunting days. Six, seven skinners came down with it and they were right poorly for a spell, sick as poisoned pups. It's a hell of a misery, and no mistake."

The sheriff stepped over to the window and glanced outside. "Still raining bullfrogs and heifer yearlings out there, John. But it's time I was making my rounds across the tracks. Those uppity lace-curtain folks expect to see a lawman now and again, and they don't make allowances for the weather."

A smile tugged at Kilcoyn's lips. Bat's idea of patrolling was to sit in parlors drinking bonded whiskey from a crystal tumbler while entertaining the fashionable young belles and their mothers with tales of his derring-do during his buffalo-killing, Comanche-dodging days on the plains.

Kilcoyn nodded, his face straight. "Best you go, then, Bat. Mayor Kelley does like us to show the flag over there. And who knows what kinds of desperate characters might be lurking around."

"I'm on my way, then." The deputy shrugged into his slicker, then pounded the side of his head with the heel of his hand. "Wait a minute. I plumb forgot. When Bob Gordon gave me a cigar yesterday, he gave me something else, a letter for you. He said a fellow paid him two dollars to deliver it and told him to make sure it got into your hands. Well, you weren't here, so I took it myself."

"Where is the letter?" Kilcoyn asked, puzzled.

"Top right drawer of the desk."

Kilcoyn opened the drawer, took out an envelope and opened it. As Bat hovered nearby he read the contents, written in a fair copperplate hand—and felt fear slide into his belly like the blade of a knife.

John,

I have Doc Wilson and his daughter. Bring ten thousand, three hundred and sixty-five dollars and eighteen cents to Black Mesa within seven days if you want to see them alive again. You know me, John—I'm not a patient man. You have seven days or I'll gun them both.

And the note was signed: Jake Pride.

Masterson saw the sudden change in Kilcoyn's face and he stepped quickly to the desk. "What is it, John? Bad news?"

The marshal tossed the note across the desk, his face like stone. "Here, read it for yourself."

A look of puzzlement knotted Masterson's forehead. He picked up the note and, as was his habit, read it aloud. After the last words died on his lips, the handsome sheriff looked stricken.

"Jake Pride," he said, his eyes haunted. "After all these years, that just doesn't seem possible."

Despite his dandified mode of dress, from the wide-brimmed white Stetson on his head to the pearl-handled, silver-plated Colts around his waist, Bat Masterson was a tough, capable lawman when he had to be. A first-class fighting man, three years before, on June 27, 1874, he'd been at Adobe Walls, down to the Texas Panhandle, when he and around thirty of his fellow buffalo hunters had fought off an attack by seven hundred Kiowa and Comanche led by the famous war chief Quanah Parker. Since his appointment as sheriff of Ford County he'd battled Comanche raiders, border outlaws, fast-gun hardcases up from the Indian Territory and arrested dozens of assorted thieves and ruffians. Those who rode with Masterson called him a brave man who was sudden and accurate with the Colt. As far as Kilcoyn knew, Bat had never taken a step back from any man—yet even he stood in awe of the legendary lawman Jake Pride.

Masterson sat on the corner of Kilcoyn's desk, the lace-curtain side of town momentarily forgotten. "You knew him, John. Tell me about him," he said. "I remember you told me once before, but I've forgotten most of what you said at the time."

Kilcoyn glanced at the clock, its slow, steady tick telling him that time was running on Pride's deadline—and he'd already lost a day.

"It's quick to tell, Bat," he said. "Jake was a first-class officer and fear didn't enter into his thinking. He began his career as an end-of-the-track lawman for the Union Pacific Railroad when they were driving west from Omaha across the plains. Jake kept order with his fists and gun in the ragged, makeshift tent towns that sprung up every sixty miles or so along the right of way."

Kilcoyn rose, crossed the office and settled his hat on his head, then shrugged into his mackinaw.

"They called those towns hell-on-wheels, and that was putting it mildly. The tent saloons were dens of iniquity that offered gambling, whores and forty-rod whiskey, and they were more than happy to unburden the tracklayers of their thirty-five a month.

"Jake worked the worst of them: North Platte, Julesburg, Cheyenne, Laramie, Corinne—hell holes where a dead man was served up with breakfast every day.

"During that time Jake Pride killed four men and earned a reputation as a hard, no-nonsense lawman. After that, he wore a town-tamer's tin star twice, rode shotgun for the Lee-Reynolds stage out of Dodge and finally was appointed a Deputy United States Marshal."

"John, it was a woman who done for him in the end, wasn't it?"

The marshal buckled on his gunbelt and nodded. "Her name was Maggie Morton. She was seventeen when Jake met her while she was working the line here in town, and that's when his troubles began.

"Maggie wanted all the good things in life: expensive clothes, a big house, a fancy carriage and a high-stepping team to haul it. Jake couldn't afford those things on the money he earned, so when Maggie threatened to leave him, he did what he had to do and stole what he needed."

"Robbed the Drover's bank in Hays, didn't he?"

"Yeah, he did. He was wearing a flour sack over his head, but maybe ten, twelve people in there, including the banker, recognized his voice and the fancy engraved pistol he always carried. Funny what desperation will do to a man's common sense."

"And you arrested him, didn't you?"

"It wasn't difficult. I went to his cabin south of town and the money was right there—ten thousand, three hundred and sixty-five dollars and eighteen cents. I put a scattergun to his head while he was asleep and took Jake into custody. He got five years at hard labor, and that was five years ago."

"And the girl?"

Kilcoyn shrugged. "Lit a shuck. Last I heard she was a fancy woman in New Orleans, working the riverboats."

"Think Jake blames you for what happened?" Masterson asked.

Kilcoyn shrugged and opened the office door, letting in a gust of cold air and rain. "I don't know, Bat. He did what he had to do and so did I. You can hardly blame a man for that."

Masterson stood. "Where you headed?"

"To talk to Mayor Kelley. Tell him I'll be gone for a couple of weeks."

"And this time I'm going with you," Masterson said, his mind made up. "Look what happened to you when you went up against the Cheyenne alone. You got shot, that's what happened. My younger brother, Ed, is a town policeman, and since the punchers are gone and Dodge has lost its snap, he can also handle things around the county, him and a new man who goes by the name of Wyatt Earp.''

It was in Kilcoyn's mind to protest, but then he recalled that Jake Pride was a dangerous man, and the chances were he'd have others with him who would be almost as gun handy. Bat could go a long way to evening the odds.

"I don't know Earp, but I hear Ed is a good officer,'' he said.

Masterson grinned. ''Damn right, he is. Takes after me.''

"I'll be glad to have you along,'' Kilcoyn said. "Now let's go talk to the mayor.''

3

Of Photographers and
Irish Kings

Mayor James H. Kelley read the ransom note Kilcoyn had handed to him, then reread it, his face turning paler with each reading. "Jesus, Mary and Joseph, and all the saints in heaven, save and preserve us," he said. "Can we take this seriously, John?"

"It's very serious," the marshal answered. "You remember Jake Pride, Mayor. He's mighty fast with the Colt, and when he says a thing, he means it. There are maybe half a dozen dead men who can attest to that."

Kelley, short and stocky, with the bright black eyes of an intelligent bird and a determined chin, chewed on his cigar, his face screwed up in thought as he sought a solution to the problem. Finally he gave up the effort and asked, "What are we going to do, John?"

"Bat Masterson and me are going after Angela and Doc. We'll be gone for a couple of weeks, maybe less."

The mayor thought that through, then his eyes slid to Masterson and he said, "If you're taking Bat along, you must be thinking of ending the thing with gunplay. He's mighty slick with the Colt on the draw and shoot."

The marshal nodded. "It's a language Jake understands."

Kelley shook his head. "No, John. We'll pay him. We'll give Jake Pride what he asks. I don't want the lives of two of Dodge City's leading citizens endangered."

Kilcoyn opened his mouth to object, but Kelley waved a dismissive hand and cut him off. "No shooting scrapes, John. And I mean that, now." He turned to Masterson. "Bat, you're a first-rate lawman, but a man who's wearing two guns doesn't intend to do much talking with his mouth."

Before Masterson could reply, Kelley turned to his office clerks, a couple of pale young men who had laid down their pens and were watching the lawmen and the mayor with keen interest.

"Tim, Bob, round up all the town's businesspeople and tell them to get here on the double. I want every one of them—Graham, the banker, the saloon keepers, even Sad Sam Nelson the undertaker, all of them." The clerks were looking openmouthed at Kelley. A full town meeting this long after the cattle season was unprecedented, and their excitement was obvious. "Go!" Kelley yelled.

After the clerks scampered out the door to spread the word, Kelley asked Kilcoyn, "Why that odd amount of money? It doesn't make much sense."

The marshal's smile was slight. "It does if you recall that it's exactly what Jake stole from the bank in Hays."

"Wait a minute. Yes, indeed it was," Kelley said, a tangle of emotion on his face as he remembered. Finally his expression cleared. "Well, I'll raise the ransom money—don't you concern yourself about that. Then you and Bat will ride to Black Mesa and pay Jake Pride what he's asking." The mayor took the cigar out of his mouth and stabbed it in Kilcoyn's direction. "Remember, no guns. Just hand over the cash and get Doc Wilson and his daughter out of there. Bring them home, John." Without waiting for the marshal to answer, he added, "Where the hell is Black Mesa, anyhow?"

"It's a chunk of lava rock that rises about five thousand feet above the flat in the panhandle of the Oklahoma Territory, Mayor," Masterson said. "All around the mesa lies desert country cut through with deep arroyos and steep ridges. I did some buffalo hunting there a spell back. It's a wild, empty place. A few other hunters and me were on a high lonesome there for nigh on a month. It's no place for a white man, or any other kind of man, come to that."

"How far?" Kelley asked.

"Four, five days' ride," Kilcoyn answered. He gave the mayor a significant look. "We can make it with time to spare if we start out real soon."

"Have some patience, John," Kelley said. "Raising ten thousand dollars takes a little while."

As they waited, the mayor asked Kilcoyn about his brush with the Indians. After the marshal recounted what had happened, Kelley nodded. "I bet them Cheyenne were part of ol' Star Blanket's band. I heard from a cavalry major that the old chief broke out of the reservation with maybe thirty warriors and a bunch of women and kids. The horse soldier officer said he expects Star Blanket to play hob until he's rounded up. That Injun's got no love for white folks."

Then Kelley said something that made Kilcoyn snap up his head in surprise. "Star Blanket has his first-born son with him, a great warrior they call Scar. And the major said he's worse than any of them."

Kilcoyn remembered the dead Cheyenne with the terrible scar down his left cheek. He could only have been Star Blanket's son, and the marshal felt a pang of unease. It seemed that the goose was flying again, and that was not a good feeling. . . .

The first of the town notables to arrive was Bill Johnson, the blacksmith, a friendly, talkative man with a host of questions on his lips as soon as he walked through the door of the mayor's office. Kelley waved Johnson into silence. "As soon as the rest get here, Bill. Then we'll all discuss it."

27

Later, while Kilcoyn and Masterson fretted outside, Kelley held his closed-door meeting with the town notables. After less than twenty minutes the door to Kelley's office swung open and a clerk stuck out his head. "Marshal Kilcoyn, Sheriff Masterson, would you both step inside, please?" he said.

When the lawmen walked into Kelley's office, the mayor stood and waved his arms around the room, taking in the assembled crowd. "We've come to a decision, Marshal Kilcoyn," Kelley said. "Mr. Graham has agreed to put up half of the money, and the rest of us will chip in the remainder."

A look of alarm crossed Kilcoyn's face. "How long will that take?"

"Not long," Kelley said. "Mr. Graham will supply the whole amount and we will reimburse him later." The mayor gave the plump banker a sidelong glance. "I, of course, will pay my share of the ransom just as soon as certain . . . ah . . . funds I am expecting become available. As to when that will be, I can't really say."

Graham, looking unhappy, fiddled with one of his bushy sideburns, his opinion of the mayor's financial wheeling and dealing a low one. The banker had often said in the past that Mayor Kelley had more than a touch of larceny in his soul, and he seemed to realize the chances of his being reimbursed by his honor were slim to none, and slim was already saddling up to leave town.

With a grand gesture, Kelley declared the proceedings over and Graham left to put together the ransom money. Bill Johnson, a dark, handsome man with Navaho blood in him, stuck out his hand and Kilcoyn took it. "Bring Angela and her father back, John," he said. "I set store by both of them and I'm looking forward to seeing you and Angela hitched."

The marshal nodded. "I'll see no harm comes to them, Bill. I'm relying on you and the others to help Ed Masterson and that new man Earp take care of things in Ford County while Bat and I are gone."

"Depend on it, John." A look of concern fleeted across Johnson's face. "I don't know if you've heard, but Star Blanket is out."

"The mayor told me." Kilcoyn hesitated, then said: "I think maybe I killed his son yesterday. He was one of the Cheyenne who murdered that sodbuster family out to Wagon Bed Springs."

"Scar?" The big blacksmith drew a line down his left cheek with a forefinger. "Had a deep knife scar runs like that. He was a Dog Soldier and a big man among the Cheyenne."

"Sounds like him. There were three warriors in the attack. Two of them were still alive when I tracked them down. The man with the scar was one of them."

Johnson's black eyes mirrored his concern. "Kilcoyn, ride careful. If Star Blanket gets the word that you killed his son, he'll come after you. I met that old man a couple of years back. His braids are gray and thin, and he has milk in his eyes, but he's a bad enemy to make, not the kind to forgive and forget."

"I'll remember that, Bill," Kilcoyn said, smiling. "And thanks. But I'm not looking to borrow trouble, so I'll figure on staying well out of his way."

"If he'll let you," Johnson said. "I'm feeling something, Marshal, something way down deep in the Navaho part of me that I don't like."

The big lawman grinned. "Like a goose just flew over your grave?"

Johnson nodded, his face like stone. "Yeah, maybe a whole flock of them."

After everyone had gone, Kelley grabbed Kilcoyn by the arm. "Step over to the Dodge House with me, John. There's somebody I want you to meet."

"Mayor, I don't have time to—"

"Nonsense, me boy," Kelley interrupted. "This will only take a minute and Graham will be that long putting the money together anyhow."

Outside, the rain was still hammering down, blown by a chill, gusting wind. Thunder rumbled to the west, coming off the distant Sangre de Cristo peaks, and the air smelled of ozone and the dampness of the surrounding wood-frame buildings.

Kilcoyn and Kelley stepped along the boardwalk, heads bent against the wind. The rain battered the mayor's cigar into shredded ruin and he tossed the dead butt into the mud of the street in disgust.

They crossed Front Street, picking their way across raised islands of firm ground amid the river of mud, and entered the lobby of the hotel, rain and wind chasing them inside.

The desk clerk smiled at Kilcoyn, then caught sight of Kelley and scowled. "He was at it again last night, Mayor," he said. "Took a couple of shots at the moon from out his window, then blew the gas lamp right off the wall. It's a miracle he didn't send the whole damn hotel sky-high."

Kelley waved an expansive hand. "You know I'm good for the damages." The mayor shook his head, his smile forced. "Ah, he's a high-spirited lad, my nephew, and no mistake. But he's a rolling stone who'll stop and steady up when he finds the kind of moss he wants to gather."

The clerk, a small balding man with an eye twitch, let that go, muttering under his breath about Irishmen in general and Mayor James H. Kelley in particular. Then, in a stage whisper, he proceeded to express the low expectation he had of ever seeing any of the mayor's money.

Kilcoyn followed the mayor up the stairs and stopped at a room at the end of the hallway. Kelley didn't knock, but yelled at the closed door, "Barry, it is your uncle James. Now don't be shooting no pistols and the like. Just open the door and be good, lad."

"It's open," a slurred voice called from inside.

Kelley's eyes slanted to Kilcoyn as his face took on

31

a long-suffering look. "Me sister Charlotte's boy. I told her I'd try to give the lad his start in life, introduce him to the right people like, but he's a heller, drunk or sober."

The mayor opened the door and Kilcoyn followed him inside. A tall young man with red hair lay fully clothed on the bed, a huge .44 Smith & Wesson Russian revolver in his hand. The man turned as Kilcoyn entered, the muzzle of the gun swinging in the marshal's direction. Kilcoyn stiffened and his hand instinctively dropped to the butt of his Colt.

Kelley saw Kilcoyn's movement and quickly stepped between him and the youngster on the bed. He walked to the bed and grabbed the revolver from his nephew. "Give me that," he said. "You'll get yourself killed, Barry O'Neil, pointing guns at people."

The mayor introduced Kilcoyn, then lit a cigar, studying O'Neil through a cloud of smoke as though he was making up his mind about something. Finally he told his nephew about the ransom demand and how the marshal and his deputy were taking the money to the outlaws, their leader once a famous lawman.

As Kelley talked, Kilcoyn looked around him. A bottle of whiskey, two-thirds gone, lay on the table beside O'Neil's bed, and the wall around the gas lamp was pitted with bullet holes. A tripod, a large camera in a mahogany case and bottles of chemicals stood in one corner of the room.

"Yes, Kilcoyn, Barry is a photographer," Kelley said as he saw the marshal's interest. "And a fine one too. In the auld country, he had his own exhibition in the fair city of Cork not a six month ago. Since he got off the boat in New York the boy's been itching for Western adventure, and that's why I want him to go with you and Bat. He can record the whole trip, and we'll get the photographs done up in all the newspapers when you come back."

Kilcoyn shook his head. "Mayor this will be a dangerous ride, most of it through hard country, and now that Star Blanket is on the prod I don't need a pilgrim fresh off the boat tagging along. He could get himself killed out there."

O'Neil, who'd been listening to this exchange with growing irritation, sprang from the bed, staggered slightly, then said to Kilcoyn in a broad Irish brogue, "Marshal, I can take care of meself. I can ride and I can shoot and I won't be a burden to you." He glanced at Kelley. "If I'm stuck in this dead town much longer, I'll go right off my rocker."

The young man looked to be in his midtwenties. He was tall and slender in the bones, and he sported a small, well-trimmed mustache. His eyes were a startling sky blue, the whites veined with red.

"How well do you shoot?" Kilcoyn asked, smelling the whiskey on O'Neil.

The Irishman shrugged. "I've been practicing."

"So I've heard." Kilcoyn nodded to the Smith & Wesson in Kelley's hands.

"How well do you shoot that?"

O'Neil thought about it, then chose truth over a lie. "Not very well. I hit the gas lamp last night, but it took me a dozen tries."

Kilcoyn nodded. "Then you stay right where you are. I'm going up against a mighty dangerous man, and neither Bat Masterson nor me will have time to wet-nurse you."

A sudden anger flared in O'Neil's face and the young man opened his mouth to speak, then shut it again. Kilcoyn could see him gulping down his pride like a dry chicken bone. "Marshal," he said finally, "give me the chance. I promise you, I won't let you down. Me father and his father before him come from a long line of Irish kings and I won't step back from an enemy, no matter how hard or dangerous he may be."

"John," Kelley said, his eyes pleading, "I'd take it as a personal favor. Give the boy his opportunity to become a man."

The marshal held himself a minute. In the past Mayor Kelley had done him a good turn or three and he owed him. Then so be it, but Barry O'Neil, descended from Irish kings or no, would have to stand on his own two feet and take his chances.

Deciding the circumstances called for some kind of dramatic action, Kilcoyn strode to the bedside table. He lifted the whiskey bottle by the neck and smashed it to pieces against the edge of the table.

"O'Neil, no more of this until you're back in

Dodge," he snapped. "If I catch you drinking just once I'll send you packing. That is, if I don't shoot you first my ownself."

"Not a single drop will pass his lips, Marshal," Kelley said. He glared at his nephew. "Isn't that so, Barry?"

The young man nodded. "I won't drink, Marshal. I promise."

"Then saddle your horse," Kilcoyn said. "We're moving out soon."

"And my pack mule," O'Neil said.

"Pack mule?"

O'Neil nodded to the photography equipment piled in the corner. "To carry my gear. It weighs a hundred pounds and I can't tote it on my back."

Kilcoyn gave Kelley a hard look. "God help us," he said.

But worse was to come.

"Before we set out I want to make a photograph of you and Bat Masterson, Marshal," O'Neil said. "Two famous constables together is one for the history books."

Kilcoyn shook his head. "We don't have time for that."

"Sure you do, John," Kelley said. "It will only take but a minute or two." He hesitated for a few moments, then added, "The boy wants to start making his mark right away. A personal favor, Marshal?"

Defeated, Kilcoyn nodded. Best to get the thing over with and then be on their way.

Because of the weather O'Neil had Kilcoyn and Masterson pose inside the livery stable. He insisted the lawmen stand with their rifles at the ready and glare unsmilingly into the camera.

O'Neil rubbed his hands and grinned. "This is going to be great. Here stand the stalwart policemen before riding out on a dangerous mission of mercy across the wild prairie."

"Get it done, O'Neil," Kilcoyn growled.

Masterson, afraid of ruining his carefully arranged pose, whispered to Kilcoyn out of the corner of his mouth, "All us Mastersons look right handsome in a camera picture, John. We take our features after our mother, you know, a beautiful woman and no mistake."

Kilcoyn sighed and shook his head, and O'Neil, buried under a black cloth behind his camera, yelled, "Damn it all, Marshal. Don't move."

O'Neil fiddled with the camera and said, "Riiight . . . hold it . . . hold it . . . got it!" Kilcoyn grimaced and turned to Masterson. "Mount up, before he takes it into his damn fool head to make another one."

4

The Dangerous Trail

Kilcoyn led his small posse over the wooden bridge across the Arkansas River, then swung to the southwest across flat, open country. The unseasonable rain continued to fall, and all three riders wore slickers, O'Neil completing his attire with a battered brown derby. Kelley had given his nephew a new, sixteen-shot Henry rifle that he carried in a saddle boot under his left knee.

Just before they left Dodge, Masterson's tall American stud had made up its mind to show no affection for the interloper mule lugging O'Neil's heavy equipment. The horse had bared his teeth and tried to take a bite out of the other animal's rump. Kilcoyn was concerned that there might be trouble between the two, a concern that grew when Masterson said, "You know a white mule is a gambler's ghost, John, don't you? That should worry us some."

As though Kilcoyn didn't have worries enough.

Thanks to Kelley's gossiping clerks and the emergency town meeting, it was no secret that he was carrying more than ten thousand dollars in his saddlebags.

Bill Johnson had seen a shady character who called himself Hank Poteet leave Dodge at a fast gallop when the news became known. Kilcoyn had seen Poteet around town, a small, thin man with the quick, sly eyes of a bunkhouse rat. He had come up from the Indian Territory at the start of the cattle season and always seemed to have money to spend, but as far as was known steered well clear of work. Poteet carried a short-barreled Colt in his waistband and Masterson said he'd seen three notches cut in the walnut handle.

Had Poteet hurried to spread the good news of the money to others of his kind?

In the Indian Territory there were outlaws who would cut any man, woman or child in half with a shotgun for fifty dollars. The kind of money Kilcoyn was carrying would keep such men in whiskey and women for a long time, and when the word got around, there were some might come looking.

It was a mighty worrisome thing, and Kilcoyn rode alert in the saddle, his eyes constantly searching the level, rain-lashed country around him.

He expected to reach Crooked Creek before nightfall, a place where they could camp and eat, and maybe find shelter from the downpour and a wind that that was now honed to an icy edge.

There seemed to be no letup in the black skies

rolling in from the west, and lightning flashed in the distance, touching the interior of the clouds with shimmering silver and orange light. The wind was rising fast, driving rain against Kilcoyn's face. Beside him Masterson rode, head down against the weather. O'Neil took up the rear. The young man's face was gray and he seemed to be suffering, but whether from the hard trail or a hangover, Kilcoyn could not guess.

Darkness was falling around them when Kilcoyn sighted the creek, its banks lined with cottonwoods and a few willows. There would be shelter of sorts under the trees, still clinging to their smoke-colored leaves though the summer was long gone. During the past hour Kilcoyn had felt the rain turning to sleet, and that was always the herald of coming snow.

The three riders unsaddled under a cottonwood, then turned out their mounts onto a patch of good grass growing along the creek bank. Masterson rigged up a crude shelter—a few fallen tree branches driven into the muddy ground, covered with a canvas tarp O'Neil had brought along. The three men huddled under its meager shelter.

The wood Kilcoyn had gathered was wet and made for a smoky, sullen fire, but it was enough to boil coffee and fry bacon and thick slices of sourdough bread.

"We made good time today, John," Masterson said, speaking around a mouthful of food. "Seems like we won't try Jake's patience."

Kilcoyn nodded. "He'll wait anyway. He'll wait because I believe it's not really the money he wants, it's me."

"I don't understand," Masterson said. "Jake was a lawman. He knows you were only doing your duty, John. He would have done the same thing if the shoe had been on the other foot."

"You'd think that would be the way of it, but Jake just didn't see it. He blamed me for Maggie leaving after I arrested him. Blamed me too for putting a Greener to his head while he was asleep, said I didn't give him an even break."

O'Neil smiled. "I'd say he was right, Marshal. The shotgun sure stacked the odds in your favor. Buckshot always means a buryin'."

"When you come up against a man as good with a gun as Jake Pride you need all the advantages you can get," Kilcoyn said. "The last thing I wanted to do was test my draw against his. The outcome would have been a mighty uncertain thing."

"Uncle James told me you're good with a gun, Marshal," O'Neil said. "This man Jake Pride is that fast, huh?"

Masterson jumped in to answer the question. "Jake Pride is that fast, boy, maybe even a sight faster than me, and that's saying plenty. It could be he's the best around this part of the country on the draw and shoot. You don't give a man like that an even break, not if you can avoid it, you don't."

"So I live and learn," O'Neil said.

"You watch your step," Masterson said. "Come up against ol' Jake Pride and you won't live long enough to learn anything else."

Later, in the crowding darkness, the three men stretched out under the leaky tarp and tried to get some sleep. The rain had now completely changed to a watery sleet, and as they got closer to Black Mesa and the foothills of the Sangre de Cristos it would turn to snow.

Kilcoyn lay awake for a long while, listening to the soft fall of the sleet on the tarp and Masterson's snores. Out on the flat the wet and miserable coyotes were calling, and from down by the creek, a horse blew through its nose and stomped the ground.

"Marshal, are you awake?" O'Neil's voice.

"Yeah, I'm awake. And for God's sake, call me John."

"John . . . do you think Jake Pride will take the money and let Doc Wilson and Miss Angela go without a fight?"

Kilcoyn smiled into the darkness. "Why? You scared?"

The marshal heard a soft rustle as the man shook his head. "No, at least I don't think so."

"You should be scared of a man like Jake Pride. He's tough and he's hard to kill."

"Are you scared of him?"

The marshal held off speaking for a few moments, thinking the younger man's question through. Then he said, "No, O'Neil, he doesn't scare me, but still, I plan on giving him all the room I can. I don't much cotton to the thought of meeting Jake Pride in a straight-up gunfight."

"John?"

"Yeah, O'Neil?"

"For God's sake, call me Barry."

"I will. When I think you've earned it."

Kilcoyn rose at first light and shook the others awake. He fed a few more sticks to the fire, grabbed the coffeepot, and stepped out from under the tarp. The sleet had stopped, at least for the time being, but the sky was heavy with black cloud that hung low over the plains, shrouding the grass in a motionless gray mist.

The marshal stretched, easing the knots out of his back, then walked down to the creek to fill the pot. The bank was high along most of its length, but a section about twenty feet wide had been trampled down by buffalo, forming a low, sandy break washed by the fast-running creek water. Kilcoyn walked through the break and kneeled to fill the pot.

It was then that he glanced to his left and saw the track.

It was part of a heel print, just a shallow arc in the sand and barely visible. Kilcoyn rose, the pot in his hand, and stepped to the print. It was not cut deep, like a boot heel would have done, and there was only one.

Turning, Kilcoyn called out to Masterson, who was saddling his horse. The sheriff left off what he was doing and stepped to Kilcoyn's side. "What do you make of that?" the marshal asked, nodding toward the print.

Masterson kneeled beside the mark in the sand, his face knotted in concentration. Finally he looked up and said, "Moccasin print, John. Sure as shootin'."

"Why only that one?" O'Neil asked, stepping beside Kilcoyn and looking around him uneasily.

"Because there was only one Indian," Masterson answered. "That's how come our scalps weren't lifted last night. I'd say this one was on the scout, checking on us." His eyes lifted to the marshal. "What say you, John?"

"I've got a good notion that's the case, and I'm betting this one was from Star Blanket's band."

"But what does all that mean?" O'Neil asked. "And who's Star Blanket?"

"He's a war chief, boy, and he's bad medicine," Masterson answered. "As to what it all means, it means we're in a whole heap of trouble. Or, to put it another way, our teats are in the wringer and it's wash day at the orphanage."

"From now on, we ride careful and check our back trail," Kilcoyn said. "That scout has reported back to Star Blanket by this time and the old man knows we're here."

Masterson nodded, looking unhappy, as icy, wind-blown sleet spattered against him. "It never rains but it pours," he said, turning his eyes to the black sky. "And that's a natural fact."

Kilcoyn and the others rode through the day as the weather around them worsened, the sleet changing to flurries of snow driven by a keening wind.

They kept the south fork of the Dry Cimarron a few miles to their south, heading into country abruptly changing from flat prairie to shallow, rolling hills that rose gradually in elevation toward the Black Mesa country. The land around them was now mostly covered in bluestem and buffalo grass, broken up by clusters of mesquite, lotebush and redberry juniper. Here and there grew yucca, prickly pear and cholla cactus, and scattered flocks of scaled quail fled at the approach of their horses.

They camped that night on the Dry Cimarron and were in the saddle again at first light, heading into a wilder, more rugged wilderness of humpbacked hills, narrow creeks and raw outcroppings of granite rock. There was no sun, just a vast roof of gunmetal gray cloud that touched the earth in places. The air was raw and cold.

Around noon, Masterson turned in the saddle, glanced behind him and urgently whispered Kilcoyn's name.

The marshal nodded. "I know, Bat. They've been dogging us for the past thirty minutes."

O'Neil, his face showing his alarm, asked, "Are they hostile Indians?"

Masterson glanced behind him again, then looked over at O'Neil. "They sure as shootin' are, boy—old Star Blanket's Cheyenne if I'm not mistaken—and there's a passel of 'em."

"How many can you make out, Bat?" Kilcoyn asked.

The sheriff took a quick look over his shoulder, then shook his head. "Hard to tell with all this cloud mist, but I'd say a dozen, maybe more."

"O'Neil," Kilcoyn said, "haul in that pack mule and close up. If we have to make a run for it I don't want you trailing behind. If the worst comes to the worst, let the mule go and hightail it."

"Do you think they'll attack us, John?" the young man asked.

"Hard to tell with Indians. They're mighty notional, but I'd say they're probably planning on it."

The Cheyenne kept their distance, staying just out of rifle range, playing such a strange game Kilcoyn had no idea what kind of hand they were about to deal him.

"Glad they're not Comanche, John," Masterson said. "If they were, they'd have come at us by now." He glanced behind him. "Damn them, what the hell are they waiting for?"

No sooner had Masterson said the words than one of the warriors broke free from the rest and galloped his gray pony toward them. Kilcoyn swung his dun around to face the danger, swiftly sliding the Winchester from the scabbard under his knee. But the Cheyenne reined his horse to a stop and loosed an arrow from his bow that sailed in a high arc over the marshal's head and thudded into the ground ahead of Masterson and O'Neil.

The Indian let out a wild war whoop, made an obscene gesture in Kilcoyn's direction, then galloped back to the others.

"What the heck was all that about?" O'Neil asked, looking around him.

Kilcoyn didn't answer. He swung out of the saddle and retrieved the arrow. It was an ordinary war arrow of dogwood, fletched with turkey feathers and tipped with a strap iron head. But what made it unique was the red lightning bolt painted down the entire length of the shaft.

It was a sacred arrow of the Dog Soldiers.

"What do you think, John?" Masterson asked.

"I think Star Blanket knows who killed his son," the marshal answered, looking toward the waiting Cheyenne. "He's just notified me."

Kilcoyn broke the arrow in half and threw it contemptuously in the direction of the watching Cheyenne. He walked back to his horse and stepped into the saddle.

"I'm sure that pleased them immensely." Masterson smiled. "What now?"

The marshal kneed his horse alongside Masterson,

leaned over in the saddle and whispered into the sheriff's ear. Masterson's face changed from a look of interest to one of shocked surprise.

"John," he said, "I'm grateful for your suggestion, but it isn't going to work. All we'll do is get ourselves killed for sure."

"Trust me, Sheriff Masterson," Kilcoyn wheedled, smiling. "Just be ready to move when I give the word."

As Masterson slid his rifle from the scabbard, doubt written large on his scowling face, the marshal called over to O'Neil. "This isn't your kind of game. When you see Bat and me make our move, you light a shuck on out of here. If everything turns out real bad, as it well might, keep on going and don't stop until you reach somewhere safe."

O'Neil looked directly into Kilcoyn's eyes, and like Bat's, his face was a study in uncertainty. "What are you going to do?"

Kilcoyn's smile grew slight. "Just sit tight, O'Neil. You'll see."

The marshal eased his horse to a walk. Masterson looked gloomy riding beside him, holding his Winchester upright, the butt on his thigh.

Flurries of snow were tumbling in the wind and the day was growing colder. Already the grass was streaked here and there with thin patches of white, and the horses were jetting steam from their nostrils.

Masterson turned in the saddle, about to glance back at the Indians, but Kilcoyn stopped him with a low, warning hiss. "No, don't look at them, Bat. You'll be seeing enough Cheyenne in a moment or two."

They rode on, the Indians following, but keeping the same distance as before.

"Star Blanket doesn't want to hurry this," Kilcoyn said. "He plans on us getting good and scared before he attacks."

The sheriff's smile was forced. "Hell, he doesn't have to wait any longer, John. He's got me good and scared already."

"That makes two of us," Kilcoyn said.

They rode on, and Kilcoyn took a furtive, sidelong glance over his shoulder. The Cheyenne had shaken into a loose line, a couple of flankers breaking out wider than the rest.

It was coming.

"Now!" Kilcoyn yelled.

He swung the dun around, conscious of Masterson doing the same with his big stud. They rode past a startled O'Neil at a gallop, Kilcoyn's rifle already firing. Ahead of the marshal an Indian went down, then another as Masterson's Winchester spat flame.

The Cheyenne were milling around, surprised and confused by the speed and suddenness of the white men's charge. As the marshal and Masterson crashed into them the Indians splintered into two groups, their ponies crow-hopping out of the way of the charging horsemen. A warrior rode at Kilcoyn, his rifle coming up to his shoulder. A gun blasted close to the marshal and the Indian tumbled off his horse, a sudden red rose blossoming on his war shirt. Kilcoyn glanced to his left and saw O'Neil lever another round into the chamber of his Henry.

"Get back!" Kilcoyn shouted.

O'Neil ignored him, firing steadily.

Kilcoyn was in a circle of Indians, not shooting, but slashing out with his rifle barrel. He caught one warrior hard across the face and the man toppled from his saddle. He hit another with a raking blow, the rifle sight laying open the man's cheek. Then he slammed the spurs to the dun and broke free, cranking another round into the Winchester. He fired to his left, where Masterson was fighting with his Colt, and a Cheyenne went down. A bullet burned across the thick muscle of Kilcoyn's right shoulder but he couldn't see who had fired at him. He saw O'Neil's horse fall, the young man's rifle spinning out of his hands.

Then, as suddenly as it had begun, it was over.

The Cheyenne were streaming to the east, taken by surprise by the savagery of Kilcoyn's attack and beaten for now. But the brutal reality was that they'd be back—and next time they would be a lot more careful and a sight more dangerous.

Five Cheyenne lay on the grass. One, the man Kilcoyn had hit with his rifle barrel, was sitting, his head in his hands. Kilcoyn swung out of the saddle, stepped to the stunned warrior and picked up the rifle that was lying close by. The eyes the man lifted to Kilcoyn were black with hate. He reached for the knife on his belt as he tried to scramble to his feet, but Kilcoyn clubbed him with a swinging blow of the rifle butt. The warrior's head was slammed to one side, his skull shattered. He fell on his back and lay still.

For a moment Kilcoyn felt sickened, but such was the harsh fact of Indian warfare on the plains, when mercy was neither asked nor given. Had he tried to spare the man, the Cheyenne would have seen it only as a sign of weakness and held him in contempt, a woman among warriors. And he would have tried to kill him at the first opportunity.

"John, over here," Masterson called.

Barry O'Neil was lying on his back, the sheriff kneeling beside him. The young man's horse was standing close by, its head down and the reins trailing. "He took a bullet in the shoulder," Masterson said as Kilcoyn stepped beside him. "Passed all the way through, but he's torn up real bad."

Kilcoyn cursed under his breath. They had to be at Black Mesa in a few more days, and a wounded man would slow them down.

"How are you feeling"—Kilcoyn hesitated a moment, then added—"Barry."

The young man managed a weak, pained smile. "Thought I had to earn that," he said.

"You just did," Masterson said. "You played the man's part today. Maybe saved our bacon."

"Think you can ride?" Kilcoyn asked.

O'Neil nodded. "Sure I can. I'm shot through and through, and the fall from my horse jolted my liver loose, but I can ride."

Kilcoyn's eyes scanned the distance ahead of them, where a shifting lace curtain of snow was drawn across the prairie. "Maybe there's a farm or a settlement up ahead," he said. "We have to get you to a place where your wound can be treated and you can rest."

"I'll be fine," O'Neil said. "I'll stick with you and Bat."

Masterson looked down at the man and shook his head. "Don't be a damn fool, Barry. Feeling as puny as you are with that shoulder of yours, you can't ride all the way to Black Mesa. Hell, boy, you could bleed to death. We've got to get you some doctoring, like John says."

Masterson made pads of grass and bound them to O'Neil's wounds using a rag he found among the man's gear. "That's about the best I can do," he said. "It might stop the bleeding."

"Let's get him on his horse," Kilcoyn said, worry tugging at him. It was still a long way to Black Mesa. And Star Blanket would be back.

5

Woman Trouble

The three riders headed west again, the snow and the waning day falling around them. O'Neil was bent over in the saddle, obviously hurting, and Kilcoyn held the lead rope of the pack mule.

The marshal felt concern. O'Neil was weak from loss of blood, and every now and then Masterson had to reach out to prevent him from toppling from the saddle. The young man's face was gray as old paint, his lips a tight white line as he silently fought back his pain. He needed help, and soon.

Darkness was gathering around them when Kilcoyn lifted his nose to the wind and detected the fleeting smell of burning mesquite. The odor was coming from the west, somewhere beyond the blowing veil of the snow.

Masterson smelled it too. He gave Kilcoyn a sideling glance and asked, "Indians?"

"Could be," Kilcoyn allowed. He slid his rifle from the boot. "Maybe we should ride careful, Bat."

"I think I'll go on ahead and take a look-see," the sheriff said. "That smoke smells like it could be real close."

In fact, the smell of the burning mesquite was much stronger now, and Kilcoyn nodded. "Yes, take a look. But if it's Cheyenne come fogging it on back here. Don't try to take them on by yourself."

"There isn't much likelihood of that." Masterson grinned. He touched the brim of his hat and lifted his horse into a fast canter.

Kilcoyn watched the sheriff disappear into the cartwheeling snow, feeling suddenly vulnerable. With a wounded man to protect, he'd be in big trouble if Star Blanket chose to attack now.

A few taut minutes passed, then Masterson emerged from the snow and the darkness, waving his arm at Kilcoyn to come on. The marshal took the reins of O'Neil's horse and kneed his dun into a trot. The pack mule, unhappy with the snow and cold, followed reluctantly.

"Cabin just over that next rise, John," Masterson said. "And they seem like right friendly folks."

"Did you meet them?" Kilcoyn asked, surprised.

The sheriff shook his head. "No, smelled them. I'd say any folks who are cooking a possum-and-onion stew for supper over a mesquite fire have got to be friendly."

"Then let's go make their acquaintance."

The rise was a low lava ridge laid down in ancient times, when volcanoes still erupted in the Sangre de Cristo. Beyond its crest the far slope fell away gradually for about a quarter mile, dropping a hundred feet in elevation to a narrow, winding stream. A cabin lay at a bend of the stream, half hidden behind the wall of the falling snow, but light glowed like welcoming beacons in windows to the front. As he sat his horse on the ridge and studied the place, Kilcoyn saw a sway-roofed barn to the left of the cabin and, closer, a corral or pigpen built hit-or-miss of pine poles.

Even with his vision obscured by the falling snow, Kilcoyn decided the place looked rundown and neglected, the homestead of a sick man, perhaps, or a woman alone.

Motioning Masterson to follow, Kilcoyn rode slowly down the slope, leading O'Neil's horse. When they were twenty yards from the cabin he yelled: "Hello the house!"

Immediately the oil lamps inside were doused, then the door opened a crack and a man's voice called out, "Mister, we got faith in rifles here and we ain't a-sittin' on our gun hands. What the hell do you want?"

"I'm United States Marshal John Kilcoyn and with me is Sheriff Bat Masterson. We've got a wounded man here."

A few moments of silence followed Kilcoyn's declaration; then the door opened wider, and a tall, stoop-shouldered man, his face partly hidden by a long black beard threaded with gray, stepped into the yard. He held a shotgun in his hands. "Heard o' you two," he said. "Ride on in."

Kilcoyn rode closer and sat his saddle. Grudgingly the man said, "Step down. And that goes for the others of ye."

Four more men, close copies of the first, but younger, stepped out of the cabin. All carried rifles and sported heavy beards, greasy tangles of hair falling over their shoulders. They wore ragged pants and collarless shirts open at the neck, revealing stained and dirty vests underneath. The five men looked shiftless and their black eyes were mean, but their rifles were clean and oiled. Kilcoyn sensed danger in them.

After the marshal swung out of the saddle, the older man said, "Name's Caleb Early, out of the Tennessee feudin' country." He waved a hand. "These are my boys. Jacob, he's the oldest. Then there's Jasper, Jeremiah and Jesse, the youngest. Got me a daughter in the house. She's seventeen, and I call her Jenny when I call her anything."

Masterson stepped beside Kilcoyn, a friendly grin splitting his face. "It's real nice of you folks to be so hospitable and all. The snow looks like it's planning to get heavier and there's a cold wind blowing."

"Like I haven't noticed that my ownself," Early said. "And don't thank me for hospitality afore it's been offered."

Masterson slanted a puzzled glance to Kilcoyn, then shrugged. "Well, a good meal and a bed will be hospitality enough," he said.

Kilcoyn helped O'Neil off his horse and he supported the young man as they stepped toward the cabin door. "I'd like to get him in out of the cold," he said. "He's shot pretty bad and he's lost blood."

"Outlaws gun him?" Early asked, his interest piqued.

Kilcoyn shook his head. "Cheyenne. Back a ways on the trail."

Early nodded. "They will do that to you." He motioned toward the door with his shotgun. "Bring him inside." Turning to Masterson, he added, "You can put up your animals in the corral. Then you can bed down out of the snow in the barn and cook your meat in there too, if'n you're real careful. There's some scraps of wood lying around."

Masterson looked at Kilcoyn again, one surprised eyebrow inching up his forehead. "I may have been mistaken, but I thought I smelled possum-and-onion stew cooking," he said.

Early nodded. "You did, but it ain't for sharing. Hell, we got barely enough for our ownselves."

A wry smile tugged at Kilcoyn's lips. It seemed Caleb Early was a downright unsociable man. The big marshal reached out, grabbed his saddlebags with the ransom money from the dun and draped them over his shoulder. Unlike Early, John Kilcoyn was a sociable man at times, but he was not a trusting one.

As Masterson led the horses toward the corral, Kilcoyn helped O'Neil into the cabin. The place was sparsely furnished—a table, benches and a battered leather wing chair beside the stove that Early must have brought all the way from Tennessee.

But the place was remarkably clean, the dirt floor swept, the few dishes and cups on the shelf sparkling. A huge, smoke-blackened stewpot bubbled on the stove and a loaf of sourdough bread was already sliced on the table, some horn cups scattered around.

The reason for the cabin's immaculate appearance became immediately apparent when a young girl stepped through the door from an adjoining room.

Jenny Early was a pretty blonde with huge baby blue eyes. Her hair lay over her shoulders in soft, shining waves and her lips were a full, luscious pink. She was dressed in a ragged dress of brown wool that looked like it had been almost worn out by a much larger woman, then passed down. But the shabby clothes did nothing to conceal the rich curves of the girl's body, and the graceful, provocative way she moved.

Only when Kilcoyn looked closer did he see the fine lines around Jenny's mouth and across her forehead, lines that should not have been there in one so young. Her lovely eyes had a hurt, haunted look to them and her hands were work-roughened, the nails short and broken, speaking of a life of unrelenting hard labor. She was, the marshal decided, a young girl being worked to death, caring for five grown men who were too bone idle and selfish to shift for themselves.

Jenny caught sight of O'Neil, who was sitting with his head bowed, nursing his shoulder, and cried, "Oh, you poor man. Let me see that wound."

"She's a fair hand at doctoring," Early said as he lifted the lid of the stewpot and sniffed. "Patched all of us up at one time or another."

O'Neil's eyes lifted to the girl and widened in surprise. Then Kilcoyn saw them fill with some kind of emotion he could not at first pinpoint. He was not by nature a romantic, but then it dawned on him— if there were such a thing as love at first sight, he had just witnessed it.

It had happened to Barry and Jenny just as it had to him and Angela and, for some reason, that pleased Kilcoyn immensely.

Jenny helped O'Neil out of his slicker, and then removed his coat and shirt. "What's your name?" she asked as she studied the bullet wound, a little frown gathering on her forehead.

"Barry O'Neil," the young man said, watching the girl's face intently, like he couldn't quite believe what he was seeing.

"Barry O'Neil." The girl tested the name on her tongue. "I like that. It has a nice ring to it."

"I'm a photographer," O'Neil said, his voice unsteady. "You're so beautiful, Jenny. I'd like to make your picture sometime."

"Only a damned, ignorant Mick would talk pretties to a gal he don't even know, and her with kinfolk close," Jacob Early snarled, anger and jealousy all tangled up in his eyes. He was a tall, rawboned man with a thin, mean mouth and huge hands that hung, fingers curled, loose at his side.

If O'Neil was stung he didn't let it show. He gave Jacob a slight smile. "I've accepted the hospitality of your home, so I will let that pass." His smile widened. "At least for now."

Jacob's eyes hardened and he opened his mouth to speak again, but Jenny cut him off, her anger flaring. "If Barry wants to make my picture, I'll let him. I've never had one made before in the seventeen years I've lived in this godforsaken place."

"Don't talk sass to your brother, girl," Caleb warned, "or you'll get the back of my hand. Now patch that boy up and we'll get him into the barn."

"You'll do no such thing, Pa!" Jenny protested. "Barry is hurt and he needs more rest that he can get in that cold, drafty barn. He can sleep in my bed tonight."

"I don't want to put you to any trouble," O'Neil said.

"It's no trouble," Jenny said. "I'll be quite comfortable in Pa's chair."

"Now the damned Mick is throwing us out of our

own beds," Jacob snarled, a wicked gleam in his eyes.

The man was on the prod and spoiling for trouble, and it was in Kilcoyn's mind to give him all he could handle and then some if he pushed it too far.

But Caleb Early defused the growing tension. "Jacob, let it be," he said, his sly eyes slanting to his son. "O'Neil can sleep here tonight, but he leaves at first light tomorrow morning."

For the next few minutes, Jenny cleaned, then treated O'Neil's wound, using something out of a bottle that stung him badly.

"No bones were broken and the wound is clean," she said finally. "I think with time you'll heal up just fine, Barry."

Then Kilcoyn saw it again, in Jenny's eyes this time, something fleeting and hard to interpret, admiration maybe . . . or a promise. His gaze shifted beyond the girl to the wall behind her, where gleaming rifles stood in a rack along with holstered revolvers.

The marshal sensed a brooding danger in the room, and not just from Jacob. His brothers—cast in the same mold, all three of them tall, hard-eyed men, raised to the feud—were regarding O'Neil with open hostility.

Right there and then Kilcoyn decided he and Masterson would move out before sunup—and they were taking O'Neil with them.

Despite his misgivings, he tried to make light of the situation. "Well, Jenny," he said, "I'll leave Barry in your very capable hands." Then, to let Early and his sons know his intentions, he added, "We're dog-tired, so we'll be leaving after we catch a few hours' sleep."

"See you do leave, Marshal," Jacob said. "You wouldn't want to overstay your welcome, now, would you?"

"I reckon it's right unsociable, John," Masterson said. "I mean, to cook possum for supper and not invite a man to take a place at the table." He gave the marshal a sidelong glance. "And that Jacob feller shapes up to be as mean as a curly wolf."

"It takes all kinds, I guess," Kilcoyn said. "Sometimes meanness becomes a habit with a man and, like milk in a thunderstorm, it turns him sour."

Kilcoyn looked through the gaping space in the sagging barn doors to where the falling snow was starting to cover the ground, ennobling and beautifying the mean surroundings of the Early homestead. Over at the cabin he heard the clink of plates and the muffled talk of Caleb and his sons.

Masterson shivered and licked his lips. "Getting right chilly, John. What do we have for supper?"

A smile touched Kilcoyn's lips. "Well, we could build a fire over there on the bare ground by the doors and boil up some coffee," he said. He jerked a thumb over his shoulder. "But the barn is full of Caleb Early's horses, so I don't reckon that's a real good idea."

"The man himself said we could."

"I know, and I've been wondering at that. Early must realize how dangerous that is, but did he have reason enough to accept the risk? Could it be he wanted us real comfortable so we'd fall asleep easy?"

Masterson nodded. "Oddly enough, I've been thinking exactly along those lines myself. At first I couldn't understand why he wouldn't let us spread our blankets in the cabin where it's warm. But it makes sense to isolate us here in the barn if he plans on robbing us."

"Maybe so. Rob us of our horses and guns, and he showed a lot of interest in my saddlebags—caught him looking at them a time or two, like he was wondering."

The two lawmen were sitting in front of an empty stall where a few stacked bales of hay sheltered them from the worst of the icy drafts that swept through the barn. Rats scuttled and squeaked in the corners, and now and then ran along the beams over their heads.

Kilcoyn turned to Masterson and waved a hand, taking in what lay beyond the doors. "Look around you out there," he said. "There's no smokehouse, no corncrib, no plow, no farm implements of any kind. And the hay around us is store-bought, or they stole it. Seems to me Caleb and his boys get money to live from somewhere, but it's not from farming, or raising stock, either."

"You think they kill and rob people for a living?"

"It's possible. Fact is, I'd say it's highly likely."

"If Caleb Early is planning a robbery, he knows he'll have to kill us." Masterson's steady gaze held Kilcoyn's. "But it's no small thing to murder a United States Marshal. Or an elected sheriff of Ford County, Kansas, come to that."

"Who would ever know?" Kilcoyn asked. "There's plenty of space around here to bury a man where he'd never be found." The marshal was quiet for a few moments, listening. "They're still eating, so we have some time before they come for us."

"Do you think the girl is in on it?" Masterson asked.

Kilcoyn shook his head. "I think they more or less use Jenny as a slave, for cooking and cleaning and the like." His lips thinned to a tight line, a normal man attempting to come to terms with the vilely abnormal. "And if I'm reading her eyes right, I reckon they're using her for other things besides." He looked at his deputy, his face bleak. "But to answer your question—no, Bat, I don't think Jenny's in on it."

Kilcoyn rose to his feet and stepped to the rear of the barn, his spurs chiming in the silence. He returned and said, "Just as I figured. I found a door back there. I'd say Caleb Early plans on a-coming at us from two directions."

The marshal pulled his Colt and thumbed a sixth

round into the cylinder. "But you and me," he said, icy promise in his voice, "we're going to throw Early and his boys a little surprise party."

Using as few words as possible, the marshal outlined his plan. Masterson nodded with each word. "Hell, I'll go along with that." He grinned.

After a few minutes, a small fire burned near the open door of the barn. The two lawmen had dropped their saddles on each side of the fire, angled their hats on them, then stuffed their blankets with straw. From a distance it looked convincing—two exhausted and trusting lawmen, hats over their faces, sacked out and sleeping after a long trail and a shooting scrape with Indians.

Or at least Kilcoyn hoped it looked that convincing.

Carrying their rifles, he and Masterson left the barn by the back door so as not to leave footprints out front where they'd be readily seen. The snow was still falling, billows of fat white flakes shredding in the wind. Out in the distant darkness the frosted muzzles of the coyotes were lifted, yapping their misery to the echoing night, and the breaths of the two lawmen smoked as they walked swiftly away from the barn and faded into the shadows.

As his eyes became accustomed to the gloom, Kilcoyn made out the rotted hulk of an abandoned farm wagon. The wagon still had its two back wheels, the body slanting away from him. Motioning Masterson to follow, the marshal stepped to the wagon and crouched behind a huge, iron-rimmed wheel. Masterson kneeled beside him, blowing on his gun hand, his eyes scanning the darkness.

"John," he whispered, "being out in this cold isn't a place for a supperless man."

The marshal smiled. "Being out in this cold is no place for any kind of man."

A few slow minutes rolled past. Once Kilcoyn thought he heard Jenny cry out angrily, then her voice was cut off by a crack that sounded like a hard slap.

One by one the oil lamps in the cabin were doused. Over in the darkened barn, the flames of the fire flickered in the wind, casting a trembling scarlet glow on the bare ground and on the bulky stuffed blankets.

If Caleb Early and his sons left the cabin and made for the barn, Kilcoyn knew that he and Masterson would have to leave their place of concealment and get closer to the five men. He liked no part of it, but there was no other way. In the uncertain light and tumbling snow any shooting would have to be up close and mighty personal.

Beside Kilcoyn, Masterson stiffened. "Look there," he whispered.

From where he was, Kilcoyn hadn't been able to see the front of the cabin, but he watched as five men, rifles in their hands, emerged from the darkness, walking stealthily in the direction of the barn.

"Get ready, Bat," the marshal said under his breath. "It's coming."

Halfway to the barn, Caleb Early stopped. He jabbed a forefinger at two of his sons, then motioned that they should go round the back. The men left, walking on cat feet through the darkness, and Early waited, letting them get in place before he made his move.

A minute ticked past, then another. Early waved on the other two and stepped toward the barn door. He stopped when he was fifteen yards away, raised his Winchester to his shoulder and cut loose. Shots slammed into the blankets by the fire. Early's sons joined in the shooting. One bullet hit the fire, sending up a shower of sparks, another thudded into the ground, but most found their targets, kicking up the blankets, scattering straw into the air.

"Let's go, Bat!" Kilcoyn said.

He rose to his feet and walked quickly through the shifting veil of the darkness and swirling snow, firing his rifle from the hip. A man went down; then, as Masterson fired, so did another.

Caught flatfooted, Caleb Early turned, his face shocked, confronting a threat from a direction he hadn't expected.

The two sons who'd gone to the back of the barn appeared at the door, one of them the gangling, angry Jacob. Both men leveled their guns at Kilcoyn and Masterson. Neither of the lawmen fired, but as a rifle shot hammered into the night, the younger of the two brothers screamed, staggered a step, then thudded onto his back. Confused, Jacob Early glanced quickly down at his brother, his face suddenly ashen. Kilcoyn fired at him as Masterson shot at Caleb. Masterson missed, but Kilcoyn didn't. Jacob was hit hard, the shot taking him low in the belly. The man bent over, turned and lurched into the gloom of the barn.

Another rifle shot crashed, kicking up a startled plume of snow and dirt at Caleb's feet. The man shrieked and threw down his rifle.

"Don't shoot no more!" he yelled. "I'm done."

"Make another move, Early," Kilcoyn hollered, "and I'll drop you like a mad dog right where you stand."

"I'm out of it," Early yelped. "For God's sake let me be." The man was badly frightened, looking around him in bewilderment, like he couldn't believe what had happened to him and his sons in just a few hell-firing seconds.

Kilcoyn glanced toward the cabin. O'Neil was standing outside, the Henry smoking in his hands. It had been he who had dropped the man at the barn door and fired at Caleb. The marshal waved to O'Neil, then said to Masterson: "Cover Early. I'm going after the one in the barn."

"Be careful, John," Masterson said. "That one's a cornered rat an' he'll be dangerous."

But Jacob Early was no longer a danger to anyone. He lay sprawled on his face near the back door and all the life that had been in him was gone.

Of the four Early sons, only one had survived the

gun battle, Jesse, the youngest, and he was gut shot and dying, lying on his back, his face a twisted mask of pain.

Kilcoyn left the barn and watched as Caleb kneeled beside the boy. "Am I dying, Paw?" Jesse asked. "I hurt so bad I can hardly stand it."

"You ain't leaving me, Jesse," Early said urgently. "You're all I got left, just you and your sister, an' she ain't much."

"I'm hurting, Paw," the boy whispered. "My whole belly's on fire."

Early's eyes lifted to Kilcoyn, standing tall and terrible as the snow wheeled around him. "You did this, Kilcoyn," the man snarled. "Damn you to hell. It was your doing. You and that damned Masterson, a lawman who ain't nothing but a hired gunfighter."

The big marshal shook his head. "It was none of my doing, Early. Or Bat's either. You wanted to kill us and take what we had. You were hunting trouble and you found it. All you got for your treachery is four dead sons."

"Jesse ain't gonna die," Early said, his face gray and tight. "I won't let him die."

"The boy is gut shot," Masterson said. "His time is short and you're his paw. Best you help him make his peace with his Maker."

It seemed to Kilcoyn that Bat was trying to spark a last, remaining act of decency in the man. Early looked up at the sheriff, his eyes unreadable, then rose to his feet. He brushed past O'Neil and stepped into the cabin. Masterson, his rifle ready, followed close behind him.

After a few moments both men reappeared, Early carrying a battered Bible in his hand. "Read the passage I showed you," Masterson said. "Can you read?"

"I can read," the man growled as he kneeled beside his son and the boy's eyes lifted to his face.

"I'm scared, Paw, real scared of dying," Jesse whispered. "I don't know what will happen to me. Remember you told us about the fires of hell—remember that?"

"You lay still, boy, and listen," Early said. He opened the Bible and began to read, stumbling over unfamiliar words.

"I am the resurrection and the life; he that believeth in me, though he were dead, yet shall he live. And whoever liveth and believeth in me shall never die . . ."

Listening, Kilcoyn thought Early was merely mouthing the words, robbing them of all meaning. He was not praying for his son, he was attempting to salve his own guilty conscience.

Maybe Jesse heard it too, because he reached up a hand and grabbed the front of his father's shirt, stopping him. "Paw, we've done some bad things, all of us. I surely regret them now I'm dying. Tell Jenny . . . tell her . . ."

But the words fled Jesse's lips as the death shadows gathered in his cheeks and under his eyes, and his hand dropped to his side.

Early knelt by his son's side for a few minutes, then slowly rose to his feet. He looked over at Kilcoyn. "What are you going to do with me and Jenny?" he asked.

"He's doing nothing with Jenny. She's coming with me." O'Neil stepped close to Early, his face stiff. "As to what the marshal does to you, old man, I don't give a damn."

Jenny emerged from the darkness and stood at O'Neil's side. Early said, "You have to stay with me, child. You're all I got left in the world."

The girl shook her head. "You mean nothing to me, Pa." She waved a hand at the scattered dead men. "And neither do they. For as long as I can remember, my life here has been mean and nasty and ugly, and the living of it a more painful hurt than the bullet in Jesse's belly because it lasted much longer." Her eyes blazing, she looked right at her father and said, "And you were the worst of them, Pa, because you stood by and let it happen and when you saw what was happening you laughed."

Anger flamed Early's cheeks with red. "Don't you backtalk me, girl. Get into the cabin. I'm going to take a horsewhip to you later."

"Touch her, Early," O'Neil said, his voice flat and hard, "and I'll kill you."

Kilcoyn stepped closer to Early. "The girl is leaving

with us," he said. "By rights I should take you with me and see you hanged in Dodge, but we have to travel fast and far and you'd be a burden. Bury your dead, Early. Then leave the territory. If I find you here on my way back, I'll arrest you."

The man touched his tongue to his lip. "I'll need a horse and a gun."

"You'll have them, when we leave here at first light." Kilcoyn turned to Masterson. "Get a rope. We'll take him inside and tie him to a chair until it's time to leave."

Masterson nodded and began to walk away, but he stopped and turned to O'Neil, grinning. "Barry O'Neil, you may be no great shakes with a hog leg, but you can sure play hob with a Henry."

6

Buffalo Soldiers

Kilcoyn and the others saddled up just before first light, Jenny riding a rangy paint pony she'd led from the barn. The girl was wearing a split canvas riding skirt, much worn, and a plaid mackinaw, a battered man's hat on her head. She looked very young and vulnerable, and O'Neil, attentive and fluttering around her like a moth to a bright light, never strayed far from her side.

The snow was still falling, now covering the ground to a depth of several inches, and the air was cold, carrying with it the raw iron smell of winter. Sullen, threatening black clouds stretched from horizon to horizon and, as the darkness began to flee daybreak, the morning was dawning gray and cheerless.

When the others were mounted, Masterson holding the lead rope of O'Neil's pack mule that now carried the guns stripped from the dead men, Kilcoyn stepped inside the cabin and freed Early from his bonds.

He nodded toward the rifle lying on the table. "There's a box of .44–40 shells for the Winchester hidden in the barn," he said. "We'll be long gone before you find them." He smiled without humor. "I wouldn't want you shooting me in the back."

The man's eyes were black with hate. "Take my advice, Kilcoyn," he said. "Kill me now, because I'm coming after you, and I won't stop until you and that Mick are dead and I've got my daughter with me."

The big marshal nodded. "Early, nothing would give me more pleasure than to put a bullet into your belly right here and now."

Early sneered. "Then what's stopping you?"

Kilcoyn opened his canvas mackinaw and pointed to the star pinned to his shirt. "This," he said. "It's the only thing stopping me—just this piece of tin."

"Then you'll live to regret it."

"You're trash, Early," Kilcoyn said, his voice even, without anger. "And you showed yellow when the chips were down and others were dying. Your kind don't scare me none, all gurgle and no guts. Now bury your dead and hightail it to some town where you'll get yourself killed soon enough."

The man opened his mouth to speak, but Kilcoyn ignored him and walked out of the cabin. He swung into the saddle and kneed his dun into motion, waving to the others to follow.

Behind them, Caleb Early stood in the yard in front

of the cabin, his hands cupped to his mouth. "You should have gut shot me, Kilcoyn! I swear to God I'm gonna kill you all, every last damn one of ye!"

Masterson turned to Kilcoyn, his eyes searching his face. "I'm not one to itch before I get bitten, John, but don't you think we should ride back and reckon with Mr. Early?"

"Still got that possum-and-onion stew stuck in your craw, Bat?" Kilcoyn smiled.

The sheriff shook his head. "No, sir, John, but I've never believed in letting a sworn enemy ride my back trail. A man can get himself killed real quick that way."

They rode through the morning, and by noon the light had changed little, the day still gray and overcast. Tumbling streaks of snow spattered against the riders who sat their saddles, heads bent against the frigid fingers of the seeking wind.

The Dry Cimarron to their south looped in a westerly direction, pointing the way to Black Mesa, and Kilcoyn followed the course of the river, traveling through hilly, desolate country. Low ridges of red rock, and sometimes shale, rose here and there like the broken backbones of great prehistoric animals. On either side of the trail grew scattered clumps of saltbush, wild plum and bunch grass, giving way to bluestem closer to the riverbank.

A stand of cottonwoods mixed in with juniper grew along a sandy bend of the river, and an outcropping of lava rock as tall as a man on a horse promised some shelter from the worst of the wind.

Kilcoyn, his feet and hands numb from cold, decided it was high time they all had coffee and something to eat from the sack of grub Jenny had brought from the Early cabin.

There was firewood aplenty lying on the ground among the trees, most of it not yet too damp, and they soon coaxed a fire into flame and set the coffee-pot to boiling on the coals. Jenny had brought a few hard biscuits and some cold antelope meat, and these lean vittles they shared, washing them down with bitter, scalding-hot coffee.

As Kilcoyn had expected, the rock cut down on some of the wind, but the flames of the fire danced when icy gusts now and then found their way into the camp.

No one felt much like talking, the events of the night before and the gloom of the day weighing heavy on them. It was Masterson who finally broke the silence. Looking to their back trail over the rim of his coffee cup, he said casually, "Riders coming, John. Looks like soldiers to me."

Kilcoyn rose and followed the sheriff's pointing finger. "Thataway, John."

In the distance a column of horsemen, guidon flapping, was riding toward them, glimpses of soldier blue showing at the V formed by the lapels of their fur greatcoats. An Indian rode just ahead of the troopers, wearing the black cloth turban of the

Pawnee. His face was painted with parallel streaks of white and red, the traditional colors of the Army scout.

The young officer in command of the ten-man detail of Buffalo Soldiers reined up opposite Kilcoyn and touched the brim of his kepi. "Second Lieutenant James Delagrange, Ninth Cavalry out of Camp Supply. I am at your service, sir."

Kilcoyn nodded. "I'd say you're a fair piece off your home range, Lieutenant."

"Indeed, sir. The needs of the service, sir. Please tell me whom I am addressing."

Kilcoyn opened his mackinaw and showed the star on his chest. "United States Marshal John Kilcoyn, recently out of Dodge City." He waved a hand toward the others who were now standing around the fire. "This is Ford County Sheriff Bat Masterson, Miss Jenny Early and Barry O'Neil."

The lieutenant, a round-faced young man with a yellow mustache and goatee, nodded to the men and touched his hat to Jenny, a gleam of interest in his eyes. "Pleased to make your acquaintance, ma'am." Delagrange looked back to Kilcoyn. "Where are you headed, Marshal?"

Deciding not to go into details, Kilcoyn answered, "The Black Mesa country."

As the Pawnee rode up beside him, the officer shook his head. "I'm afraid that's impossible." Without waiting for the marshal to respond, he added,

"The Cheyenne have broken out. They've cut the trail west of here, and just yesterday killed and scalped three buffalo hunters at their camp on Beaver Creek. My orders are to move any and all white people I can find to T. J. Pettyman's stockade on the north fork of the Dry Cimarron."

Kilcoyn had heard of Pettyman, a fur trapper, buffalo hunter, sometime whiskey trader and all-round rogue who had built what he optimistically called a fort on the Cimarron. Pettyman had killed several men, lived with an Assiniboine woman, and why he had escaped the rope this long was a mystery, not only to Kilcoyn but also to most lawmen of his acquaintance.

"Thanks for your concern, Lieutenant, but I reckon we'll take our chances," the marshal said. "We have pressing business at Black Mesa."

"Then your business will have to be delayed until the Army rounds up the Cheyenne. I'm sorry, Marshal, but those are my orders."

The Point's spit and polish was still evident on Second Lieutenant Delagrange, and Kilcoyn realized the young officer would not be turned aside. If it came right down to it, he had a sufficient number of tough, gun-savvy and battle-hardened Buffalo Soldiers to make his demand stick, to say nothing of the Pawnee, sitting stone-faced and aloof on his paint pony.

"I will escort you to the settlement, Marshal," the

lieutenant said. "And along the way pick up any farmers, buffalo hunters and other waifs and strays we might find."

"Now just you hold on there a minute, soldier boy," Masterson said, stepping beside Kilcoyn. "Didn't the marshal tell you why we're headed for Black Mesa?"

Delagrange shook his head. "No, he didn't, but I doubt it will make any difference."

"Tell him, John," Masterson said. "Tell him how we've got about three days and maybe less to save Angela Wilson and her father. And how if we go to this Pettyman place, that will use up more daylight than it took for Noah's flood to dry."

The young lieutenant looked perplexed, and Kilcoyn said, "The sheriff has a point. We have to be at Black Mesa in three days or the lives of two of the most prominent citizens in Dodge could be in danger."

Before the officer could say anything, Kilcoyn told him of the ransom note from Jake Pride and about the ten thousand dollars in his saddlebags.

Delagrange listened intently, as did the Pawnee, but after Kilcoyn had finished speaking, the young officer straightened in the saddle and said, "That is a matter for the civilian law and doesn't countermand my orders, Marshal. I must still insist you accompany me to the settlement. Right now we have three cavalry troops out looking for the Cheyenne. The renegades will be rounded up very soon, possibly today. You have my assurance of that. Once the hostiles are caged you can be on your way."

Annoyance flashed across Masterson's face. "Lieutenant, " he said, "it seems to me you're trying to straddle the fence, and the only thing you get from that is a sore backside."

The soldier opened his mouth to speak, decided against it and swung his horse away, calling on his men, most of whom had dismounted and were standing around the dying fire, to get ready to ride out.

"Hell, I hadn't near finished with that soldier yet," Masterson grumbled.

Kilcoyn smiled. "Let it be, Bat. Lieutenant Delagrange has his orders." He turned and looked right at the sheriff and gave him a wink.

"What's on your mind, John?" Masterson asked.

"Later," Kilcoyn said. "After we get to Pettyman's stockade."

The two lawmen were stepping to their horses when the lieutenant rode up beside them. "Something I forgot to tell you, Marshal. A chief called Spotted Horse has his Sioux at Pettyman's settlement, thirty lodges of them. He says he's afraid of Star Blanket and his Cheyenne renegades and he wants his people to have Army protection."

Delagrange looked uncomfortable. "I'm telling you this because I don't want you, and especially the young lady, to be alarmed when you see so many bronco Indians right off the plains up close. It is a disturbing sight to those who have never encountered such a thing before."

"Thanks for the warning, Lieutenant," Kilcoyn said, his bland face revealing nothing. "Coming on all those bloodthirsty savages all at once would have scared us for sure."

7

Kilcoyn Gets a Grim Warning

Flanked by two columns of soldiers, Kilcoyn and the others headed toward the north fork of the Dry Cimarron, the trail to Black Mesa falling behind them. O'Neil and Jenny stayed close together, stirrups touching. Every now and then they punctuated their conversation with fleeting kisses, much to the grinning amusement of the soldiers who rode near them.

It seemed to Kilcoyn that O'Neil was no longer in great pain from his shoulder, and the color was returning to his cheeks. He was even talking to Lieutenant Delagrange about making a picture of him and his men when they reached Pettyman's settlement.

Jenny seemed more alive than ever now that she was free of her father and her brothers. When Kilcoyn turned to look at how she was holding up, she was openly flirting with the young lieutenant, basking in his attention as he talked to her about what the fashionable New York belles had worn to dances at the Point and what it was like to chase down Apaches along the Texas border country.

Despite the increasing cold of the darkening day and the ceaseless fall of the snow, Jenny's laugh rang like a silver bell, a small, feminine sound against the masculine clink of soldiers' equipment and the creak of saddle leather.

It was about four in the afternoon when the Pawnee rode in from a scout and reported directly to Delagrange. Kilcoyn saw the young officer's face turn pale as he listened to what the Indian had to say.

After the Pawnee stopped talking, Kilcoyn kneed his dun close to Delagrange. "What's happening, Lieutenant?"

The officer turned haunted eyes to the marshal. "The Pawnee found a farm a mile ahead of us. The—the people there are all dead."

"Cheyenne?"

Delagrange nodded dumbly, shaken by what he'd just heard. He turned in the saddle. "First two pairs, come with me."

"I'm riding with you," Kilcoyn said. "And Sheriff Masterson if he's willing. Those Cheyenne might still be hanging around."

"Suit yourself, Marshal," the lieutenant said, "though I must warn you both that you join us at your own risk." He waved on the four soldiers who had formed up behind him and kicked his horse into a fast trot, the Pawnee passing him at a gallop to take the point.

"Care to join me, Bat?" Kilcoyn asked, turning in the saddle. "We've got more Indian trouble."

The sheriff nodded, shucked his rifle from the scabbard and laid it across his saddle horn. "Ready when you are, John."

Kilcoyn gathered up the reins of his horse and said to O'Neil, "Barry, keep that Henry of yours handy until we get back. There's no accounting for what Indians will do next."

O'Neil grinned and waved a hand in response. A soldier wearing corporal's stripes rode closer to Kilcoyn and said, "Don't you worry none, Marshal. I'll see that the young lady comes to no harm."

The corporal looked tough and capable, and Kilcoyn nodded. "Thanks, Corporal. I'm beholden to you."

Kilcoyn swung his horse around. He and Masterson galloped after Delagrange.

The gray day was shading into darkness as the Pawnee left the trail and led the cavalrymen west, toward a narrow valley hemmed in by a pair of low lava ridges, stunted stands of juniper and mesquite, starved of root soil and harried by summer heat and winter cold, growing on their slopes. The wind had shifted, driving strong off the Greenhorn Mountains to the northwest, shredding the falling snow into ragged lace curtains of white.

A cabin lay at the far end of the valley, backing up to another steep ridge. Kilcoyn followed the Pawnee and Delagrange across what had been plowed land, now iron-hard and streaked with patches of snow, then into a small meadow of tall grass.

They found the first body there.

A tall, lanky lad, no more than sixteen, lay sprawled facedown on the ground. He'd been shot several times, then scalped. His right hand had been severed. It was the Cheyenne way of making sure the boy would enter the afterlife maimed, unable to take revenge on the warriors who had killed him as he wandered among the misty lodges of the Cheyenne, forever grieving for his lost hand.

The Indians believed they had enough enemies in this life with gun hands and didn't need any more in the next.

Kilcoyn and Delagrange rode to the front of the cabin as Masterson and the soldiers took up positions close by. The door swung on its rawhide hinges in the wind, banging like a muffled drum, and from somewhere close by the windlass of a well creaked. A tattered gingham curtain waved at the two men from a broken window, beckoning them inside.

Kilcoyn swung out of the saddle and slid his Winchester from the scabbard. He and the lieutenant stepped to the door as the other men dismounted and scouted the area. Delagrange hesitated at the door, then turned to the marshal, his face ashen. "I don't want to do this," he whispered, looking over his shoulder as though someone might overhear his weakness. "The Pawnee said there are three dead people in there."

Kilcoyn nodded. "I know how you feel, Lieutenant, but we got to do it. Look around you—right now there's only us."

The marshal stepped into the cabin, but it was too dark to see anything clearly. He fumbled in the pocket of his vest, found a match and thumbed it into flame. An oil lamp hung above a pine table, and he reached up and touched fire to the wick. An orange glow spread through the room as Kilcoyn heard Delagrange step to his side.

"Where are they?" he asked.

"Look under the table," Kilcoyn answered.

A bearded man had fallen on his back and rolled partway under the table. His eyes were wide open but he was seeing nothing. Like the younger man outside, no doubt his son, he had been shot and then horribly mutilated.

Kilcoyn took down the oil lamp and walked with it to the bedroom door, his boots scattering empty rifle shells. The sodbuster had sand and he'd made a fight of it before he'd been overwhelmed and killed.

Behind him, Kilcoyn heard Delagrange retching, whispering, "My God, my God," over and over again. With the muzzle of his rifle the marshal pushed on the door and it creaked open. Kilcoyn stepped inside the room, holding the glowing lamp above his head. Light spilled onto the bed where a middle-aged woman still sat upright, her back bolstered by pillows. An open Bible and a few medicine bottles stood on a table by her side. The front of the woman's nightgown was stained scarlet, and the horror of her death and the manner of her dying were still frozen on her face. She had been too sick to get up and help her husband, that much was clear, and she'd been shot where she lay. On the floor at the foot of the bed was a young girl of about eleven or twelve. Once she'd had long hair the color of corn silk, but most of that was now gone, the top of her head a red, raw cap of blood.

Kilcoyn stepped back to the main room of the cabin. "In there?" Delagrange asked, his eyes red in a chalk white face. A thin strand of drool hung from his chin.

The marshal nodded. "His wife and daughter. The girl was scalped."

Delagrange's face turned even sicker, but his anger flared when the Pawnee, his own face as unexpressive as carved mahogany, stepped into the cabin. "Damn you!" the lieutenant yelled, directing all his anger and pent-up horror on the scout. "Why do you do that? Why do you scalp and mutilate that way?"

His eyes calm, the Pawnee shrugged. "Scalping we learned from the white man. He taught us much."

"Let it go, Lieutenant," Kilcoyn said. "It wasn't the Pawnee's fault. He wasn't here."

Delagrange fought a visible battle with himself,

then took a deep breath and said, "I'm sorry, Kuruk. I—I was just upset with the deaths, I guess."

The face of the man called Kuruk, the Pawnee name for bear, remained without expression. "When a man dies, he goes only from one room to another. Death is not to be feared."

The Indian turned on his heel and walked outside.

"Lieutenant, you'd better get used to this kind of thing real fast," Kilcoyn said without rancor. "If you don't, you'll end up drinking yourself to death or putting a bullet in your brain like a lot of other frontier officers who couldn't take it have done before you."

Delagrange tried to speak, but the words would not take shape. After a while he collected himself and said stiffly, "Thank you, Marshal. I'll take your advice under consideration." But the young lieutenant seemed to have a need to explain his reaction to the deaths of the farmer and his family. "I guess I vented my spleen on Kuruk because he was the only Indian within hearing distance."

"I have the feeling you'll be seeing plenty more soon," Kilcoyn said. "I hope you have enough spleen to go around."

"After this, I believe I'll have enough and plenty to spare." Delagrange stepped toward the door. "I'll organize a burial detail. At least we can lay these people away decent."

Kilcoyn shook his head. "Ground's too hard for that. It would take you all day and most of tomorrow to dig holes deep enough. Have your men bring the boy's body in here and lay him out on the table."

For a moment the officer looked puzzled, but then understanding dawned on his face and he did as he was told. As a couple of soldiers carried the dead youth into the cabin, Kilcoyn stepped outside. He and Masterson searched a shed behind the smoke house. They found what they were looking for and returned to the cabin.

As Delagrange watched, the two lawmen splashed the coal oil they'd found over the floor and walls. That done, Masterson looked around and found an old newspaper. He tore off a strip, set it alight and threw it on the floor, then another. Immediately the oil burst into flame, and he and Kilcoyn stepped quickly outside.

Despite the snow, the timbers of the cabin were tinder-dry and they caught fire quickly. The roaring flames splashed shifting shades of gold and scarlet across the grim faces of the watching men.

"You have any words, Lieutenant?" Kilcoyn asked.

The officer shook his head, still looking sick. "None that I can find."

"Me neither," Kilcoyn said. He glanced around at Masterson and the troopers. "Anybody got words?"

There was no answer and Kilcoyn nodded. "Then we'll take it that if we knew the right words we'd gladly say them. I guess that's enough."

Delagrange watched the cabin burn for a few minutes, then mounted up and motioned his troopers and the Pawnee to follow. Kilcoyn and Masterson stayed a while longer. Then they too swung into the saddle and went after the others.

About fifty yards from the cabin, at the edge of the grass meadow, the lieutenant and the Pawnee suddenly stopped and looked back at Kilcoyn. Delagrange stood in the stirrups and beckoned the marshal forward.

Kilcoyn reined up beside them and saw something he had not noticed earlier because of the heavy snow. A buffalo skull, some shreds of meat still clinging to the bone, had been impaled on a post oak branch stuck into the ground. On the forehead were painted a red diamond and beside it what looked like some kind of black insect. Two jagged streaks of yellow lightning completed the picture.

"What does it mean?" Kilcoyn asked, his eyes sliding from Delagrange to the Pawnee. The Indian's eyes were guarded as he pointed to the diamond with the muzzle of his rifle. "Star," he said. The rifle muzzle moved to the insect. "Black grasshopper means death." The rifle shifted again to the lightning streaks. "This means the enemy will be struck down."

"Is it Star Blanket's *carte de visite*?" Delagrange asked, his eyes nervously moving toward the burning cabin.

The Pawnee answered. "Yes, it is Star Blanket, but he left this for another star man."

Delagrange looked confused. "I don't understand."

Kilcoyn nodded, now realizing what the symbolism on the skull meant. "I do, Lieutenant. The diamond represents me. I'm the other star man because of the badge I wear on my chest. The old Cheyenne wanted to tell anyone who might happen this way why he attacked the cabin and murdered the settlers. He's taking his revenge because a white man killed his son. And that white man was me."

The Pawnee smiled. "All this I know. Now Star Blanket will kill you very soon, I think."

"He's tried before," Kilcoyn said. "I'm still here."

The Pawnee's smile widened into a grin. "Faugh, the marshal is a mighty warrior. He killed Scar, and Scar too was a great warrior. The marshal does not fear Star Blanket?"

Kilcoyn shook his head. "I do not fear Star Blanket. He is nothing to me."

"Then it is good. A man who is afraid hears a rustle in every bush."

Suspicion fleeted across the face of Delagrange. "Kuruk, how did you know the marshal killed Star Blanket's son?"

"Such news travels on the wind," the Pawnee said. "I know what I know."

Later, as they rode back toward the others, Masterson was silent, but every now and then his eyes slanted speculatively to Kilcoyn.

"Out with it, Bat," the marshal said. "I know you've got something stuck in your craw."

"All right, John, then I'll say my piece. First thing,

do you trust that Pawnee? And second thing, did you mean it back there when you told him you weren't scared of Star Blanket?

"First answer . . ." Kilcoyn smiled. "No, I don't trust the Pawnee. I think he's hiding something, or maybe he knows about the money we're carrying. It was him who led the lieutenant right to us, remember? That's quite a feat in wide-open country like this, even for an Indian."

"And what about Star Blanket? Does he scare you?"

Kilcoyn smiled again. "What do you think?"

The sheriff shrugged, snow turning his mustache white so that he looked like an old man. "I know I'm scared of him, John. That's what I think."

"Then there's your answer," Kilcoyn said, leaving Masterson still puzzled and no wiser than he was before.

8

The Vultures Gather

When Kilcoyn and the soldiers rejoined the others, Lieutenant Delagrange insisted they ride for Pettyman's stockade at once rather than risk getting caught in the open by the Cheyenne.

Kilcoyn saw the logic in the officer's decision, and he told O'Neil to rouse Jenny from sleep and get her mounted. The girl protested at first, but, walking stiffly from the cold, she was soon swayed by Delagrange's assurances of a hot bath and soft bed when they reached the stockade.

They rode through the night, heading into a razor-sharp gale driving a wall of snow. The Pawnee took his place well ahead of the column. Around them the dark land was silent but for the ceaseless talk of the wind and the lonesome calls of hunting coyotes. The soldiers sat slumped in their saddles, their heads nodding in sleep, and their wet guidon slapped at the air with the noise of a stranded fish.

The riders reached the north fork of the Dry Cimarron just as the gray dawn was breaking. The river was low from the long summer drought, a domed sandbank rising out of the water in midstream, and thin ice had begun to lace along both banks. The snow had slowed to a few random flakes tossing in the breeze, but the morning was bitter cold, the breaths of men and horses smoking in the frosted air.

Kilcoyn sat his horse and looked across to the other side of the river. To his left an Indian village sprawled along the bank, wood smoke rising from the tops of tall lodges made either of painted buffalo hide or brown government canvas. A pony herd of around two hundred animals grazed on sparse bunchgrass beyond the encampment and lean dogs, their ribs showing, wandered everywhere.

Kilcoyn calculated there were as many as forty or fifty warriors in the camp and three times that number of women and children.

He let his gaze shift to T. J. Pettyman's settlement, a spawning annex of hell scattered from the river to the base of a volcanic ridge a couple of hundred yards beyond the bank. Dozens of sod shanties were built without order of any kind, as though they'd decided to wander off into the prairie and lost their way. Close to the riverbank were a livery stable and a timber warehouse built to house buffalo hides. To their right stood a larger sod shack with a rickety false front, a roughly painted sign nailed to its warped planks that read T. J. PETTYMAN'S SALOON AND

GENERAL STORE. And shoulder-to-shoulder with the saloon stood another low building, with sod walls and a peaked canvas roof. A wooden board tacked to the front of the canvas bore the word HOTEL.

Of Pettyman's stockade, little remained except for a grassy mound and a few wood posts slanting out of the ground here and there. Kilcoyn guessed that the fort had been cannibalized over time for its timbers, hard to come by in this part of the country. For a number of years there had been little by way of Indian attacks here on the Dry Cimarron and Pettyman probably felt justified in dismantling his stockade, no doubt turning a large profit for the lumber.

"Not much of a place is it, Marshal?" Lieutenant Delagrange asked as he reined up his horse alongside Kilcoyn's dun. "But there's usually a hundred buffalo hunters and fur traders here at any given time, so you'll be safe until the Cheyenne hostiles are rounded up and Star Blanket is hanged."

Kilcoyn ignored the young officer's statement and nodded toward the Indian encampment. "What about them? Some of those ponies are painted for war."

Delagrange shrugged. "Pettyman has been appointed acting Indian agent until we can move the Sioux to the new reservation at Fort Peck in the Montana Territory." The lieutenant smiled. "Paint or no paint, those are beaten blanket Indians, Marshal. They won't give you any trouble."

"I've heard that kind of assurance from a soldier

before, a lieutenant like you," Kilcoyn said. "He was
talking about a band of beaten Comanche he was
chasing down to the Staked Plains country." He
paused for a few moments, remembering, then said,
"As I recall, it didn't work out the way he planned.
Those beaten Indians turned on him at Yellow House
Canyon and he ended up lucky to escape with his
hair. As it was, he had to hightail it and leave his
seven dead on the field."

Delagrange smiled. "That won't happen here, I assure you. Spotted Horse isn't Comanche and he isn't
hunting trouble."

"Maybe, maybe not," Kilcoyn said. "I just want
you to know how I feel."

The young officer waved his small command forward across the river, and Kilcoyn and the others
followed. Jenny looked exhausted and O'Neil didn't
seem to be in any better shape. It was difficult to tell
about Masterson. The sheriff rode slumped in the
saddle like a sack of grain, seemingly too tired to
even look at the sights around him. But all that was
deceptive. Masterson was a man with bark on him,
and in the past Kilcoyn had seen him endure hard
trails that forced stronger men to fall by the wayside.
He was already gaining a reputation in the West as
a brave, competent lawman and a named gunfighter.
The marshal knew that when the chips were down
he could wholly depend on Masterson and, to Kilcoyn, that was the measure of a man.

Lieutenant Delagrange dismounted his troopers

behind the livery stable, and while the soldiers made camp the officer left in search of Pettyman.

After leaving the horses at the stable, Kilcoyn and Masterson went looking for breakfast, O'Neil and Jenny following behind. All three men carried their rifles and Kilcoyn had slung his saddlebags over his shoulder.

Jenny spoke briefly to O'Neil, and the young man ran to catch up with Kilcoyn and said, "Jenny says she needs sleep more than she needs breakfast. We're going on to the hotel."

The marshal smiled. "Barry, I don't know that Pettyman's hotel is used to accommodating young ladies, but I guess you can go along and see what it's like."

O'Neil touched the brim of his plug hat. "We'll meet up with you later."

After the young man left, Kilcoyn and Masterson stepped into the saloon. It was a single, narrow room with a bar along one side made from timber planks and empty beer barrels. The only furnishings were a few tables and chairs, and a surprisingly expensive silvered glass mirror behind the bar that Pettyman must have brought up the trail from Texas. Beyond the bar there was a door covered with a canvas cloth that Kilcoyn guessed opened to the general store.

The hour was early and there was no one at the bar except the bartender, a prosperous-looking plump man in a brocade vest with five-dollar gold pieces for buttons. The man's round face was framed by enormous mutton-chop whiskers, and he was polishing a glass, ready for business, when the lawmen entered.

"Name's Hennessy—at least that's the name my mama told me I owned. What can I do for you gents?" he asked as the two lawmen stepped to the bar.

"We're looking for some grub, if you have any," Masterson said, his eyes doubtful.

"Well, you've come to the right place," the bartender said. "Andy Wilson, who runs the general store, was a range cook for ol' Richard King, down at the Santa Gertrudis. He's got a game leg, but he's a fair hand with buffalo steak an' eggs. You like buffalo steak?"

Masterson nodded. "Sets fine by me. How about you, John?"

"Sounds about right."

"Tell Andy to burn us each a steak and half-a-dozen eggs over easy," Masterson said.

"And we'd surely appreciate some of that coffee you have on the stove behind the bar there," Kilcoyn said.

The bartender nodded and poured coffee for both of them. "The chuck will cost you two bits, each," he said. "That sound reasonable to you?"

"Hungry man doesn't have much choice," Masterson said.

"Then I'll go talk to the cook." Hennessy disappeared into the store and Kilcoyn and Masterson took places at a table.

When the food came it was good, and Wilson had also provided some thick slabs of buttered sourdough bread and half a dried-apple-and-soda-cracker pie.

"This is excellent," Masterson said around a mouthful of steak. "Or is it just that hunger is the best sauce? I always say a man can't go wrong with prime steak and—"

The sheriff's eyes slid over Kilcoyn's shoulder, widening in surprise. "Well, I'll be," he whispered.

Kilcoyn turned and studied the two men who had walked into the saloon. One of them was Hank Poteet, his black eyes sly and knowing, the notched gun stuck in his waistband. The other was a small man with protruding front teeth in a thin-lipped mouth that seemed to be twisted in a permanent sneer. He wore two long-barreled Colts in crossed belts, an unusual gun rig at that time in the West, the holsters hanging low on his thighs.

Both men passed Kilcoyn's table, Poteet's crafty eyes moving to the saddlebags on the chair beside Kilcoyn, then sliding away again as though they were oiled. The other man gave the marshal a direct, bold stare, his pale blue eyes hard and challenging, letting Kilcoyn know that he was someone to be reckoned with.

Kilcoyn watched both men disappear into the general store, and Masterson let his pent-up breath hiss through his teeth. "John, know who that two-gun ranny is?" he asked. "I recognized him right off, saw him one time when I was freighting a load of buffalo robes into Wichita. Those who were with me told me who he was. They said he was pure poison and to have no part of him."

The big marshal shook his head. "No, I don't know him, but he sure thinks a lot of himself."

"Hell, John, an' so he should. That there was Frank Ivers as ever was."

Now the name sounded a sudden warning bell in Kilcoyn, and he brought to mind what he knew about the man.

Frank Ivers was a fast, deadly gunman who had discovered early that the Colt symbolized power and the ease with which a man could acquire money and instill fear in lesser men, whose only wish was to survive in a harsh, unforgiving environment.

At a time when every male Western citizen carried or owned a gun, named men of reputation were few and far between, perhaps as few as fifty or sixty out of the tens of thousands who lived in and around the booming cattle and mining towns. After Frank Ivers killed his fourth man, the word got abroad that he was a shootist of reputation and his name began to be mentioned in the same breath as Hickok, Wes Hardin, Bill Longley, Cullen Baker and Clay Allison.

As Kilcoyn recalled, Ivers was something of a child

prodigy. In 1866, when he'd just turned sixteen, he'd come up the trail to the New Mexico Territory with twelve hundred head of Goodnight-Loving cattle, and killed his first man at Fort Sumner in the spring of that year.

But the hard work of the cattle drive did not appeal to Ivers, and he quickly discovered he could kill and get paid for it if he was efficient and discreet.

He'd signed on as a range detective for big outfits in Texas and Montana and for several years had drifted into the country before disappearing again, like a puff of smoke, leaving dead men behind him, usually ragged nesters, sodbusters and flat-footed sheepherders.

Ivers was a man without a sense of right or wrong, and he thought no more of killing a man, woman or child than he would a rabbit.

It was said, Kilcoyn recalled, that Frank Ivers had killed twenty men and probably many more than that. Away from the open range, where he shot his victims down at a distance with a rifle and worked with admirable discretion, he was a loud, arrogant bully, quarrelsome in drink, and not a man to be trifled with.

Recently he had outdrawn and killed Jim Goode, a deadly Texas gunfighter, and Kilcoyn recalled that just a few weeks ago Ivers had killed a man named Rafton in a saloon in Amarillo.

The fact that Frank Ivers was here at Pettyman's with a lowlife like Hank Poteet was bad news. So far

Ivers had managed to use the law and work within it, but ten thousand dollars could tempt a man to cross the line.

This was also a fact that was not lost on Masterson. "John," he said, his voice low and urgent, "do you reckon Ivers knows what we're carrying?" He moved across the table, closer to Kilcoyn, his voice dropping to a whisper. "The ransom money, I mean."

Kilcoyn nodded. "I'm sure of it."

"But how could he know we were here?"

"He didn't. I think he was on our trail and came by Pettyman's for supplies. It was just our bad luck that he showed up when we did."

"What do we do now?"

"We just sit tight, Bat. I reckon it's gonna be real easy to get yourself killed around here, so don't stick your neck out."

The sheriff was taken aback. "Hell, John, I don't intend to, not with Frank Ivers in town I don't. I'm fast on the draw, as you know, but I don't think I'm in his class."

Kilcoyn was just finishing a last cup of coffee when Ivers and Poteet stepped out of the general store and entered the saloon. Poteet was walking ahead, carrying coffee, sugar and a slab of bacon, but Ivers' hands were free.

The two men walked past Kilcoyn and Masterson, but then, as he reached the door, Ivers turned so he was facing them. He backed out, a sneer on his face, and let the door swing shut behind him.

It seemed Frank Ivers was a careful man.

Kilcoyn rose and stretched, and threw some money on the table. "Come on, Bat, let's go. I don't like the look of the hotel; too crowded and close. But what say you we head back to the livery and grab some shut-eye?"

"Shut-eye! John, we can't sleep with Ivers and Poteet in town."

The marshal smiled. "Oh, yes, we can. Just sleep with one eye open."

"I'll have both eyes open, because I won't sleep a wink."

As Masterson snored beside him in the empty stall where they'd bedded down, Kilcoyn lay on his back, worries large and small nagging at him. By nature a man who took each day as it came, he knew that to worry about tomorrow was to worship at the altar of a false god, yet the thoughts crowding into Kilcoyn's brain would not let him be.

How were Angela and Doc? Would Jake Pride kill them at once if he refused to pay the ransom and went to the gun instead? And what of Frank Ivers? When would he make his move? It wouldn't happen here at the settlement with the Army close, so Ivers must plan to strike somewhere between Pettyman's and Black Mesa. Ivers was good with a gun, the best there was some said—could he match that kind of skill? Bat Masterson didn't scare easily, but even he didn't relish the idea of bracing Ivers, and Bat, too, was one of the best.

Kilcoyn shook his head, clearing his gloomy thoughts. He had bridges to cross, but there was no point in stopping to build houses of worry on them. When the time came, he'd do what had to be done. He knew he wasn't afraid of dying. If he were, he'd have gotten out of the law enforcement business a long time ago.

It was all this not knowing that was the problem.

Kilcoyn tilted his hat over his eyes and willed sleep to come. Beside him, Masterson was snoring like a ripsaw running through a pine knot and Kilcoyn jabbed the sheriff hard in the ribs with his elbow. Masterson snorted and snuffled and fell silent. But only for a moment. He started snoring again, his mouth wide open, and Kilcoyn decided sleep was going to be impossible and rose to his feet.

The marshal stepped to the door of the livery stable and glanced outside. The wind had died to a thin whisper and flakes of snow were slowly drifting to the ground. It was not yet noon and the sun was nowhere in sight, the sky covered in thick, gray cloudbanks, building higher and blacker to the west. The air was ice-cold and smelled of wood smoke and the rank buffalo hides from the warehouse by the river.

Behind the stable, Lieutenant Delagrange's men, looking wet and miserable, huddled under rubber groundsheets, coaxing flame from small, reluctant fires. Of the young officer there was no sign.

Kilcoyn strolled to the corner of the building and studied the Indian encampment. The tall lodges were wreathed in shifting ribbons of blue smoke, and here and there blanket-wrapped warriors watched as women with babies on their backs kneeled to tend cooking fires. Maybe Delagrange had been right. The Sioux seemed content to remain where they were, unwilling to incur the wrath of the Army by becoming identified with Star Blanket and his renegade Cheyenne.

When he stepped back to the front of the stable, a cluster of men in deep conversation outside the saloon caught his eye. Frank Ivers was doing the talking, his head lowered confidentially, Poteet standing beside him, grinning like a predatory rodent. Listening in rapt attention was the Pawnee, who every now and then seemed to ask a question. But it was the fourth man who made Kilcoyn look, then look again.

That man was Caleb Early.

The presence of Early at the settlement dismayed Kilcoyn. Had he come after Jenny? Or was he throwing in with Ivers? That seemed to be the case when the gunman laughed, slapped Early on the back and ushered him into the saloon. Poteet and the Pawnee remained outside. Perhaps warned by a sixth sense that many Indians possessed, the Pawnee's black eyes slanted to Kilcoyn, aware, but revealing nothing.

The man called Kuruk whispered to Poteet, and

the other man turned and looked at the marshal. His mouth widened in a grin and he raised his right hand to eye level, pointed at Kilcoyn, two fingers extended. Poteet's thumb came down on the base of his forefinger like the hammer of a gun, then he laughed and stepped into the saloon. The Pawnee remained where he was for a few moments, gauging the marshal's reaction. Then he too walked inside.

Kilcoyn shook his head, badly irritated by Poteet's aggressive gesture. He couldn't very well arrest a man for pointing a finger at him. The marshal fought down the primitive urge to go after the little outlaw and smash him to a bloody pulp. As he calmed himself, he realized his hesitation had probably been just as well—because at that moment he'd wanted to kill Poteet real bad.

Kilcoyn let the gray day wear on until three, then he woke Masterson and told him what he'd seen outside the saloon.

"John, so you reckon Early has thrown in with Ivers?" the sheriff asked, settling his hat on his head.

"I'm sure of it," Kilcoyn answered. "That's why we're pulling out tonight."

"What about the soldiers?"

"We'll waken O'Neil and Jenny. Then, as soon as it gets dark, we'll take the horses to the other side of the settlement, near the old stockade. We'll move one horse at a time. Attract less attention that way and maybe, with a bit of luck, we won't arouse suspicion."

Masterson nodded. "Get us a head start on Ivers and the rest, especially the Pawnee. I believe that Indian could track a minnow through a Louisiana swamp."

"And that's why we're going to need a head start," Kilcoyn said, his frowning face revealing his growing concern. "And the longer the better."

9

A Woman for Sale

The hotel was a series of tiny rooms arranged shotgun-style along the length of the building. Each room had a canvas door curtain and was separated from its neighbors by a partition of the same material. Several oil lamps hung from ceiling beams, though their pale glow did little to lift the gloom of the place. The hotel smelled of man sweat, buffalo hides, chewing tobacco, unwashed clothing and the rank odor of the lamps, fueled by either coal or skunk oil. Someone sleeping off a drunk snored loudly, and as Kilcoyn and Masterson stepped through the warped timber door a rat scuttled away from under their feet. Halfway along the hallway, O'Neil squatted outside Jenny's room, his Henry across his knees, head bent in sleep. Wary of waking an armed man from uneasy slumber, Kilcoyn stopped when he was a couple of yards from O'Neil and called the Irishman's name.

O'Neil woke instantly, his hands tightening on the

rifle. But then he turned and saw the marshal, and climbed to his feet, groaning slightly as his cramped muscles worked loose. "I thought I'd better keep guard outside Jenny's room," he said. "There's a lot of men around who haven't see a pretty woman, or any other kind of woman, in a long while."

"Guard stays awake, Barry," Masterson chided, his smile taking the barb out of it. "We could've snuck up on you and cut your throat quicker'n scat."

The young man nodded. "I guess I dropped off a while back."

"The time for sleep is over," Kilcoyn said, his face grim. "Caleb Early is here."

"Early, here?"

"Indeed he is," Masterson answered. "And from now until we leave this place, you step real careful, Barry. Early is a cold-blooded killer who means you harm. Believe me, there's nothing more dangerous than a coward with a gun."

"Maybe he'll mean me even more harm when he hears I plan on making Jenny my wife," O'Neil said. "When are we leaving?"

"As soon as it gets dark," Kilcoyn said.

Quickly he told O'Neil about Frank Ivers and how the man had been seen talking to Early and the Pawnee. Then he outlined his plan for leaving the settlement without being seen.

"Now wake Jenny," Kilcoyn said. "You two are bound to be hungry, but I don't want you going anywhere near the saloon. Bat and me will buy supplies at the general store and meet you at the livery stable in thirty minutes."

"Do you think that's wise, John?" O'Neil asked. "You're carrying the saddlebags with the money in them. If Ivers is at the saloon and is as bad a man as you say, he might be tempted to go after you right there and then."

"I'll take that chance," Kilcoyn said. "Now wake Jenny."

"How's the weather outside?" O'Neil asked.

"What difference does it make?" Masterson asked. "We still have to leave."

O'Neil shook his head. "Bat, it's not about leaving. I want to make a picture of the settlement and real Indian-fighting soldiers before I go. When places like this and men like those are gone, they're gone forever, and we'll never see their like again, not in our lifetime or in any other."

Kilcoyn's first inclination was to refuse, but when he thought it through he realized it could work to their advantage. Outside of the towns, photographers were rare in the West, and when one appeared with his camera and tripod, he was bound to attract a curious crowd. It was unlikely that Early would try anything with so many onlookers and soldiers near, and O'Neil could occupy Delagrange and his men while the horses were quietly taken from the stable.

"You make your pictures, Barry," Kilcoyn told him. "But you're going to be real busy and your head will be under a black cloth most of the time, so Bat and me will take Jenny with us. I want her close, where we can protect her from her father. Now go wake her like I told you." The marshal smiled. "And by the way, congratulations on your upcoming marriage. Jenny will make a wonderful wife."

"That is, if she says yes," Masterson said.

O'Neil nodded, smiling. "She surely did already. She said as soon as she set eyes on me she knew we'd be married one day. Told me she sees things like that before they happen."

"Heard of that," Masterson said, looking uneasy as he shifted from one foot to another. "Never did cotton to the idea much."

After O'Neil left to fetch Jenny, Kilcoyn and Masterson waited outside until she appeared. The girl's eyes were full of sleep and her hair was tousled, but Masterson gave her an elegant little bow and declared her to be "as pretty as dollar cotton." And Kilcoyn was inclined to agree.

With Jenny between them, the two lawmen stepped into the saloon. Frank Ivers, Early, Poteet and the Pawnee stood at the bar, sharing a bottle of Old Forrester bourbon. At a time in the West when whiskey was delivered to saloons in fifty-five-gallon barrels and then decanted into bottles by the bartender, Old Forrester was the first bourbon to be sold already bottled. It was wildly expensive and still something of a rarity on the frontier, and indicated to Kilcoyn the importance Ivers placed on himself.

Another man, in a black broadcloth suit and

striped silk vest, sat at a table, a china coffeepot and cup and saucer in front of him. He was tall and flashily handsome, with curled, perfumed hair that fell to his shoulders and a well-trimmed mustache. He regarded Kilcoyn and Masterson with mild interest, then his eyes moved to the girl and lingered.

Ignoring the sidelong glances in his direction of the men at the bar, Kilcoyn hitched his saddlebags higher on his shoulder and he and Masterson made to walk past the man at the table toward the general store.

The man's voice stopped them. "Just hold on there, lawmen," he said. "I'm T. J. Pettyman. Welcome to my humble establishment. The soldier boy told me you'd probably be stopping by. I'm sorry. He didn't tell me your names."

Kilcoyn turned to Pettyman. "I'm Deputy United States Marshal John Kilcoyn."

"Sheriff William B. Masterson," Bat said.

"Would that be Bat Masterson?" Pettyman asked. "Out of Dodge?"

"The same," Bat said. "Dodge and other places."

At the bar, Ivers turned and studied the sheriff for a few moments, the presence of a named gunfighter piquing his interest. Kilcoyn saw the man's calculating eyes move from Masterson's expensive Texas boots to his white Stetson. Not one to wear a mackinaw, Masterson had changed out of his slicker into an ankle-length box coat made by Dunn and Simpson, Gentlemen's Tailors of Savile Row, London.

Sometimes called a coach coat, the garment was of heavy, gray English wool, with several layers of short capes at the shoulders. The coat covered Masterson's guns, but Ivers had seen all he'd wanted to see. His contemptuous eyes dismissed the sheriff as nothing more than a frontier dandy with an inflated reputation and he went back to his bottle, smiling to himself.

Kilcoyn had been watching Ivers closely; now he became aware that Pettyman was talking to him again. "And the pretty young lady is?"

"Miss Jenny Early," Kilcoyn said as he gauged the man's reaction.

If Pettyman knew the girl's father was standing at the bar, watching Kilcoyn with ill-concealed hatred, he didn't let it show. "Good to make your acquaintance, Miss Early," he said.

The man sat in thought for a few moments, then said, "Marshal Kilcoyn, I've had dealings with the law before, and lawmen like to hear things straight up, no shilly-shallying around if you know what I mean."

Kilcoyn felt Caleb Early's eyes on him and he was tense and ready. But to Pettyman he said sociably, "What you say sounds about right."

"Then I'll get right to the point, Marshal. How much for the girl? Come, man, be plain. Give me a figure. I assure you, I can be generous."

Kilcoyn shook his head. "She's not for sale."

Pettyman sighed and waved an expansive hand.

"Look around you, Marshal Kilcoyn. This settlement is full of men just in from weeks, sometimes months, on the plains, and every man jack of them badly needs a woman." The man smiled, making an effort to show his sincerity. "I can go as high as two hundred dollars, though I fear at that price you'll be taking advantage of me."

"Nothing doing, Pettyman," Kilcoyn said. "Like I told you, she's not for sale."

Pettyman tried to hide his disappointment. "If you change your mind . . ."

"You'll be the first to know."

Kilcoyn turned and stepped toward the store. Early had been drinking heavily, and when he deliberately stepped into Kilcoyn's path the effect of the whiskey had loosened his tongue and showed in his bloodshot, belligerent eyes. "Damn you, Kilcoyn, the little slut is mine to sell. I'll take the two hundred and—"

Kilcoyn threw a left from the shoulder, his big, hard-boned fist crashing into the point of Early's chin. The man's head snapped back and he collapsed, rushing to join his shadow on the floor.

Masterson whirled to face the men at the bar, his hand on his gun. But Ivers had made no move, except to lift his glass to his lips. He carefully laid the glass back on the bar and looked down at the groaning Early with a noticeable lack of compassion. "Talkative feller, ain't he?" he said to no one in particular.

Masterson ignored Ivers and followed Kilcoyn and

113

Jenny into the store, backing up all the way, his blue eyes never leaving the grinning gunman.

The purchases Kilcoyn made were few—a slab of salt pork, flour, coffee and a little tea. Jenny caught Masterson by the arm and pointed to a jar filled with red-and-white-striped sticks of candy. "What are those?"

Masterson smiled. "Peppermint candy sticks. Haven't you seen those before?"

The girl shook her head. "I've never had candy. How is it?"

"It's sweet," Masterson said. "Like sugar."

"Like molasses?"

Masterson nodded. "Yes, something like molasses."

"Can I have one?" Jenny asked.

Andy Wilson, the storekeeper, opened the jar and handed a stick of the candy to the girl. "Yes, you can have one, little lady. It's on the house."

Jenny licked the candy and her eyes widened in surprise. "It's good," she said.

Masterson slapped his hands and did a little jig of delight. "Hot dang, so it is! I think I'll try one myself."

"Yours," Wilson said, opening the jar again, "will cost you a nickel."

When Kilcoyn and the others left the store and walked into the saloon, Early was sitting groggily at a table, his eyes rolling in his head.

"My offer for the woman still goes, Marshal,"

Pettyman said as Kilcoyn walked past. "Anytime you want to reconsider, just say the word."

Kilcoyn nodded. "I'll bear that in mind."

Masterson again backed out, covering Kilcoyn.

"Hey, Marshal," Ivers called.

Kilcoyn turned. "What do you want, Ivers?"

The man shrugged, a grin on his small, mean mouth. "Me, I want nothing, at least not right now. I'm being polite, like. I just wanted to say I'll see you around."

"Not if I see you first," Kilcoyn said, his warning plain.

Outside the snow had stopped, but the wind was rising again and the light had changed, crowding gray and murky over the settlement. A mule wagon loaded with reeking hides, its wheels churning black mud, rolled past the saloon toward the warehouse. Out among the surrounding shacks men were beginning to stir. Dignified buffalo shooters in fringed buckskins, each carrying a Sharps big fifty, rubbed shoulders with lowly skinners in rough work boots and plaid shirts crusted with dried blood. Fur trappers in coonskin hats stopped to talk with a couple of men who might have been professional gamblers, the sartorial grandeur of their frock coats patched and faded, like they'd recently fallen on hard times. Stepping warily were a few hard-eyed men with guns on their hips, their careful gaze falling on nothing in particular, but seeing everything. And there were others; ragged, hollow-eyed men, the flotsam and jetsam of the frontier, men who had drifted into the settlement and, whether from lack of funds for a good horse or because of whiskey or sheer apathy, had never left.

It was a volatile mix that could explode into violence at any time and often did.

One by one, or in twos and threes, men were walking toward the saloon, eyes turning to Jenny, some in open admiration, others hot with lust, undressing her in their minds.

Kilcoyn and Masterson ushered the girl toward the livery stable, in time to see O'Neil walk toward them, looking hunched and dejected, his hands in his pockets, the Henry dangling from the crook of his left arm.

"It's no good," the young man yelled when he was still some distance away.

"Look at this light. Even I can't make a picture in the dark."

Kilcoyn glanced at the sky. There was still an hour of daylight left, but the building black clouds hung low over the settlement, dark, dreary and ominous. Confused by the waning light, the coyotes were already talking on the plains and the night birds were calling.

Kilcoyn stepped close to O'Neil. "Barry, make a picture of Delagrange and his men." The young man opened his mouth to object, but the marshal rolled over him. "Light or no light, go through the motions.

116

You must keep those soldiers occupied until we get the horses out of the livery stable."

O'Neil glanced miserably at the sky. "All right, I'll do it, but the picture won't turn out. I can tell you that."

"Delagrange won't know. Tell him it's going to be great. Now get your stuff and round up those soldier boys. Just keep them away from the front of the barn. Just say the light is better at the back. Say anything, but get them there."

O'Neil's eyes moved to Jenny and softened. "I see you got a candy stick," he said.

"Yes, she does, and me too," Masterson said. "It's been a long time. I'd say I haven't eaten peppermint candy since I was a kid growing up in Canada." He extended the candy to O'Neil, the end of it sucked to a point. "Want a lick?"

The young man smiled and shook his head. "Thanks all the same, Bat, but I think I'll pass."

The sheriff shrugged. "Your loss. It's right tasty."

Kilcoyn badly wanted to tell Masterson that the variety of loud smacking noises he was making as he sucked on the candy was irritating the hell out of him, but he let it pass. There was no point in getting Bat riled when what lay ahead called for a cool head.

Kilcoyn led Jenny and Masterson into the barn while O'Neil went in search of Lieutenant Delagrange. A few minutes later the young man came back and lugged his camera and tripod outside.

"Delagrange mentioned the light to me," he

warned the marshal. "He may be an officer but he isn't dumb."

"Just keep him busy for a while," Kilcoyn said urgently. "As soon as you get him posed, we'll lead out the horses."

After a wait of ten minutes to allow O'Neil time to get set up, Kilcoyn walked to the corner of the stable and looked back at the soldiers' encampment. O'Neil had assembled Delagrange and his men well behind the rear wall of the livery, where they couldn't see what was going on at the front.

The young officer stood with his grinning men clustered around him. Delagrange was self-consciously striking a heroic pose, his right hand thrust into his coat in a military posture. O'Neil had his head buried under a black cloth, his left arm on the lens of his camera, confusing the milling soldiers by yelling instructions that no one seemed to understand.

Masterson was suddenly at Kilcoyn's shoulder, amusement in his eyes. "Delagrange looks like that famous Yankee general I saw in a newspaper one time. What's his name?"

"George B. McClellan," Kilcoyn supplied absently, his eyes on the assembled soldiers.

"Yes, him. So you see it too, John. I reckon he's a dead ringer. He's got the same—"

"I suggest we get started, Bat," Kilcoyn said, cutting the man's ruminations short. "We don't have much time."

Kilcoyn quickly saddled his dun and then helped Jenny with her horse. Masterson led his stud to the front of the barn, O'Neil's pack mule in tow.

Making little sound, Kilcoyn and the others led the animals from the livery stable and walked them to the ruined stockade. They had not been seen, and the night was now beginning to fall around them, drawing a dark veil over the settlement. And the snow had started to come down again.

Now all they had to do was wait for O'Neil to get there and they could leave.

Ten minutes passed, then fifteen. But there was no sign of O'Neil. Kilcoyn's annoyance grew. Where was the man? Across at the Indian camp, fires were winking in the dark, and from somewhere among the pony herd a horse whinnied, then immediately fell silent.

Five more minutes agonizingly ticked by. Where was O'Neil?

Pettyman's saloon was doing a roaring business. Men came and went, a rectangle of yellow light splashing off and on across the muddy entrance as the door opened and closed. The hide wagon rolled past, empty now, the driver smoking a smoldering pipe that threw tiny red sparks into the air.

Suddenly there was a commotion down by the livery stable. Kilcoyn heard Delagrange yelling orders, and equipment clattered as men ran to saddle their mounts.

"Damn it all, John," Masterson said. "Now our

biscuits are burning. George B. McClellan knows we're gone!"

Kilcoyn nodded. "Mount up. We're getting out of here."

"Without Barry?" Jenny asked, concern tangled in her face.

"We'll leave his horse here and he can catch up later," Kilcoyn said, swinging into the saddle. "Now get on your pony."

The marshal watched as Jenny mounted. "Right, follow me," he said. But O'Neil's urgent yell stopped Kilcoyn and he reined in the dun.

His pants spattered with mud, the young man came running. "They've gone," he panted. "Just about every last one of them."

"Who?" Kilcoyn demanded.

"The Sioux. As soon as it got dark, the warriors just up and left. Took the pony herd and the young women and children and left everything else behind, including Spotted Horse and the rest of the old people."

"Where's Delagrange?" Kilcoyn asked.

"He's gone after them, and he's madder than hell."

10

Death in the Snow

As Kilcoyn and the others crossed the Cimarron, the shallow water was brown with silt, churned up by the passage of the Indian pony herd and the pursuing soldiers. Kilcoyn and the others crossed the river and rode south for a couple of miles before looping to the west.

After an hour the snow began to fall heavier, driven by a north wind that shrieked across the buffalo grass, and the four riders rode with their heads bent against the worsening weather, their breaths misting in the cold air.

A few miles to the south lay the lower fork of the Cimarron, and it was in Kilcoyn's mind to seek shelter there among the cottonwoods if the snow got any heavier.

The cold was intense, and getting worse by the minute. No one spoke, each wrapped in a personal cocoon of freezing misery.

Finally Masterson rode alongside the marshal and yelled against the pounding wind, "I reckon we should find a place to hole up, John, till this storm passes."

Kilcoyn turned in the saddle and looked back at Jenny and O'Neil. Their fronts were covered in a thick layer of snow. O'Neil, still weak from his wound, was gray-faced, hunched and silent. Jenny didn't look to be in any better shape and her pony was breathing hard, its head hanging.

Ahead of him, Kilcoyn saw only darkness and an impenetrable wall of snow, the distance hidden and the way made hazardous by cold and by the relentless, ravaging wind. The Sioux and Delagrange's soldiers were out there somewhere, and were probably faring no better than themselves. Even Masterson, a tough, enduring man, looked exhausted.

Reluctantly Kilcoyn decided they would have to seek the slim shelter of the riverbank and hope the blizzard would soon blow itself out.

He led the way south toward the Cimarron, and only knew he had reached the river when his dun balked on the edge of the bank, refusing to go further. Kilcoyn stood in the stirrups and looked around him. He could see little in the darkness and the wildly wheeling snow, but he was able to make out that there were no trees in sight, or anything else that might provide shelter. Angry at himself as a sudden feeling of helplessness swept over him, Kilcoyn told the others to remain where they were and swung his horse to the west along the bank, alert for the smallest sound, especially the wind talking among tree branches.

The storm tore savagely at him, and several times he felt the big dun falter and stumble. This stretch of the riverbank was bare of trees; only clumps of bunchgrass grew here and there, snow tangled among their roots.

Kilcoyn rode on for a few more minutes, finding no trees, only a barren wilderness of snow and wind, the dull gleam of water reminding him that he was very close to the river. If the dun stumbled and fell into the water, he would never get his clothes dry and would freeze to death. It was a worrisome thought and one that gave the marshal pause. This part of the river was obviously bare. Was there any point in risking his life by going farther?

Kilcoyn reined in his horse and his eyes searched ahead of him, trying to penetrate the darkness. Then, for a brief instant, the rampaging wind parted the snow . . . and he beheld a miracle.

Miracles come all by themselves, they cannot be summoned, and they usually arrive at unexpected moments and to those who least expect them. And right then John Kilcoyn was not expecting a miracle. Yet there it was, a ruined sod cabin, its roof fallen but its walls intact, squatting on a slight rise about thirty yards from the bank of the river.

Kilcoyn urged the dun forward and when he reached the cabin he swung out of the saddle. He left his horse with its reins trailing, and stepped to the doorway. Another miracle—the buffalo-hide door was dry and cracked but still intact. Kilcoyn swept it aside and walked into the ruin. It looked like the timber roof had collapsed several years before, and some of the beams were charred, probably the result of an Indian attack. The roof had broken in the middle and then both ends had fallen to the dirt floor, forming a V shape.

Bending over, Kilcoyn worked his way to the corner where the sidewall met the front. He thumbed a match into flame, and by its guttering light moved some debris out of the way, saving a dry packrat's nest, and soon cleared an area big enough for him and the others to sit. The corner was sheltered from the worst of the wind and the fallen roof gave some protection from the snow—and there was dry wood enough for a fire. Kilcoyn smiled, a welcome vision of salt pork, pan bread and hot coffee swimming into his head.

It was time to get the others.

More dead than alive from cold, Jenny, O'Neil and Masterson unsaddled their mounts and let them loose around the cabin, where there was grass in sheltered areas that were not yet covered by snow. O'Neil did the same for his pack mule, relieving the animal of its heavy burden. The animals would not wander far, being used to humans and needful of their closeness, and the cabin itself would give them shelter from the wind.

As the others crowded into the corner of the cabin, Kilcoyn started a fire against the wall, using the dry packrat's nest as kindling, and fed the blaze with fallen timbers from the roof.

The fire caught, spreading its warmth, and Kilcoyn grabbed the coffeepot. "I'm going down to the river for water."

Jenny looked at him gratefully. "I could sure use a cup," she said.

"Let me do it, John," Bat said, extending his hand, but Kilcoyn saw by the drawn expression on the sheriff's face that his heart wasn't in the offer.

The marshal shook his head. "Best you stay put and warm up, Bat. Besides, I need you here if there's Indian trouble."

Kilcoyn didn't expect an Indian attack, but it was his way of letting the man down gently. Masterson accepted it at face value. "If those redskins come anywhere near, I'll be ready for them, John," he said. "Depend on it."

Kilcoyn nodded. "I know you will."

He worked his way out of the cabin and then walked to the riverbank. The wind had shifted, now driving out of the west, but the night was still bitter cold, the snow slanting from a pitch-black sky.

The bank was broken down in places where animals had come to drink, and Kilcoyn worked his way onto a narrow strip of sand and dipped the coffeepot in the water. He held there for a few moments while the pot filled, then rose to his feet. He was about to walk back up the bank but froze in his tracks as the wind brought a fleeting sound to his ears.

Kilcoyn listened intently. There it was again, the faint *crack-crack* of rifles, far-off and indistinct. Had Delagrange caught up with the fleeing Sioux? But if he had, why was he shooting at them? An uneasiness in him, the marshal made his way back toward the cabin. Then another thought came to him—had the soldiers run into trouble, an ambush maybe?

Indians, the Cheyenne and Sioux included, were not much inclined to fight at night, but they would if pushed to it, especially if they thought the darkness and falling snow would give them a tactical advantage.

The Sioux were running in front of him with their women and children, and Delagrange would not have expected trouble—and the weather was against a pitched battle. But the warriors could have hung back from the rest, laid for him out in the darkness and opened up when the column appeared.

It was a possibility—a possibility that brought Kilcoyn a deal of concern and no comfort.

When he reentered the cabin he decided against saying anything to the others, including Masterson. Right now they all had enough to worry about without concerning themselves with the soldiers.

*   *   *

A new set of problems arrived with the dawn.

The horses had wandered off during the night, only Masterson's big stud staying close. The falling snow had covered their tracks and it took Masterson an hour to round them up, all but O'Neil's pack mule.

"I don't know where in tarnation she's gotten to," Masterson told Kilcoyn. "But she's wandered far, that's for sure. Damn gambler's ghost . . ." His voice died away into a string of muttered curses.

The decision was made to stash O'Neil's camera and other gear in the cabin and pick them up on the way back. The arrangement didn't set well with O'Neil, but Kilcoyn assured him there was no other way. They couldn't spare a horse to pack his equipment.

After a hasty breakfast, Kilcoyn and the others mounted up and headed west. The snow had stopped, and the sky was the color of washed-out denim and clear of cloud, but the bright morning was bitter cold. Snow lay four inches thick on the flat. Frost crusted the spiking leaves of the yucca and as the sun topped the distant Sangre de Cristo and began its climb, the light transformed the mesquite and wild plum bushes into delicate sculptures of glittering crystal.

The breaths of the four riders smoked in the frigid air, icy cold nipping at their cheeks, painting them red as though they were wearing rouge.

An early morning silence hung over the group, and for an hour the only sounds were the soft crump of hooves on the snow and the creak of saddle leather. Once they saw a small herd of bighorn sheep, down from the mountains to graze on the flat, and black-tailed jackrabbits ran from them in a panic, bouncing across the snow like rubber balls.

Kilcoyn estimated they were a day's ride from Black Mesa, but they would camp that night and make contact with Jake Pride the next morning, honoring the man's deadline with a day to spare. He reached inside his coat and found his watch. It was almost nine o'clock. All they had to do now was follow the Cimarron west and they would see the outline of the mesa before nightfall. As Masterson had described it, Black Mesa was a steep wall of granite almost five thousand feet high, capped by a black layer of iron-hard, volcanic rock.

Around the mesa lay wild, rugged country, hostile and unforgiving, a wilderness of craggy ridges, cone-shaped hills and deep canyons that even the Indians shunned. It was no place for a woman, and Kilcoyn wondered how Angela was holding up. He consoled himself with the fact that she was strong-willed, and that she'd spent most of her life around men and knew how to handle them. There was within Angela an enduring spark that flamed and grew bright in the hour of darkest adversity, whether while assisting her father with surgery or caring for cholera victims. It was a fire that Kilcoyn had not yet seen extinguished by fear or any other reason.

Angela would survive. She had to survive because Kilcoyn couldn't imagine his life without her.

The riders crossed the stark and empty land, talking little, each trying to cope with the cold and the raw wind as best they could. After an hour Masterson caught sight of the red-and-white pennon of Delagrange's cavalry guidon fluttering behind a low, hump-backed rise.

"I guess the soldiers are camped," he said, looking at Kilcoyn. "Must have given up on catching the Indians on account of the weather."

Kilcoyn reined in his bay and raised a hand, halting the others. His eyes scanned the rise, missing nothing, and his hand moved to the stock of the Winchester under his knee.

Masterson gave the marshal a sidelong glance and grinned. "John, I swear you look like an old hound dog on the prod, with its neck hair all raised up. What are you seeing?"

"It's what I'm not seeing that's bothering me, Bat. Delagrange knows there are hostiles around, but where are his pickets?"

The sheriff's gaze swept the rise, his face suddenly concerned. "I don't hear anything, either, John. It's almighty quiet."

Kilcoyn turned in the saddle. "Barry, shuck your rifle and stay here with Jenny. Bat and me will go on ahead to take a look-see."

O'Neil saw the urgency in the marshal's eyes and nodded. He slid his Henry from the scabbard and levered a round into the chamber.

"Let's go, Bat," Kilcoyn said.

The two lawmen approached the rise at a walk, rifles across their saddle horns.

A single cloud passed over the face of the sun, casting a brief, scudding shadow on the surrounding snow. Kilcoyn's dun tossed his head and snorted, the bit jangling loud in the taut silence. A coyote suddenly emerged from behind a cholla and trotted toward the fluttering guidon, then stopped, catching sight of the two riders. The skinny little animal remained where he was for a few moments, undecided, then turned tail and fled, scarring the virgin snow with tracks that were quickly filled with blue shadow.

Kilcoyn and Masterson topped the rise and reined in their mounts—and looked down on the scattered bodies of Lieutenant Delagrange and his detail.

Eleven men lay sprawled in death, four of them, including the young officer, lying in an almost straight line, shot off their horses at the same instant as they rode one behind the other. The seven survivors had dismounted and formed a circle around their fallen lieutenant, and tried to make a fight of it. But, as Kilcoyn kicked away snow from around the troopers' bodies, he saw only a handful of empty shells from their Springfield carbines. It looked like a large force of Indians, the fifty or so warriors who had fled Spotted Horse's village, had overwhelmed these men very quickly.

The Pawnee, the one man whose scouting skills could have perhaps saved them, was not among the dead. It seemed pretty clear to Kilcoyn that the scout had thrown in with Frank Ivers and had not ridden out with the soldiers.

The Indians had not stayed to mutilate the bodies, but Delagrange and a couple of his troopers had their heads crushed by war clubs. Reading the signs, it appeared to Kilcoyn that the lieutenant and the others had probably been wounded in the first volley and were no longer able to fight. But they were still very much alive when their brains were scattered.

Kilcoyn, standing amid the carnage, looked down at Delagrange, lying ghastly white. Frozen snow had collected in the hollows of his eyes and open mouth. He had been a West Point graduate, by act of Congress an officer and gentleman in a thoroughly modern army. Yet all his high-dollar education had brought him was death at the hands of a skin-clad savage wielding a stone war club.

Kilcoyn had seen this kind of thing before, but the stark reality of the brutal plains warfare never ceased to horrify him.

Masterson turned haunted eyes to the marshal. "These poor boys never stood a chance, did they, John?" He shook his head. "And I was starting to take a real liking to the lieutenant. He meant well, I guess."

The guidon had been stuck in the snow by one of the troopers who had made his last stand around Delagrange. Kilcoyn forced it deeper into the frozen ground, where it might serve as a marker for an Army burial party, if one ever came.

Masterson stepped closer to the marshal. "John, you reckon the Sioux will join up with Star Blanket's Cheyenne?"

Kilcoyn nodded. "Probably with them right now."

Masterson whistled through his teeth. "That's a right scary passel of Indians."

The marshal looked across the white prairie to the horizon and shivered. Later, remembering, he could not tell if it was from cold or if the goose had again taken wing.

11

Death in the Darkness

Kilcoyn and the others made camp that night in a shallow arroyo a couple of miles from the base of towering Black Mesa. The canyon was hemmed in by high ridges of volcanic rock, and juniper and sage grew along its narrow bottom where a stream bubbled, coming off the high mountains further to the west.

Kilcoyn was uneasily aware that the tracks of their four horses were cut deep into the frozen snow, an arrow pointing straight at their location for any curious Indian who happened to be passing by. But there was no way to cover the tracks and they could only live with the risk.

Masterson built a small fire among some fallen talus rocks close to the almost vertical north wall of the arroyo. A stunted juniper had forced its way through the tumbled boulders. Its branches would scatter the small amount of smoke from the flames and the smooth wall itself would act as a reflector for the heat.

They were now very close to Jake Pride and there were hostile Indians around, reasons enough for Kilcoyn to tell Masterson and O'Neil that the three of them should take turns standing guard throughout the night.

After they'd eaten and drank coffee, O'Neil took the first watch and headed for the mouth of the arroyo with his rifle.

There was little snow lying in the canyon. Masterson and Kilcoyn gathered enough grass from where the horses were grazing to make a soft bed for Jenny near the fire. The girl gratefully lay down, her head on her saddle. She pulled her blanket to her chin and her eyes lifted to Kilcoyn. "Marshal, do you think your friends are still alive?" she asked.

Kilcoyn looked at the girl across the guttering fire and nodded. "I'm sure of it. Angela is a strong woman, and Doc is tough and in the past he's proved his courage more than once."

Jenny was silent for a few moments, then she said quietly, "Yet one among us will die. And quite soon."

Masterson, who had retrieved the last inch of his stick candy from the pocket of his box coat and had been busily cleaning it of fluff and hair, glanced over at Jenny in shock. "Girl, that's a right scary thing to say. You sound like one of those black-eyed witch women they say live in the Tennessee hills."

The girl had an almost dreamy expression on her

face, her eyes fixed and distant. "My ma was born and raised in the Tennessee hills, Bat," she said. "And she had the gift. She knew when a body was going to die, knew it for certain sure long before it happened."

"No one's goin' to die, Jenny," Masterson said, the candy forgotten in his hand, "excepting maybe Jake Pride." He turned to Kilcoyn. "Isn't that a natural fact, John?"

Kilcoyn nodded and smiled at the girl. "Jenny, Bat and me won't let anything happen to you or anyone else. And I know Barry will back me up on that."

The girl shook her head. "What I see, I see. It can't be changed. Strong dreams always come true."

"Well, if that isn't enough to make a man swallow his tobacco and freeze his blood," Masterson said. He looked at the piece of candy in his hand for a few moments, then threw it into the fire. "All of a sudden I don't want any more of that."

Kilcoyn couldn't bring himself to chide Jenny for upsetting Masterson. After all, hadn't a goose been flying back and forth over his grave since he killed the Cheyenne Dog Soldier? But he felt something too, a vague, undefined uneasiness that kept clamoring at him, sounding a warning.

"Jenny, best you get some sleep," he said finally. "One way or another, tomorrow's going to be a long day."

"Not for one of us," the girl said. She gave Kilcoyn a slight smile. "Who knows? Maybe me."

Jenny closed her eyes, and around Kilcoyn and Masterson, the crowding darkness settled into a brooding silence, weighing on the two lawmen like the folds of a heavy cloak.

It was two in the morning when Kilcoyn relieved Masterson and took his turn at watch.

A moon had risen, haloed with frost, and a few lonesome stars showed in the night sky. Beyond the arroyo the land was dark, moonlight gleaming like dull steel on the snow lying on top of the rises, leaving the slopes inked in deep indigo blue. Nothing moved, not even the wind. It was as if the earth were holding its breath, waiting for what was to happen.

Out on the prairie and among the echoing, shadowed canyons the coyotes were calling, talking their hunger to all who would listen, and the icy air lay around Kilcoyn, sharp and brittle as shattered glass.

He moved his rifle to his left hand, flexing the numb fingers of his right, then stepped closer to the talus rock that stood waist high to a man at the mouth of the arroyo, its smooth surface rimed with frost.

Kilcoyn's breath smoked and he stamped his feet, trying to warm them, aware only when it was too late that his spurs were chiming loudly in the quiet.

A bullet *spaaanged!* off the top of the rock where he was standing and rebounded, viciously splitting the air close to Kilcoyn's head. Dropping quickly to one knee, he knew he had paid for his mistake.

He looked around the edge of the boulder and his

eyes searched the darkness. He had not seen the flash of the rifle, and nothing was moving out there. Kilcoyn got to his feet, lifted the Winchester chest high and waited.

A few moments later Masterson and O'Neil were at his side. "Heard the shooting, John," Masterson whispered. "Is it Indians, or Jake?"

Kilcoyn shook his head. "I don't know, but I'm guessing it's Indians." He waved to O'Neil. "Barry, find some cover at the other side of the arroyo. We don't want to bunch together."

The young man crouched low and ran. When he reached his position, he called out in a hoarse stage whisper, "I'm here, John."

"Just lay low and watch for a target," the marshal answered.

A minute ticked past, then another.

Masterson turned to Kilcoyn. "Whoever it was is gone. Maybe just a passing redskin trying his luck."

"Could be," the marshal answered, his eyes on the snow-streaked darkness. "But right now I'm not counting on it."

Masterson hesitated a few moments, then said, "Do you set store by what Jenny said? I mean, about one of us catching a bullet."

Kilcoyn shook his head. "I don't know. I don't know the right or wrong of a thing like that. Maybe one day I'll speak to a preacher and ask him."

"Jenny's from the hills," Masterson said. "And her mother was a witch woman before her; she said so herself. You know, when the Comanche had me and a bunch of other buffalo hunters penned up at Adobe Walls back in seventy-four, there came a break in the shooting. Well, Billy Dixon took to reminiscing about this and that and where he'd been and such. Billy told us about the Tennessee hills and the witch women, and he said they can see things the rest of us can't."

Kilcoyn smiled. "Then we should bring Jenny out here. Maybe she could see where the Indians are at."

"This isn't a heap of hilarity, John," Masterson said, his voice faintly chiding. "It's a big mistake to take a woman like Jenny too lightly. She has the gift."

A bullet thudded into the side of the arroyo, followed a split second later by the flat report of a rifle. Once again, Kilcoyn failed to see the flash of the gun and held his fire. But across from him O'Neil shot once, then again.

"See anything?" Kilcoyn yelled.

"Thought I saw a shadow," O'Neil replied. "Could be I did."

The marshal swore under his breath. Shooting at shadows wasn't going to get the job done. All O'Neil was doing was spitting on the handle of the axe.

A couple of guns fired out in the darkness, the bullets kicking up spiteful spurts of dirt and snow around Kilcoyn and Masterson. This time Kilcoyn saw a flash. He fired at the spot where he'd seen the rifle flare, then dusted two fast shots to the left and right of the location. He was rewarded by a sudden shriek of pain and surprise.

Masterson let out a whoop of triumph. "That got a double-danged hair-lifter's attention right quick, and no mistake."

A fusillade of shots hammered around the entrance to the arroyo as the Indians opened fire. All three men shot at the orange gun flares. Then, as quickly as it had begun, the firing stopped and darkness again descended on the land beyond the canyon.

"Did we get any?" Masterson asked, as gray gunsmoke drifted around him. "Hell, they were all spread out like a sneeze through a lace curtain."

Kilcoyn shrugged. "I don't know." He called out to O'Neil, "Barry, are you all right?"

"I'm fine," the young man answered. "Jenny's with me."

"Then tell her to keep her head down," the marshal yelled, irritated. "Or she'll get it blown clean off."

"Not much chance of her laying low," O'Neil answered, a smile in his voice. "She's got my forty-four Russian."

"I can shoot, Marshal," Jenny hollered. "Pretty soon you're going to need all the guns you can get."

"Hell, is that witch gal seeing stuff again?" Masterson grumbled. "I've already got goose bumps all over me as big as nickels."

The darkness deepened as a cloud passed in front of the moon, then another. One by one the stars winked out as the sky grew blacker, the clouds building, rolling in fast from the west. The wind rose, blowing cold, and a few flakes of snow tumbled to earth. The coyotes had fallen silent when the gunfire started, but now they were talking again . . . and quail were calling from the mesquite thickets where there should have been no quail.

Kilcoyn was instantly alert. The birdcalls were very close. He whispered a warning to Masterson, his eyes probing the pitch-blackness.

An arrow flew into the arroyo and thudded into the hard ground inches from where Masterson was standing. Another whirred through the air in a high arc and vanished into the gloom behind them.

It seemed Star Blanket's warriors had been stung by Kilcoyn and the others firing at their rifle flares, and now they'd gone to the bow, a deadly and noiseless weapon that did not burn its brand on the night.

But the Cheyenne, and probably the Sioux with them, were shooting blind, no more able to see their enemy than could Kilcoyn and the others.

To be effective, they would have to get closer. A lot closer.

The marshal fed fresh shells into his rifle and waited, his breath clouding in the cold air.

A couple of minutes passed, the slow, dragging time before a gunfight when a man's senses sharpen and what he can see around him stands out in stark detail. Kilcoyn was aware of Masterson's steady breathing, the glint of his rifle barrel as he adjusted and readjusted his grip on the stock and forearm. He heard the soft splash of runoff water hitting a rock back in the arroyo and the small sound of an animal rustling through the frosted grass.

The Indians came out of the darkness. They were mounted and rode past the mouth of the arroyo at a fast gallop. Arrows whistled through the air and thudded around Kilcoyn and Masterson. The marshal heard the angry bark of O'Neil's Henry and a sharper report as Jenny cut loose with the Smith & Wesson.

Kilcoyn fired at a shadowy rider, the white splashes of a paint pony just visible in the darkness. A miss. The Indian rode past the arroyo and was soon out of sight. Beside him Masterson fired and fired again at fleeting glimpses of mounted warriors, but as far as Kilcoyn could see Bat scored no hits.

The snow in front of the canyon was scarred by the passage of hooves, but not a single Indian was down and the rest had faded into the night.

"We're all right over here, John," O'Neil yelled. "Didn't hit anything though."

Masterson thumbed shells into his rifle and looked at Kilcoyn. "I reckon Star Blanket wants us dead real bad to be attacking at night like this," he said. "I know Indians are notional, but this is strange as a sidesaddle on a sow. Why doesn't he just wait until sunup?"

"He realizes by now there are other white men at Black Mesa. Could be he figures they'll come a-running to help us as soon as it's light."

Masterson snorted. "Just as well he doesn't know that it's Jake Pride and his boys. I don't reckon ol' Jake would come a-running for anybody."

"He might," Kilcoyn said. "If he thinks he could lose his ten thousand dollars—and me."

Masterson opened his mouth to speak, but Kilcoyn's shout cut him off. "Here they come again!"

The Indians were fast-moving shadows that were there, then gone. But several arrows had streaked into the arroyo and Kilcoyn heard O'Neil cry out like a man in mortal agony.

"Barry!" the marshal yelled. "Are you all right?"

"Jenny's been hit," O'Neil said. "She's hurt real bad. Jesus, Mary and Joseph . . . there's . . . there's blood everywhere."

"Stay here, Bat," Kilcoyn said. He sprinted across the mouth of the arroyo and found Jenny lying on her back, O'Neil on one knee beside her. The girl was unconscious, and she'd been hit hard. The arrow had penetrated her upper chest, just where the breastbone meets the neck, and the strap iron point was deep.

Kilcoyn, a sudden, clutching sickness in him, gave Jenny three or four minutes of life. No more than that.

O'Neil's eyes glinted white in the darkness. "Can we pull the arrow free?"

Kilcoyn shook his head, realized it was a gesture O'Neil couldn't see, and added words. "Jenny's time is short, Barry. There's nothing we can do for her."

"No!" O'Neil yelled. "You're lying! We can save her."

Jenny stirred, raised a hand and caught the front of O'Neil's mackinaw. "Barry, I heard what John said," she whispered, scarlet blood staining her pale lips. "And he's right. I'm dying."

"You can't die," O'Neil pleaded. "I just found you and I can't lose you so soon."

"I saw it, Barry," the girl said. "I knew there would be a death. I have the gift."

"You saw us getting married, Jenny. You saw that, so it's bound to happen." O'Neil's face turned to Kilcoyn, a white blur in the gloom. "Isn't that right, John? Say it's so. Say it's right."

Jenny's eyes lifted to Kilcoyn, and even in the darkness the marshal could see the death touching her face. "John, you are a United States Marshal. You are an important man and the law has given you great powers. You can marry us." Her hand sought Kilcoyn's, and he reached out and took it, feeling it very small and frail within his huge paw. "Marry us, Marshal. Do it now, before it's too late."

Kilcoyn knew he had no such authority. But Jenny's life had been difficult beyond belief, and he would do what he could to make her dying easier, even as the last few grains of the sands of her life ran fast through the hourglass.

He reached out, took O'Neil's arm and placed Jenny's hand in his. "By the powers vested in me by the president of the United States I pronounce you man and wife," he said.

It was an untruth, and quickly and hastily spoken, but it was a small untruth that gave Jenny what she needed.

"You see, we are husband and wife," she whispered to O'Neil, her lips parted in a smile. "I saw it all. Now we're not two people, but one."

Then she died, with no more fuss than a wounded songbird dying on the prairie. She simply closed her eyes and her life left her.

"They're coming again, John!" Masterson yelled.

12

Kilcoyn's Torment

The Indian attack, like the ones before, was brief and no hits were scored on either side. But Star Blanket had surely noticed that the guns firing at his warriors had been reduced from four to just two. Jenny was dead, and O'Neil, loudly grieving over her body, was out of the fight.

A small anger had been growing in Kilcoyn, and now, with the girl's death, it blossomed into a full-blown rage. He was all through being trapped like a rat in the arroyo. Up until now Star Blanket had directed the course of the battle, dictating when and how it would be fought, and that had to change.

Now it was time to take the fight to the Indians.

Kilcoyn drew his Colt, thumbed a round into the empty chamber under the hammer and urgently whispered a few words to Masterson.

The sheriff had sand and fear was not part of his makeup. He knew what had to be done and that

Kilcoyn's plan was as good as any. He made no protest.

Masterson pulled one of his own revolvers and, following the marshal's example, filled all six chambers, then passed the gun to Kilcoyn. "Ready, John?" he asked.

"Ready. Let's get it done," the big marshal said.

Masterson picked up his rifle and the two lawmen stepped into the darkness in front of the mouth of the arroyo. They stood back-to-back, Masterson's Winchester held at high port, Kilcoyn's Colts up and ready.

Like two fashionable New Orleans bucks about to fight a duel, they stood without talking and waited.

The snow was falling heavier, the gloom of the night deepening. Around them the wind was talking among the canyons, and somewhere in the arroyo a horse whinnied, made uneasy by the crash of guns and the smell of death.

A couple of slow minutes passed and snow settled on the hats and shoulders of the lawmen. Behind him, Kilcoyn heard Masterson restlessly move his feet and adjust his hold on his rifle.

Where were the Cheyenne?

There was no depth to the blackness in front of Kilcoyn. It was like his eyes were trying to probe a solid wall of basalt lashed by cartwheeling snow. Standing still in one place as he was, the cold was intense, his smoking breath instantly snatched away by the howling wind.

Masterson gave voice to Kilcoyn's thought. "Where in tarnation are they, John?" he whispered. "I'm going to freeze to death if I'm out here much longer. It's as cold as a mother-in-law's kiss."

"They'll be here," Kilcoyn said. "I can smell 'em."

The Indians attacked a few moments later. But they didn't come in the direction Kilcoyn had expected—they were riding straight at the arroyo.

"On your right, Bat!" Kilcoyn yelled.

"I see them."

Kilcoyn turned and crouched, his six-guns hammering. Beside him he heard the flat statement of Masterson's rifle followed by the sharp clank of the lever working.

The Indians were riding right at them, but lead was tearing into their ranks. It was as dark as the bottom of a well and there was no question of aimed fire. In the faint moonlight Kilcoyn caught a quick glimpse of a gray pony going down, the rider rolling clear. At a range of ten yards, Masterson shot the man, then shot him again as he tried to stagger away. An Indian went over the back of his horse as Kilcoyn fired, the arrow from his bent bow flying into the air. Kilcoyn fired, fired again, and another Indian tumbled into the snow. The Cheyenne had not expected a stand out in the open, and some of them desperately tried to reverse direction, their ponies buck-jumping and scared.

A warrior in a horned headdress came on fast and bumped Kilcoyn with his pony. The big marshal staggered back a few steps, then sat down hard on the snow. The Indian came at him again, the feathered lance in his right hand lowered, its long, iron head aiming for Kilcoyn's head. The marshal raised his gun, holding it straight out in front of him at eye level, and fired. The Indian took the bullet in the chest. He dropped the lance and rode past, fading into the night. Now the Indians were all around them, yelling and determined. Masterson used his rifle as a club and swept a brave from the back of his mount. A Cheyenne came at Kilcoyn and swung a stone war club. The marshal took the blow on his upraised right arm, his Colt dropping from his hand as he suddenly went numb from shoulder to fingertips. Several horsemen were coming right at him, and he fired with his left hand. Two shots, both of them missing clean. Masterson spun and went down, his hat flying off his head. Kilcoyn had no time to see where the sheriff had been hit. He was fighting for his life, cutting at the Indians surrounding him with his gun barrel.

Something hard crashed into his head. He sank to his knees, then felt strong arms grabbing him. He tried to fight back, but his strength was gone. He was thrown facedown over the back of a horse and under him he saw the snow-covered ground rush past. . . . Then he knew no more.

John Kilcoyn woke slowly. It was cold, very cold, and as his eyes adjusted he saw a rock overhang above him, streaks of green and brown moss veined on its smooth surface.

He was lying on his back. He tried to move, but found it impossible. His hands and feet were tied. He was trussed up tighter than Dick's hatband and he knew right then that his tail was in a crack.

Kilcoyn turned his head, pain instantly hammering at him. There were Indians all around him, both Cheyenne and Sioux judging by the beadwork on the war shirts and the women's braids. A few smoky campfires burned, falling snow sizzling on the coals, and near the tethered ponies children played with hoops of bent willow and rawhide.

Kilcoyn calculated there were at least eighty or ninety warriors in the camp and one of them, a tall, blanket-wrapped man with gray braids, suddenly glanced in his direction. The man's entire face was painted white, the color of mourning among the Cheyenne, and deep lines ran from the corners of his wide mouth to his chin.

The warrior, who John guessed could only be Star Blanket, said something sharp to a plump woman who was standing near a fire. The woman nodded and walked purposefully toward Kilcoyn. She bent over and tested the ropes that bound him, then grunted and slapped him across the face with the back of her work-hardened hand.

The crack was loud in the silence and people turned the marshal's way, a few of them laughing. Encouraged, the woman grinned and slapped the marshal again. But Star Blanket yelled something to her and she glared at Kilcoyn, sniffed, then turned on her heel and stomped away.

Kilcoyn's cheeks stung from the woman's blows, and he knew when the time came, the task of torturing him would fall to her and the other women. He realized it was all up with him, and that his dying, when it came, would be slow and painful.

Where was he?

Kilcoyn looked around him. As far as he could tell he was in some kind of wide, shallow canyon, juniper and sage growing on its eroded slopes. Above him the sky was gray, here and there shading into black, and the snow was falling steadily. It was hard to tell without sight of the sun, but he figured it was not yet noon.

Only then did memory of the fight at the arroyo come back to him. His head was pounding, and he recalled going down after being hit, probably by a war club. The Cheyenne had wanted to take him alive, saving him for torture. He remembered O'Neil sobbing over Jenny's body and then, after the fight started, Masterson getting hit. Was Masterson still alive? Was O'Neil?

Kilcoyn had no answers for those questions, and the not knowing felt like a knife twisting in his belly.

He lay where he was under the overhang for several hours. No one came near him except for the children, who jeered and threw snow and rocks at him until they were chased away by their elders.

Time dragged by slowly. And Kilcoyn, having time only to think, wondered about the manner of his dying. Would he cry out like a woman in childbirth when the fire burned and the knives cut? Or could he stifle his screams and die like a man, like a warrior? He had always thought of himself as being as brave as any other man but, when put to the test, would he give the lie to that belief and shriek like a rank coward for mercy?

Kilcoyn closed his eyes, willing such questions to leave him. He would soon know the answers and the kind of man he really was would become abundantly clear.

But right now he was already in torment. He had no idea what had happened to Masterson and O'Neil, and what of Angela and Doc? By tomorrow Jake Pride's deadline would be up, and what then? Angry at not getting his ransom, would he kill them both? Pride was a hard, uncompromising man, and not a patient one. He would not wait longer than he needed and then he'd act.

A terrible sense of defeat in him, Kilcoyn looked up miserably at the rock above his head, knowing the deaths of Angela and Doc would be of his own doing. He had led Masterson and O'Neil to disaster and Jenny to her death—and in doing so he had also failed Angela and her father. Soon he was going to die himself, and his conscience would hurt much worse than anything the Indian women could do to him.

The gray day was just beginning to shade into a grayer dusk when they came for him.

Several warriors grabbed Kilcoyn and dragged him to a fire where most of the Indians—men, women and children—were clustered around, waiting.

The bonds were cut from Kilcoyn's wrists and ankles and he was thrown on his back. Quickly and roughly his coat was stripped from him, he was spread-eagled and his hands and feet were staked to the ground. The warriors stepped back as Star Blanket walked to his side and stood over him.

"I am Star Blanket," he said. "War chief of the Cheyenne."

"Pleased to make your acquaintance," Kilcoyn said, raising his head, determined not to show fear. "Sorry I can't get up right now."

Star Blanket's milky eyes glittered with hate, burning in his painted, chalk white face. "You make a joke, but soon you will not joke, I think. I had a first son, a Dog Soldier who was mighty in war and whose voice was respected in council. The young women looked at him in admiration and many times called his name, and his name was Scar." The Indian waited a few moments, then said, "It was you who killed him."

Kilcoyn nodded. "Your son died bravely and well. In battle, as a warrior should."

Star Blanket gave an answering nod, his face grim. "And you, white man who wears the morning star on his chest, will you die as bravely and well?"

Having no ready answer to that question, Kilcoyn said only, "I will."

The Cheyenne shook his head. "I think not. You will die screaming like a woman. You will die like a dog, foolishly begging the Cheyenne for mercy. And you will die a thousand little deaths before your spirit leaves you. Your dying will be long, with great pain."

"Star Blanket," Kilcoyn said between gritted teeth, "you go to hell."

"This much I will give you," the Indian said, ignoring the marshal's outburst. "You will see death come at you, wearing the faces of women, but one eye will not see, and that is the only mercy the Cheyenne will allow you."

Star Blanket stretched out a hand and a woman placed the end of a slender, burning stick in his palm. The Indian bent over Kilcoyn, the flaring stick poised above his left eye. Kilcoyn arched his back, prepared to bear the pain. The stick came closer, charred black and smoking, small red and yellow flames fluttering at its pointed tip. Kilcoyn closed his eyes.

From somewhere a rifle slammed.

Star Blanket jerked under the impact of the bullet, straightened up and fell across Kilcoyn, the burning stick dropping to the snow, where the flames sizzled briefly, then died.

Horsemen burst into the canyon, firing wildly, and the Indians, surprised, scattered in all directions, the men running to reach their weapons.

As guns banged, Star Blanket's body was roughly rolled off Kilcoyn by a tall, thin man in a black hat, amused wrinkles creasing the corners of his eyes.

"How you doing, John?" the man asked.

The big marshal recognized his rescuer at once. He was older, a little grayer, but the hard-eyed, lined face was unmistakably that of Jake Pride.

13

Jake Pride's Promise

Pride's knife slashed Kilcoyn's ropes and the man helped him to his feet. He picked up the marshal's coat and threw it at him. "Quick, get up on your horse," he said.

The dun had been led into the canyon by one of Pride's riders. Kilcoyn swung into the saddle, bullets cutting the air around him. Pride stepped into the leather and yelled to his men, "Let's get the hell out of here!"

One of Pride's riders was down, sprawled and dead on the ground. The four others turned their horses around and galloped out of the canyon. As Kilcoyn followed them, Pride turned in the saddle, his Colt slamming lead. An Indian fell, then another.

Suddenly they were in the clear, galloping through the gathering darkness in the direction of Black Mesa.

Kilcoyn glanced over his shoulder, but there was no pursuit. Shaken by the death of their leader, the

Cheyenne were confused and uncertain, the warriors milling around, some of them vehemently arguing with the Sioux.

A new war chief would step forward soon, but until then the Indians would not mount another attack. Star Blanket had been killed and, for now at least, their medicine was bad.

Pride, seeing they hadn't been followed, slowed down his horse and rode alongside the marshal. "Been a long time, John. Five years." In the gloom Pride smiled, but his eyes were hidden, hollows of darkness. "I can't say it seems just like yesterday since we last met. Time passes slowly in a territorial prison."

"You brought that on yourself, Jake," Kilcoyn said, no give in him. The man opened his mouth to speak, but the marshal cut him off abruptly. "How are Angela and Doc Wilson?"

"They're just fine, so far. And so is Masterson and the other man—what's his name—"

"Barry O'Neil."

"Yeah, him. We buried his woman in the arroyo at first light this morning before we came looking for you."

"How did you know what had happened?"

"Masterson came looking for me last night, his head all bleeding and banged up. Said you'd been taken by Cheyenne, then they'd pulled out and left him and O'Neil alone. The snow had covered most of the tracks, but it wasn't real hard to find you." Pride waved his hand toward one of his men, a sullen, silent rider with a mane of greasy black hair falling over his shoulders from under a low-crowned hat. "That's Luis Garcia. He's half Apache, half Mexican and all son of a bitch, but he can read sign like nobody I ever met. He led us right to you."

"Well, I want to thank you, Jake. You saved my life back there."

"Think nothing of it, John," Pride said pleasantly. He hesitated a few moments then added, "I didn't want the Indians to kill you, because that's something I plan on doing myself."

Kilcoyn's eyes sought Pride's in the gloom. "Still blaming me for something that was all your own doing, Jake?"

"Uh-huh. My horse was outside the cabin. You could have taken back the money and let me ride."

"You know I couldn't do that. My job was to uphold the law, and that's what I did."

"Was I a good lawman, John?"

"One of the best."

"An honorable career that ended the day you put a scattergun to my head."

"No, Jake, your career ended the day you rode into Hays and robbed the Drover's bank. That's when it ended."

The marshal saw a slight motion of Pride's head in the darkness. "I spent five years in hell, and the only thing that kept me going was the thought that one day I'd kill you, John. Nothing you can say will take that away from me."

"Then give me my gun, Jake. Let me have an even break."

Pride laughed without humor. "I can shade you, John, always could. You were never fast with the iron. But that would be too easy. I'll kill you when you least expect it. Maybe like I did, you'll wake up one morning, could be tomorrow, maybe the next day, with my gun pointed at your head. As soon as your eyes open and you realize what's happening, I'll scatter your brains."

"It was never about the ten thousand dollars, was it, Jake?" Kilcoyn asked. "It was me you wanted all the time."

"What do I care about the money now Maggie is gone?" Pride asked in turn. "Yes, you're right, John, I wanted you. I kept track of you when I was in prison, and that's when I was told you were sweet on a doctor's daughter called Angela Wilson. I knew if I ever took her, you'd come after her. Sure, I demanded money, but that was just a way of proving my bona fides. The money is nothing. After I deal with you, I plan to share it out among the low-life scum who are riding with me."

Jake Pride was insane. The marshal knew that with sickening certainty. Maybe his five years in prison, or losing the woman he'd adored, had warped the man's mind. Whatever had tipped him over the edge into madness had made Pride unpredictable and dangerous.

Kilcoyn gathered up the reins of his horse. He had no gun, but he had to get away from Pride. The only way he could help Angela and the others was to remain free and find a way to strike when the time was right.

But Pride stopped him. "Don't even think about it, John," he said, looking straight ahead of him, smiling slightly. "You light a shuck and I'll kill them all: Angela, Doc, Masterson and the young Irishman. You know I will."

Kilcoyn turned in the saddle and looked at Pride, both of them riding through a moving veil of snow. "Angela never did anything to you, Jake. You have me, so let her go."

Pride nodded. "She's a real nice young lady. Reminds me of Maggie sometimes. But it doesn't make no never mind, John. I plan to keep her until I do what I have to do."

The marshal knew further talk was useless. He'd only be wasting words on a man whose mind was no longer rational, unable to differentiate between right and wrong. Jake Pride was a mentally sick human being, and that made him a hair trigger looking for a finger.

When they rode up on Black Mesa it took Kilcoyn a few minutes to make out its looming bulk, dark against the lighter dark of the sky.

Pride led the way around the north slope of the

mesa and past a high, cinder-cone volcano that stood near the mouth of what appeared to be a small box canyon, just a narrow, wedge-shaped cut in a rawboned ridge of sandstone. A fire glowed inside the canyon and Kilcoyn saw the flickering shadow of a short, stocky man who looked like Doc Wilson step past the flames, then disappear into the darkness.

When he was still a distance from the canyon mouth, Pride reined up and yelled: "Dave, you hear me?"

A voice answered from the darkness. "I hear you."

"It's Pride. I'm coming in."

"Come ahead."

Kilcoyn followed Pride and the others to the canyon mouth, and he swung out of the saddle when the rest did. Pride was suddenly beside him, his Colt leveled. "Move up to the fire, John. Don't try any fancy moves or I'll gun you right where you stand."

The marshal nodded and stepped toward the fire.

"John!"

It was Angela's voice, and Kilcoyn stopped in his tracks as the woman ran into his arms. "I knew you'd come," Angela whispered, her tears wet on Kilcoyn's cheek. "I knew you'd find us."

Angela lifted her face to his, and Kilcoyn kissed her, the woman's lips soft and yielding on his own. They clung together for long moments, melting into each other, becoming one, then Angela whispered, "Take me away from here, John. Take me home."

The woman's plea was like a knife in Kilcoyn's belly. He drew back his head and said softly, "Angela, you must be brave, braver than you've ever been before in your life."

Firelight glowed on Angela's tear-stained face. "But why, John? Jake has the money. It's over now."

Kilcoyn shook his head. "He didn't want the money, Angela, not really. He wanted me."

"But . . . but I don't understand. . . ."

Pride stepped beside them. "It's easy to understand, Angela," he said. "It's payback time—payback for all those years I rotted in a stinking jail cell. I have scars on my back from the lashes I took, but the worst scars are deeper, buried way inside me, and they hurt like the fires of hell."

Angela turned frightened eyes to Pride. "Jake, what do you mean?"

"I mean I'm going to kill your intended," the man answered, a flat, emotionless statement. "That's why I kidnapped you and your father. To flush John out of wherever he was and bring him here."

"You have the money—let us go," Angela said, color draining from her face.

Pride shook his head. "When I say I'm going to kill a man, I kill a man. There's no arguing the point."

"And how many men have you killed, you damned butcher?" Doc Wilson stepped beside Kilcoyn and Angela, his eyes blazing.

Pride smiled, his cold blue stare lifeless. "How many fingers you got, Doc?"

"Damn you, and you want to kill even more?" Doc yelled.

"Just one. Just John Kilcoyn."

"Listen, you have me," Kilcoyn said. "You've got what you wanted. Let Angela and the others go."

Pride touched his chin with a forefinger. "Ah, but therein lies a wee complication. See, Luis Garcia wants Angela for himself—real hot for her you might say. When this is over, he plans to take her with him down Sonora way." Pride smiled. "Garcia is quick-tempered and even quicker on the draw. I don't want to upset him, John. So you see how it is with me."

Doc Wilson, a man strong in the arms and shoulders, swore and made a lunge at Pride, but Kilcoyn held him back. "No, Alan, he'll kill you."

Pride smiled. "He's right, you know, Doc. Another inch or two closer and I'd have put a bullet into you."

"Damn you," Doc yelled. "You're not a man, Pride. You're some kind of wild animal."

"You shut your trap, or you'll find out just what an animal I can be," Pride said, his eyes angry and savage.

Kilcoyn took the raging Doc by the arm and led him to Angela. "Make him stay here," he said. "He's walking on some mighty dangerous ground."

Kilcoyn stepped back to Pride and for a few moments his eyes searched the man's face. Finally he said, "Jake, you told me the men riding with you are low-life scum. Well, none of them are lower scum than you. They don't even come close."

If Pride was stung he didn't let it show. "Set by the fire, John. Have some coffee. And don't worry, I won't gun you tonight. Maybe in the morning, when you don't see it coming, but not tonight." He looked at Angela and her father, then waved a hand toward Masterson, who was standing near the fire. "Tonight we're just a bunch of good old friends who've gotten together again after five years. That's how it's going to be."

Kilcoyn ignored the man. He took Angela by the arm and walked her to the fire. Coffee was simmering on the coals and Masterson found him a cup. The sheriff opened his mouth to speak, but Kilcoyn hushed him. "Later," he said. Kilcoyn threw out the old dregs, and filled the cup to the brim with boiling coffee. "Want some?" he asked Angela.

The girl shook her head. Kilcoyn squatted by the fire and Angela sat beside him. There was shelter in the canyon mouth from the cold wind, and only a few flakes of snow were falling. The slopes of the canyon were steep, juniper growing here and there, and the start of a switchback game trail was just visible at the base of the rise to Kilcoyn's left. Talus rocks were piled up at the foot of the slopes, suggesting erosion and washouts. The trail would have plenty of loose rocks underfoot and Kilcoyn made a mental note that any attempt to use it to get away from

Pride and his men would be difficult, if not down-right impossible.

Kilcoyn's intent gaze lifted to Garcia, who was standing in the shadows watching him and Angela with hard black eyes. The man wore a gun low on his right thigh and was on the prod, measuring Kilcoyn, deciding on his move.

He made it.

Garcia shouldered away from the rock he'd been leaning against and sauntered to the fire. He stopped, straddle-legged, close to the big marshal, his thumbs tucked into his gunbelt. The black eyes glittered, trapping the guttering flames of the campfire in their depths.

A smile touched the gunman's thin lips, then he said, "You, get the hell away from my woman."

The men standing around, including Pride, stopped; watching, waiting to see how the big law-man would handle it.

They didn't have to wait long.

There's a time for talking and a time for doing, and Kilcoyn was a doing man. He didn't try to rise, but moved quickly, throwing the boiling-hot coffee in his cup in Garcia's face. The half-breed screamed and staggered back, his fingers clawing at his eyes. Kilcoyn rose, stepped swiftly to Garcia and hit him with a hard, straight right, punching through the man's splayed hands. The gunman's lips flattened against his teeth and a scarlet fountain of blood erupted from his nose. Garcia stepped back, his hand

164

dropping for his gun. Kilcoyn backhanded the man across the face, then followed up with a looping left that crashed into Garcia's chin. The gunman's head snapped back, spraying a wide fan of blood, and he fell flat on his back and lay still.

Anger spurring him, Kilcoyn bent, caught Garcia by the front of his mackinaw and dragged him to his feet. He held the glassy-eyed gunman at arm's length, then pulled back his right fist, planning to end it.

A gun roared and a bullet kicked up snow and dirt at Kilcoyn's feet.

"Let him be," Pride said. "He's a piece of human trash but I may need him alive."

Kilcoyn turned and glared at Pride, his blood up, but the triple click as the hammer of the man's Colt eased back sobered him. "I mean it, John," Pride warned. "Let him go or I'll drop you right now rather than later."

The marshal opened the fingers of his left hand. Immediately Garcia's knees buckled and he slumped to the ground, then fell flat on his face.

"I'd say you've made a bad enemy there, John." Pride grinned. "Now Garcia will try to kill you if he can."

"Before you, Jake?" Kilcoyn asked, his voice bitter.

The man shook his head. "I won't let that happen."

The marshal looked from the fallen gunman and back to Pride, two mad dogs who wanted to tear him apart at the altar of vengeance.

It was not a good feeling.

14

The Coyote and the Cougar

Kilcoyn led Angela to a space between a pair of large talus rocks that had rolled down the slope during some ancient earthshake. They were far from the thin warmth of the fire, but at least he and Angela had some small measure of privacy.

The marshal looked around him. Apart from himself and Garcia, Pride had four other men, by the look of them run-of-the-mill hardcases out of Texas or the Indian Territory. But they were a tough-looking bunch and Kilcoyn had come up against their kind before, professional hired killers who were not seeking a reputation like Frank Ivers was, but would coolly gun anybody just so long as they were getting paid for it.

Garcia was kneeling by the fire, blood trickling over his chin from his smashed mouth and nose. The half-breed threw Kilcoyn a look of intense hatred, and the marshal knew it was only the presence of

Jake Pride that was stopping the gunman from killing him.

Masterson, looking sheepish, stepped in front of Kilcoyn and Angela. He had the marshal's hat in his hands and he extended it to Kilcoyn. "Brought you this, John. It came off during the fight with the Injuns."

Kilcoyn nodded his thanks and settled his hat on his head. "Been missing this," he said. "It cost me thirty-five dollars, and that was a fair spell back when stuff was a lot cheaper than it is today."

Masterson shifted his weight from one foot to the other, looking uncomfortable, his eyes moving between Kilcoyn and Angela. Kilcoyn recognized the signs and said, "Out with it, Bat. What's on your mind?"

"I've got us in a hell of a fix, John," Masterson said. "After you were carried away by the Indians, and me with my head nearly blown off"—his fingers strayed to his bloody right temple where he'd been creased with a bullet—"I knew we needed help bad, and the only person I could think of was Jake. I didn't think the whole thing was going to blow up in my face, kind of like stealing a watermelon from the sheriff's patch."

Kilcoyn smiled. "Bat, you did what you thought was right. I'm not going to kick about that, and neither should you." He looked around him, at the guard with a Winchester standing alert and ready a few yards away, and Pride and the others squatting by the fire. "What we have to do is find a way to get out of here."

"John, this might help," Angela whispered.

The marshal felt the woman's hand move furtively down her side and behind her back. Kilcoyn reached around behind Angela and his hand met hers. She passed him something small and cold with a familiar and unmistakable shape—a Remington .41 caliber deringer.

Kilcoyn palmed the little gun and shoved it into the pocket of his mackinaw.

"Dad passed it to me after we were taken by Pride and his men. He knew they wouldn't search my purse," Angela whispered. "Or at least he hoped they wouldn't."

The deringer was a close-up and personal gun, not much good at anything over tabletop distance, but it was better than nothing and Kilcoyn felt less naked with its reassuring weight in his pocket.

For the first time since he'd arrived in camp, Kilcoyn noticed O'Neil. He was curled up in a fetal position on a bare patch of ground, snoring, a whiskey bottle clutched tight to his chest.

Doc Wilson, who had stepped away from the fire and had been watching Kilcoyn's eyes, shook his head. "He's been that way since he got here. Drunk as a pig. At least I got a chance to look at his shoulder. It's healing well, though God knows why."

"Who gave him the whiskey, Doc?" Kilcoyn asked.

Doc waved a hand toward the fire. "One of them.

They're liberally supplied with rotgut and I guess they think it's funny to see the young man drink himself insensible."

The night was falling around them, made blacker by the clouded sky. The snow had quickened its pace, and wet, white flakes were tumbling into the canyon. The fire spat as snow fell on the flames. A man rose and threw on a few more branches, sending up a dancing shower of sparks that glowed scarlet for an instant and then died into darkness.

Kilcoyn looked across at Garcia and saw the trouble coming.

The gunman had never taken his eyes off Angela. Now he rose and wiped dried blood off his chin with the back of his hand. He walked toward where Kilcoyn and Angela were sitting among the rocks, the amused eyes of Pride and his men watching his every move.

Doc Wilson stepped into the gunman's path and said angrily: "You leave my daughter alone, you damned scoundrel."

Garcia snarled and roughly pushed Doc aside, then pulled his gun as Kilcoyn rose to his feet, his hand on the deringer in his pocket. The gunman loomed over Angela, the woman lifting a pale, frightened face to him. "You," Garcia said, "come with me. It's time to sleep."

A man by the fire guffawed and yelled, "Hell, sleep ain't what you got in mind, Louie boy."

Garcia grinned, then winced as the red cracks in

his split lips opened. "On your feet, woman. Tonight you will sleep in my arms and you will keep my belly warm."

Kilcoyn's voice was low and flat, heavy with barely suppressed anger. "You leave her alone, Garcia."

The gunman swung on Kilcoyn, his Colt coming level with the marshal's belt buckle. "And if I don't, lawman, what are you going to do about it?"

"Just leave her be," Kilcoyn said. "You damned half-breed lowlife."

Garcia shook his head, as though he couldn't believe what he was hearing. "The hell with Pride. I think I'll kill you now," he said, his black eyes narrowing.

A gunshot tore apart the stretched fabric of the night.

Garcia staggered back, unable to believe what was happening to him, staring stupidly down at the black blood blossoming on his stomach just above his gunbelt. He tried to bring his gun up, and Kilcoyn shot him again. The marshal's first bullet had ripped through the canvas pocket of his mackinaw. But he'd pulled the deringer clear for the second and he hit Garcia in the middle of his chest.

The gunman's Colt fell from his hand and he backed off a couple of steps, his horrified eyes on Kilcoyn, unwilling to believe the fact of his dying. Garcia opened his mouth, tried to say something, then toppled forward on his face.

Garcia's gun was lying on the ground only a couple of feet from the marshal. Kilcoyn tensed to make a dive for it, but Pride's voice cutting across the silence stopped him. "Don't try it, John, or I'll kill you."

Pride's Colt was level and steady, and anger flared in Kilcoyn. "Damn you, Jake. Then shoot and get it over with."

"Too easy, John, way too easy. I'll shoot when the time comes. See how it is with you, you're already starting to fall apart, and that's how I want it, how I planned it for all those years. Soon you'll beg me for mercy, to let you ride out of here, like when I asked you the same thing." Pride shook his head. "Well, it didn't happen then and it won't happen now. I'll kill you, John, but, like I told you, it will be in my own good time and when you least expect it."

Pride turned to one of the men by the fire. "Len, pick up that Colt and relieve the marshal of his stingy gun." He nodded to Garcia. "And drag that back into the canyon somewhere." He gave another shake of his head. "That boy never did learn that a coyote doesn't brace a cougar, did he?"

Kilcoyn and Angela lay close to each other and slept until the night darkness began to shade to a cold gray dawn. Above them, rugged parapets of black cloud were building in the sky, hugging the crests of the surrounding hills, and the snow was falling steadily.

Kilcoyn rose and stepped to the fire, a man with

a rifle and hard green eyes watching him closely. He lifted the coffeepot, shook it to gauge its contents, then poured himself a cup. Angela was still asleep. Doc and Masterson were lying close to the fire, the sheriff, an arm thrown across his eyes, snoring softly. Masterson was one of a rare breed, a man who had ridden so many rough trails he could sleep like a pup using only his belly as a cover and his back as a mattress.

O'Neil was awake. He drained the whiskey bottle, held it up to the gray light, studying the lack of contents with bloodshot eyes, then tossed it away in disgust.

Kilcoyn walked over to the man and said, "Barry, want some coffee?"

"Hell no, I don't want coffee. I want whiskey," O'Neil answered, his voice slurred and thick with morning-after hoarseness. He looked over to the guard and yelled: "Hey, you! Where's the damn whiskey?"

The man's green eyes glinted in amusement. "Hell, I dunno, boy. Look around."

O'Neil staggered to his feet and pulled away from the hand Kilcoyn had reached out to steady him. "Let me be," he said. "I need a drink."

"You need to drink some coffee," Kilcoyn said. "We all feel bad about Jenny, but you're not grieving for her, Barry, you're wallowing in self-pity."

"Damn you, Kilcoyn!" O'Neil yelled. He threw a punch at the marshal's chin, but Kilcoyn easily side-

172

stepped the blow and O'Neil fell flat on his face. The young man lay stunned for a few moments, then struggled to his feet. Kilcoyn already forgotten, he staggered to where Pride and his men were getting out of their blankets and yelled, "Whiskey!"

One of the outlaws, a sour-looking man with a huge walrus mustache that covered his entire mouth, reached beside him and tossed a half-empty bottle at O'Neil. "Here, take that and quit yer yammering," he said. "And be damned to ye for a drunken Mick."

The bottle had fallen at O'Neil's feet and the young man dived on it. He raised the whiskey to his mouth and his throat bobbed as he swallowed greedily. O'Neil took the bottle from his lips and wiped the back of his hand across his mouth.

"We each grieve in our own way," he said, turning to Kilcoyn, his bleary eyes bleak. "This is mine."

The marshal shook his head. "Then God help you, Barry, because I can't."

O'Neil staggered back to where he'd been lying, then stopped and threw back his head, the old song wrenching out of him cracked and tuneless.

The minstrel boy to the wars has gone.
In the ranks of death you will find him.
His father's sword he has belted on,
And his wild harp slung around behind him. . . .

The outlaw who'd given O'Neil the whiskey swore and hurriedly looked around where he sat in his blankets. He found the rock he'd been searching for, drew back his arm and hurled it at O'Neil. The rock thudded into the young Irishman between the shoulder blades. O'Neil's back arched and he groaned, then sank to his knees. He didn't even turn. He just tilted back his head, put the bottle to his mouth and drank deep.

"The minstrel boy . . ." O'Neil muttered. "The minstrel boy . . ." He fell on his side, the bottle clutched to him, and was instantly snoring again.

"Stupid, drunken Mick," the outlaw snarled. He looked over at Pride. "I swear, Jake, next time he sings like that, I'll put a bullet in his damn back."

Pride sat up in his blankets and shrugged. "You do what you have to, Bill. Makes no never mind to me." Pride donned his hat and was pulling on his boots when Kilcoyn stepped next to him. The man's cool eyes lifted to the marshal, his hand on the handle of the Colt lying beside him. "Back off, John, not too close."

Kilcoyn stayed where he was. "Jake, I've taken care of what you called your wee complication. Garcia's dead. Now let Angela and the others go."

Pride smiled. "How long do you reckon they'd last out there with the Cheyenne and Sioux on the warpath?"

"It's me the Cheyenne want," Kilcoyn said. "And probably you, since you're the one who killed Star Blanket. I think Angela and her father's chances are better out there than they are here with you."

Pride shook his head. "Harsh words, John, and unkindly spoken. I've got no quarrel with Angela and her father, nor with Bat Masterson or the Irishman either. When it's over—and you're dead—I'll turn them loose."

"Do it now, Jake."

"Later," Pride said, his voice hard and flat. "They will be witnesses to your execution and testify that justice was finally done."

Kilcoyn opened his mouth to speak, but Pride waved him into silence. "No more talk, John. This early in the morning, before I have my coffee, conversation tires me, it surely does."

As he'd done before, Kilcoyn knew he was trying to reason with a man who was touched in the head and no longer could think straight. Kilcoyn turned on his heel and began to walk away, but Pride's cold voice stopped him in his tracks.

"John," he said, "I got to be moving on, so this will be the last day of your life." Pride grinned as he stood and buckled on his gunbelt. "So make the most of it, *mi amigo*."

John Kilcoyn felt a chill run down his back. The goose had again taken wing.

15

A Daring Dash for It

"**G**et up, you damned, lazy Mick."

Kilcoyn had been talking to Angela and her father. Now he turned as the outlaw with the walrus mustache kicked the snoring O'Neil, the toe of the man's boot thudding viciously into the young Irishman's ribs.

Kilcoyn's long legs took him quickly to where O'Neil lay. He faced the outlaw and said, "Let him be."

"We need wood for the fire," the man snarled. "He's been sleeping long enough."

The outlaw drew back his foot to kick again, but he was destined to never complete the motion—the arrow that slammed into his throat instantly adding the final period to the last sentence of the last chapter of his life.

Guns slammed and another of Pride's men went

down, falling across the fire, his coffee cup spilling from his hand.

The Indians were charging across the open ground in front of the canyon, firing as they came. Pride and his two surviving gunmen took up positions behind the tumbled talus rocks and their guns roared.

Kilcoyn had time to see a horse go down, hurling the Sioux on its back to the ground before he bent and stripped the dead outlaw at his feet of his Colt. He ran to Angela, hustling her further into the arroyo. A bare outcropping of eroded sandstone jutted several feet from the canyon wall like the prow of a ship, and Kilcoyn pulled Angela behind its sheltering bulk.

"Stay here," he told the girl. "And don't move until I come for you."

"John, what are you going to do?" Angela asked, her face pale and frightened.

The big marshal gave her a brief smile. "See if I can reach more guns and get us out of here alive."

He turned as Doc Wilson stepped to his side. "John, there's a lot of Indians out there. I don't think Jake Pride can hold them off with just two men. I don't want my daughter falling into the hands of the Cheyenne."

Kilcoyn nodded. "Stay here with her, Alan. I'm going to round up Bat and see what we can do."

Despite Angela's tearful pleas for him to stay behind the relative safety of the rocks, Kilcoyn walked quickly to where Masterson was crouched, hugging the canyon wall. A few yards away, O'Neil was either dead or still sound asleep.

"You all right, Bat?" he asked.

The sheriff nodded. "So far Jake is making the redskins keep their distance. But I don't think he can keep them away for much longer."

Kilcoyn's eyes moved to the canyon mouth, where Pride and his men were shooting steadily. They had broken up the first charge, but now the warriors had shaken out into a loose skirmish line and bullets were thudding into the canyon. A wild shriek, and a man wearing a sheepskin vest toppled back from his position behind a rock, the entire top of his head blown away.

Kilcoyn saw the remaining outlaw throw Pride a frightened glance, then yell something to him that was lost in the roar of the guns.

Gunfire erupted behind him and Kilcoyn turned swiftly, his Colt coming up and level. But there was no one there. The cartridges in the belt loops of the man who had fallen across the fire were exploding as the flames heated them, erratic bullets zipping around the canyon.

Masterson sprinted to the outlaw and tried to relieve him of his gun, but the man's body was burning and the Colt was trapped beneath him.

"Where are the rifles?" Kilcoyn yelled.

Masterson looked around him and ran to the far wall of the canyon, where Pride had slept. He bent down, then came running back with Kilcoyn's Winchester and gunbelt, O'Neil's Henry, and his own holstered Colt and rifle.

"They were just lying there, all piled up where Jake left them, as neat as you please." He grinned.

A bullet thudded into the wall near Kilcoyn's head and another kicked up dirt at Masterson's feet as the Indians found the range. At the canyon mouth, Pride and the other man were still firing, and several Cheyenne and Sioux warriors lay sprawled and still on the ground.

Pride crouched low behind his sheltering rock and began to feed shells into his rifle. His eyes slanted in Kilcoyn's direction and he cursed savagely. "John Kilcoyn, damn you to hell!" he yelled. "Now is your time." He threw the rifle to his shoulder and fired. But Kilcoyn was already moving and the bullet whapped into the canyon wall where he'd crouched only a split second before. Kilcoyn snapped off a quick shot at Pride, then he and Masterson were running for the rear of the canyon.

Pride rose to his feet, levering the Winchester at his shoulder. But the other outlaw shouted a warning, and Pride swore and turned, firing, as the Indians launched another attack.

Kilcoyn and Masterson joined Angela and her father, but the marshal ignored their shouted questions and worked his way to the rear of the canyon. All the horses were picketed back there, including Kilcoyn's dun and Masterson's big American stud.

Doc's surrey had been pushed to one side, and suddenly Kilcoyn had an idea.

He sprinted past Masterson and the others, again not stopping to answer their questions, and ran to where O'Neil was still curled up in a fetal position on the ground. A quick glance told the marshal that O'Neil had not been hit, but he was snoring in a drunken stupor.

Kilcoyn cast a worried glance toward Pride, but the man was fully engaged with the Cheyenne and Sioux, who had once again drawn off a distance and were sniping at the canyon.

It seemed to Kilcoyn that Indians were not pressing home the attack with their customary determination. With the Army on the prowl, were they concerned about the women and children they'd left unprotected back at their camp? And now that the vengeful Star Blanket was dead, had no other war chief stepped forward to keep them worked up and on the prod?

The snow was falling heavier, and by now the Cheyenne and Sioux should already be in winter camp, well away from the barren and hostile Black Mesa country. If he was right and the Indians were not fully committed to the attack, it would suit Kilcoyn's plan perfectly.

But if he was wrong . . . well, that was something he didn't want to think about.

Kilcoyn shoved O'Neil's plug hat on the man's head, grabbed him by the collar of his coat and dragged him toward the rear of the canyon. O'Neil stirred and muttered something in protest. The big marshal ignored the Irishman and pulled him behind the outcropping where Angela and the others were waiting. Kilcoyn jerked O'Neil to his feet and said, "Bat, you and Doc saddle your stud and O'Neil's horse, then put Doc's mare in the traces of the surrey. You're all getting out of here."

"What about you, John?" Angela asked in alarm.

"I'll follow later." Kilcoyn turned to Masterson and Doc Wilson, who were watching him openmouthed and had made no move toward the horses. "Why are you still standing there? Do what I told you!"

The two men rushed away to follow Kilcoyn's orders, and the marshal pushed O'Neil to a split in the canyon wall where a trickle of icy water from deep inside the ridge fell like a pestle into the mortar of a hollowed-out rock, making a small splashing sound.

As bullets buzzed like angry hornets overhead, some of them whining off boulders on the slope, Kilcoyn shoved O'Neil's head under the water. It took a few moments before O'Neil's whiskey-fogged brain realized what was happening to him. The man coughed and spluttered and kicked out at Kilcoyn, but the marshal was relentless, forcing O'Neil's face into the deeper water of the rock hollow.

"John," Angela protested, "you'll drown him."

"I'll kill him or cure him, that's for sure." Kilcoyn grinned.

After a few moments he yanked O'Neil's head

from the water and shoved the man hard against the rock wall. "O'Neil, sober up," he said. "I need you. I need your Henry."

O'Neil's head rolled on his shoulders and he blinked at Kilcoyn, trying to get his eyes to focus. "Wha—wha . . . you say?"

Kilcoyn shook his head, swore with a great deal of feeling and again plunged O'Neil's face into the water. This time the man's struggles were stronger, his splutters and outraged yells louder.

Once again, Kilcoyn hauled the man upright and slammed him so hard against the wall that O'Neil's teeth rattled. His face only inches from O'Neil's, he said, his voice hard, "Barry, listen to me. We're in a hell of a fix. I need you sober."

The young man tossed wet hair from his eyes and gasped: "Let me grieve, damn you."

"The time for grief is over, Barry. Now your concern is for the living, not the dead."

Kilcoyn made to drag O'Neil to the water again, but the man threw up a hand and stopped him. "What the hell do you want from me?" he asked.

The big marshal looked intently into O'Neil's bloodshot eyes. "Do you understand what I'm saying to you?" The young man muttered something Kilcoyn couldn't hear and he shook him hard. "Do you understand, damn it?"

O'Neil nodded, his eyes focusing on the marshal. "I understand. I don't need the cold bath."

"I need your Henry," Kilcoyn said again. "I need you sober and able to shoot."

"I can shoot," O'Neil whispered. "I'm sober and I can shoot."

Angela, a warm, caring woman, reached out and threw her arms around O'Neil. "Barry, Bat told me what happened. I'm so sorry."

The man shook his head. "I thought Jenny would be with me for the rest of my life. I had her for just a moment, then she was gone. She was like a golden fairy gift that fades away in the morning light."

"I'm sure she was a wonderful girl," Angela said. "I'm so sorry, Barry."

Kilcoyn had no intention of letting O'Neil wallow in female sympathy. He grabbed the man by the front of his coat and thrust his face close to O'Neil's. "Barry, you fail me today and I swear I'll hunt you down and kill you. Is my meaning clear?"

"I won't fail you, Marshal," O'Neil said. He looked around him. "John, maybe just one drink to steady my hands."

"No more whiskey," Kilcoyn said. "When you get to Dodge you can drink yourself to death for all I care, but until then you stay sober."

The firing from the mouth of the canyon had died away to the occasional offhand shot from Pride and the other outlaw. Kilcoyn's time was running out fast. Masterson and Doc stepped beside the tall marshal. "Barry's horse is saddled, and so is mine," Masterson said. "And the mare is hitched up to the surrey and ready to go."

Kilcoyn nodded. "Give Barry his Henry, Bat." The marshal paused. "And Bat, thank you for everything. Now I have one last favor to ask of you—please take them home."

"I'll do my very best, John," Masterson said. He opened his mouth to speak, then shook his head. "I don't have the words. Just . . . just take care of yourself, huh?"

O'Neil took his rifle from the sheriff and levered a round into the chamber with a hand that seemed reasonably steady.

"Barry, mount up. You too, Bat," Kilcoyn said. "Angela, you and your father get in the surrey." He motioned to the canyon wall. "I'm climbing up there, to the top of the ridge. When I start firing, you all hightail it out of here. Hit the flat running, and if need be, don't stop until you reach Front Street in Dodge."

"But, John, you'll be left behind," Angela protested. "We can't run out and leave you here."

"Yes, you can. Like I told you earlier, I'll catch up. I'm gambling that the Cheyenne won't chase you because it's me and Jake Pride they want. Well, I plan to let them see me real clear up on the ridge so they know I'm still here."

"It's thin, John," Doc said. "Mighty thin. How do you think you'll get out of here yourself? If the Indians don't stop you, Jake Pride will."

"There's a reckoning to come between Jake and me—better now than later. As for the Indians, I'll take my chances."

From the canyon mouth a rifle slammed, fired again, then silence.

"Better get going, Doc," Kilcoyn said. "The Cheyenne and Sioux might be fixing to charge again." He turned to O'Neil and Masterson. "I'm depending on you two to keep the Indians well away from the surrey. Barry, use that Henry well. And Bat, once again, thank you."

O'Neil, his face gray and sick, said, "John, I'm sorry about—"

"You don't have time to be sorry," the marshal interrupted. "Just get on your horse and be ready to make a run for it as soon as you hear me cut loose up there on the ridge."

Angela ran into Kilcoyn's arms and they kissed passionately, like lovers about to be parted forever. Then the marshal watched as she and her father climbed into the surrey, Masterson and O'Neil mounting on either side of them.

Kilcoyn touched his hat to the others, picked up his rifle and walked to the wall of the canyon. He took the switchback game trail, climbing through scattered stands of juniper and sage. As he'd suspected earlier, the path was treacherous, with a lot of loose rock underfoot, and it rose almost vertically. This was an old bighorn sheep trail to the top of the ridge and it looked like it had not been used in some time. Large boulders had fallen on the trail years back, and here and there juniper grew right in the middle, forcing Kilcoyn to take one careful step at a time around the trees. He was uncomfortably aware that if the Indians decided to give up the fight he'd be an open target for Jake Pride up there on the bare ridge wall, the stunted trees giving only scant cover.

It was not a prospect calculated to bring comfort to a man.

After ten minutes of steady climbing Kilcoyn reached the top of the ridge and walked onto a barren expanse of volcanic capstone that measured a scant ten yards across before dropping off abruptly on both sides. He figured he was about a hundred feet above the flat, and behind him the ridge took a sharp, U-shaped turn, forming the walls of the canyon. Up there the wind was blowing hard and cold, driving the snow, yet Kilcoyn shrugged out of his canvas mackinaw and laid it on the ground. When he stepped to the edge of the ridge he wanted the Cheyenne to see the star on his vest and know who he was.

A few boulders littered the smooth surface of the capstone, bunchgrass growing in any nook and cranny it could find. Kilcoyn picked his way through the obstacles to the edge of the ridge and looked down.

Below him the Indians were spread out under a falling veil of light snow, sniping at Pride and the other outlaw. Now the morning was brightening, visibility was only fair, but good enough that the Cheyenne would be able to see him when he started firing. All the warriors had dismounted, their ponies a ways behind them, held by young boys.

This pleased Kilcoyn immensely. If Masterson, O'Neil and the surrey moved out smartly, they'd be well clear of the Indians before they got a chance to mount.

Of course, he was gambling that Pride wouldn't fire on them, and that was a mighty uncertain thing, a chance they'd have to take. But it was better to dodge Pride's bullets than be trapped in the canyon by the Indians—or by the insane Jake himself.

Kilcoyn levered a round into the chamber of the Winchester and got down on one knee. He threw the rifle to his shoulder, sighted on the closest Cheyenne and squeezed the trigger. The rifle butt slammed against his shoulder as he watched the man fall. Working the gun rapidly, Kilcoyn fired again and again, dusting along the Indian skirmish line. He scored no more hits, but the Indians were gesturing toward him and guns were fired in his direction, one bullet whining off the cap rock a few inches from his knee.

Masterson's wild rebel yell echoed from the canyon as the surrey clattered from its mouth and onto the flat. Doc Wilson was slapping the ribbons on the mare's back, urging her into a fast gallop, and Masterson and O'Neil were firing their rifles at the surprised Indians.

A warrior went down, then another. A Sioux with an angled feather in his hair leaped at the surrey, trying to catch hold of the mare's bridle. He missed and fell to the ground, and the surrey's left wheel bounced over him. The warrior staggered to his feet, but Masterson turned in the saddle and shot the man down.

Kilcoyn fired, fired again, making no hits but scattering the Indians, some of whom were running for their ponies. A warrior dropped, followed by another. Pride and his remaining outlaw had run from the canyon and were pouring a steady fire into the Indians. Pride's rifle ran dry and he went to his Colt, slamming off shot after shot. He dropped another warrior, then shot a second off his pony.

The man with Pride screamed as he took a belly hit. He doubled up and dropped to the ground on his knees, his face ashen. Another bullet crashed into the man's temple, and he fell over on his side and lay still.

Pride was backing up toward the canyon, loading rounds into his rifle. Kilcoyn gave the man covering fire, shooting into the mass of Indians who were now bunched up around their ponies. A warrior fell. Then another.

The Indians mounted, but they'd had enough of this fight and started to stream away to the south. A couple of them stopped and shot at Kilcoyn and Pride, but the range was long and their bullets went nowhere. Then they too turned their ponies and were gone.

Close on a dozen bodies, mostly Sioux but a few Cheyenne, littered the ground. The Indians had paid a high price for an attack that they had not pressed home with any enthusiasm. Their driving force, grim old Star Blanket, was gone and this had not been *Hashtai kola, hoka hey*—A day to walk the good path, a good day to die. Tomorrow, or the day after, or the day after that, their medicine might be stronger.

Kilcoyn's eyes lifted to the flat where the surrey and its outriders were rapidly disappearing into distance and the white screen of the falling snow.

"Good luck, Angela," Kilcoyn whispered, his eyes on the surrey. "Keep your wagon between the ditches."

"Hey, John! Can you hear me?" Pride's voice came from the mouth of the canyon.

"I hear you, Jake."

"The Indians are gone, John, and Angela and the others. It's only you and me left."

"I know that, Jake."

"Your time is up," Pride yelled. "I'm going to kill you now, John."

"Jake, you can surely try."

"Hey, John!"

"What?"

"No hard feelings, huh? We remember the good old times."

"No hard feelings," Kilcoyn said, but so quietly, Pride would not be able to hear him.

16

Blizzard of Lead

Kilcoyn couldn't stay where he was. The top of the ridge was flat and open. Up here he'd be a sitting duck. If Pride took the game trail he'd be vulnerable, but Kilcoyn knew he'd have to expose most of his body at the edge of the canyon wall to get a shot at him. That would be a very dangerous thing, given Pride's skill with a gun.

He had to find a way down from the ridge and meet Pride at a place of his own choosing, where he could find cover and even the odds.

Kilcoyn buttoned into his mackinaw, then walked along the ridge, putting space between himself and the canyon. After about three hundred yards, the bluff rose gradually upward and narrowed, and he followed it until he was a hundred and fifty feet above the flat. He looked around him. There had to be a way down.

The snow was falling heavier now and the wind

was rising rapidly, tossing the branches of the juniper on the slopes of the surrounding hills. To the west, Black Mesa was lost behind a shifting mantle of snow, and though it was not yet noon, the darkness of the threatening blizzard was crowding in fast over the surrounding land.

Kilcoyn glanced over his shoulder toward the wall of the canyon where the game trail ended. Nothing stirred back there but the wind and the madly cartwheeling white flakes.

Snow covering his hat and the front of his mackinaw, he stepped along the edge of the ridge, looking for a way down, and after a few minutes he found it. At this point the eroded northern wall of the ridge dropped a sheer twenty feet, then sloped outward to the flat like a buttress. The slope itself was not gradual, just a little less steep than the wall itself, but it was thickly covered in mesquite, lotebush and a few, clinging redberry junipers. A couple of inches of snow smeared part of the incline, and around the white patch was plenty of loose rock and shale.

Kilcoyn would have to jump, hit the slope and trust to the bushes to slow his descent. He knew he would have to do most of the trip sliding on his rump, but he had little choice in the matter. If Jake Pride climbed up here he'd be caught flat-footed in the open, and would be forced to match the man's gun skill. The falling snow would play into Pride's hands, dictating a close-range battle where Pride's flashing speed and deadly accuracy might make all the difference. There was always the possibility, however slim, that Kilcoyn could shade him. But it was not something he cared to put to the test, especially since Angela and the others were out in the wild country and might need him.

His decision was made. He would jump and meet Jake Pride on his own terms.

Kilcoyn stood at the edge of the ridge, gathered himself and jumped.

He dropped twenty feet and hit the slope hard. His boots sank into loose sand and rock, and he slammed forward on his face. His rifle wrenched loose from his hand and tumbled down the slope away from him, dislodging a shattering shower of shingle. Kilcoyn followed the Winchester, tobogganing down the steep slope on his belly. He rapidly dropped fifty feet, sixty, seventy, then his right shoulder slammed against the thin trunk of a juniper. The tree bent against the big marshal's weight, but it held him in place.

Gingerly, Kilcoyn rolled on his back, then eased himself into a sitting position, one foot on the tree trunk. He took a deep breath, kicked himself away from the juniper and immediately slid the rest of the way on his rump, hitting the flat with a thud that he was sure made Black Mesa jump three feet in the air.

Kilcoyn rose slowly to his feet. He was aching all over and somewhere along the way he'd collected a cut just above his left eye. The marshal wiped away the blood with his fingers, then got a handful of snow and laid it on the cut to slow the bleeding. He looked around and found his Winchester. The rifle barrel was scratched and the stock gouged, but otherwise it was undamaged.

Now there was one question uppermost in his mind—where was Jake Pride?

A bullet provided the answer.

Snow and dirt spurted a few inches from Kilcoyn's feet as Pride's rifle roared. Kilcoyn dived for the meager shelter of a small talus rock. His eyes lifted to the top of the ridge and he saw Pride up there, his Winchester at his shoulder.

Kilcoyn raised his own rifle and fired. A miss, but it was enough to make Pride step quickly away from the edge and vanish from sight.

Kilcoyn figured the man was heading back to the game trail leading down the canyon wall. The steep, prow-shaped cliff that formed the end of the ridge was quite close, and for a moment, the marshal thought about rounding the ridge, then running fast for the canyon before Pride climbed down. But he knew he'd never make it in time. The chances were he'd be caught out in the open while Jake fired at him from the plentiful cover of the canyon mouth.

Better to let Pride come to him.

Kilcoyn studied the landscape around him. To his right a stand of juniper grew close to the base of a low, flat-topped mesa, the ground around the trees level, with a scattering of cholla, yucca and red prickly pear. There were tumbled sandstone rocks showing among the juniper and some darker, wrinkled boulders that were probably chunks of basalt coughed out by an ancient volcanic eruption.

Among the trees seemed like a good place to hole up, offering as it did a clear field of fire to the west and east. Pride would have to come from one of those directions, since the ridge blocked the way to the south and the mesa behind the juniper was a barrier to the north.

Kilcoyn made his way toward the trees just as the snowstorm increased in intensity, giving all the warning signs of a full-blown blizzard. The wind was shrieking now, driving ice-cold from the north, and the snow was falling much heavier, cutting down visibility to a few yards.

His head bent against the wind, Kilcoyn reached the trees and looked for a place where he could find shelter and still watch the open land around him. Here the juniper grew fairly close together and their branches gave some cover from the snow. But at the edge of the tree line, Kilcoyn found a basalt rock crowned by a flat slab of sandstone that had fallen on top of it. The angled sandstone slab jutted out over the basalt, forming a roof of sorts, and it was high enough that Kilcoyn could stand under it and watch around him.

Here he would stay until he got Pride in his sights—or until he froze to death, whichever came first.

Thirty minutes passed and the blizzard grew wilder, whiting out the land in every direction, until the only thing Kilcoyn could see on all sides of him was a barrier of snow. He shivered in the cold, his breath smoking in the air. If there was no letup in the storm he would not be able to stay where he was. He'd have to work his way back to the canyon, where there was shelter.

The only problem was that the blizzard and Jake Pride stood in the way, and right now one was as dangerous as the other.

In an effort to stay warm, Kilcoyn stamped his feet and pulled the sheepskin collar of his mackinaw close to his face. But it brought him little relief. The cold was a living thing that gnawed at him with tearing fangs of ice.

He shoved his hands deep in his pockets to keep them warm for the gunfight that would surely come, and fervently wished for hot coffee and a fire.

But wait. Could he start a fire in the shelter of the rock?

It was unlikely, but worth a try.

The marshal looked around him, at the ground at his feet. There was fallen wood aplenty under the junipers, and some of it was sheltered from the snow by the surrounding rocks. Kilcoyn stepped deeper into the trees and began to gather what dry wood he could find. After a few minutes he had an armful and he walked back to the sandstone overhang.

He stripped off tiny shards of bark, and these he piled together at the base of the basalt rock. Then, his body blocking the worst of the wind, he bent low and thumbed a match into flame. The match sputtered and went out instantly. Kilcoyn reached in his pocket and found another. Crouching closer to the kindling, he lit the match, only to have it again blown out by the wind.

It had been his last match.

Disappointment tugging at him, he now had no alternative. If he wanted to survive the night, he must somehow reach the canyon.

Kilcoyn picked up his rifle and looked into the storm, considering his chances. If he crossed the open ground he'd eventually reach the wall of the ridge. Even if he couldn't see because of the snow, all he had to do was follow the rock wall to where it ended. He could then loop around with the wall and let it guide him back to the canyon and shelter.

It was an uncertain course of action, and fraught with danger, but it was better than the alternative— staying where he was and freezing to death.

Above Kilcoyn the sky was iron gray, and the thick, falling snow spun crazily in the screeching wind. He stepped out of the shelter of the rock and started to make his way across the open ground toward the ridge. He could not see the wall of rock behind the snow, and he knew if he got turned around and lost his way, he'd die out there for sure.

By his own reckoning he was halfway to the wall when he saw Jake Pride emerge from out of the snow like a terrible, gray ghost.

The man was riding a tall horse, but there was no telling its color, covered as it was with snow. Pride too looked like a marble statue, every inch of him white, small icicles clinging to his mustache and eyebrows.

Pride and Kilcoyn saw each other at the same instant. Pride's arm came straight up, a Colt extended at eye level. He fired and Kilcoyn heard the bullet whine as it shredded the air close to his head. Kilcoyn brought the Winchester to his hip and fired, missed and fired again. Another miss, his target obscured by the whirling snowfall.

Pride stiffly set spurs to his horse, but the exhausted animal refused to move any faster than its present shambling walk. The man opened his mouth and yelled something to Kilcoyn that was quickly snatched away by the wind.

The distance between Kilcoyn and Pride closed as the man's horse plodded closer. The marshal levered a round into the chamber of the Winchester but hesitated to shoot. Pride was swaying in the saddle, snow crusting his face. Even his eyes were hidden behind a glaze of ice.

The man was freezing to death. He must have been caught by the worst of the blizzard after he left the canyon, and had kept riding, his insane hatred for Kilcoyn driving him on and on. He was a living corpse, and Kilcoyn could not bring himself to shoot him.

Pride's gun came up again. He fired but the bullet went wide. He rode toward Kilcoyn, firing steadily as he came, bright orange flashes winking in the deepening gloom. None of Pride's bullets were even close, and now the hammer of the man's Colt was snapping on spent rounds.

"Jake, stay right there!" Kilcoyn yelled. "Come any closer and I'll drop you for sure."

Pride rode on, his revolver aimed at Kilcoyn, time after time triggering a gun that mocked him with its hollow, metallic clicks.

Could he let Pride any closer?

Kilcoyn decided he could not. Pride was a dangerous man and at any moment he could go for the rifle in the scabbard under his knee.

The marshal brought the Winchester to shoulder level. "Throw down your pistol and climb off the horse, Jake!" he yelled above the scream of the wind. "I swear to God, if you don't I'll kill you."

Pride reined his faltering mount and his eyes sought Kilcoyn through the thick barrier of the snow. "Did I get you, John?" he hollered, the words coming stiff and spaced out from his frozen mouth. "And did you get me? Are we both in hell already?"

"Toss the gun away and climb down, Jake," Kilcoyn said as Pride urged his horse closer. "Don't make me kill you."

"Hell on wheels," Pride muttered. He climbed awkwardly out of the saddle and stood facing the marshal, his Colt hanging loose in his hand. "This is hell on wheels for sure, ain't it, John? Like in the good old days."

The storm raged around both men, plastering them with snow, the raging wind tearing at them. Kilcoyn and Pride stood looking at each other, united in a strange bond that only the death of one of them would release.

"Hell on wheels," Pride said again. Then his knees buckled and he fell to the ground.

Kilcoyn stepped to the man's side. Pride's breathing was quick and shallow and his face was a grotesque, frozen mask. The marshal got his arms under Pride and lifted him. He caught a glimpse of the junipers through the snow and carried the man toward them, staggering unsteadily now and then as the blizzard hammered at him.

The marshal laid Pride under the shelter of the rock overhang where he was shielded from the worst of the wind. The man's eyes fluttered open and he whispered, "I missed my chance, John. I should have gunned you right away."

"You could have tried," Kilcoyn said. "I don't kill easy."

A smile touched Pride's lips. "Damn right you don't. You're a good lawman, John, always were. Gunned your share, too."

"I took no pleasure in any of them, Jake. I was doing my job was all."

Pride's hand touched Kilcoyn's chest. "Was I a good lawman, John?"

The marshal smiled. "The best, Jake."

"Just wanted to hear you say that. Sounds good."

Life was rapidly leaving Jake Pride. His hand dropped and his eyes closed. "Hell on wheels," he whispered. And then he was gone.

Kilcoyn looked down at Pride and nodded, his face bleak. "You were the best, Jake. Maybe the best that ever was. Then you hitched your wagon to a dark star and threw it all away." Kilcoyn's smile was thin. "And that's just about all the preachifying you're going to get from me."

The marshal rose to his feet, just as Pride's horse walked warily into the junipers. Kilcoyn stepped to the horse and brushed snow from the animal's eyes and neck. "I know you're plumb tuckered out, but do you think you can carry us both to the canyon, boy, huh?"

The horse bobbed its head, the bit jangling, and Kilcoyn grinned. "I'm going to take that as a yes."

He led the horse from the trees, but the animal was reluctant to leave the shelter of the junipers and balked, trying to turn back. Kilcoyn held the reins and soothed his reluctant mount, then swung into the saddle.

Falling snow masked the ridge, and everything else, but Kilcoyn urged the horse forward, trusting to his instincts that he was headed in the right direction. After a few minutes he was able to make out the looming shape of the wall. He swung the horse to the east and rode on, keeping the ridge close to him.

The ridge ended abruptly, a clean, vertical cliff, tumbled talus rocks scattered around its base. Kilcoyn swung the horse around the end of the ridge then headed toward the west, in the direction of the canyon.

It seemed to Kilcoyn that the snow had eased, though the wind was still blowing strong and icy cold. Above him, a small break in the gray clouds appeared, revealing a smear of blue sky, before the gap quickly closed up again.

He rode through some scattered juniper and mesquite, snow lying heavy on their branches, then skirted a huge boulder that had fallen from the ridge in ancient times. The horse had been walking with its head low, tugging on the bit, but suddenly its ears went up and Kilcoyn felt the animal's muscles stiffen. The horse let out a soft whinny and quickened its pace, sensing that the canyon and shelter were near.

Kilcoyn gave the animal its head and it broke into a shambling trot. Through a gap in the snow he saw the mouth of the canyon a couple of minutes later. And there was a man standing there with a rifle across his chest, watching him.

17

A Mysterious Summons

Kilcoyn reined in the horse and levered his Winchester with numb fingers. A man out here could only mean an enemy because, ever since Angela and the others left, he had mighty few friends. The marshal was caught out in the open, an easy target, and having little to lose, he decided on the unexpected.

Kilcoyn yelled, dug his spurs into the horse's flanks and charged at the rifleman.

The tired horse managed to force itself into a shambling canter, and driving snow careened around Kilcoyn as he rode at the man, his spurs flying. But to his surprise, the rifleman dropped his gun and waved his hands, yelling something Kilcoyn could not hear.

The marshal had covered half the ground between himself and the rifleman when he at last heard the man's voice, sounding thin and alarmed above the noise of the wind and the horse's pounding hooves.

"John Kilcoyn, it's me! It's O'Neil!"

Through the curtain of the snow, Kilcoyn recognized O'Neil by his battered plug hat and red hair. He rode up to the man and pulled his mount to a skidding stop, high plumes of snow kicking up from the animal's flailing hooves.

"Why are you here?" he called out, the blizzard forcing him to raise his voice. "Where is Angela?"

"Gone!" O'Neil said, stepping closer to the marshal. "Angela, her father and Bat, they've been took again."

Kilcoyn swung out of the saddle, grabbed O'Neil by the front of his coat and shook him violently. "Who took them? Tell me, who?"

O'Neil opened his mouth to speak again, but Kilcoyn waved a hand to cut him off. The snow and the roaring wind were tearing at them, and he motioned toward the canyon. "We'll find shelter," he yelled. "Then you can tell me what happened." Cold blue eyes bored into O'Neil, hard and threatening. "And for your sake, the part you played had better be real good."

He and O'Neil walked past dead men as Kilcoyn led the horse to the back of the canyon, where other mounts were grazing on what little grass remained. The wind was not as strong here, and the high ridge on three sides kept out the worst of the snow.

Kilcoyn wanted to speak to O'Neil urgently, but he knew the needs of the horse must come first. He unsaddled the gelding and rubbed as much snow off him as he could with the saddle blanket. The horse seemed to like the attention and stood until the marshal had finished, then he wandered off to join the others in the lee of the ridge wall.

Kilcoyn found a spot clear of snow and spread out the saddle blanket to dry. He walked back to where O'Neil was standing beside the projecting column of rock where Kilcoyn had led Angela during the fight with the Indians.

"Before you say another word, Barry, let me first warn you good," Kilcoyn said, his mouth a grim, tight line. "You tell me you found a bottle and started drinking again and I'll gun you right where you stand."

The young man shook his head. "I didn't, John. On me word of honor, in front of all the saints in heaven, I didn't."

Kilcoyn's searching gaze scanned O'Neil's eyes and found no lie there. "All right, what happened?" he asked.

O'Neil swallowed hard, then answered, "We were an hour from here, maybe a little more, and we were keeping the Dry Cimarron in sight all the way when it happened. Bat had been worried about Indians and he kept dropping behind to check our back trail. Finally he rode up to the surrey and told me to ride out and take the point.

"I guess I was a mile ahead of the others when I heard shooting. I rode back and saw six or seven men surrounding the surrey. Bat was lying on the ground, but then they picked him up and threw him in the seat beside Angela and Doc Wilson." O'Neil turned haunted eyes to the marshal. "They saw me then, John, and started shooting. There were too many of them and their bullets were coming real close, so I turned my horse around and ran. Ran all the way back here in fact. I couldn't think of anyplace else to go. I was just hoping that you'd still be alive."

"Did you recognize any of the men?" Kilcoyn asked. "Who were they?"

"That Pawnee with the black turban for sure. And Caleb Early was there. No mistaking that Old Testament beard of his."

"Frank Ivers? Did you see Frank Ivers?"

The young man shook his head. "I don't know. I don't know Frank Ivers."

"Think. He wears two guns, low on his thighs. He's a strutting little guy and he'd be the one doing all the talking."

"I don't know, John," O'Neil said, his face miserable. "I didn't exactly stay around to watch."

Kilcoyn had no doubt that Ivers was leading the bunch. The gunman hadn't made much of a secret about his interest in the ten thousand dollars he was carrying. A frustrated anger gnawing at him, the big marshal realized everything he'd done so far—the gunfight with Jacob Early and his sons, the bloody Indian battles, the death of Jake Pride—had been for nothing. All he'd done was swap one set of kidnappers for another—and this bunch was probably even more ruthless.

At least Jake Pride said he liked Angela, her father and Bat, but Frank Ivers, a cold, emotionless killer who liked no one, would not hesitate to shoot all of them.

"John, I'm sorry," O'Neil was saying. "Maybe I should have stood my ground and tried to make a fight of it."

"You did the right thing, Barry," Kilcoyn said. "All that would have happened is that you'd be dead, and Angela, Doc and Bat would still be captives."

"What are we going to do, John?"

A slight smile touched the marshal's lips. "Right now we're going to start a fire. That is, if you have a match."

The blizzard blew itself out during the night, and Kilcoyn and O'Neil woke to a crystalline world of hard-frozen snow and frost. The surrounding ridges and mesas were crowned with white, and on the flat the buffalo and grama grass was hidden under a glittering blanket that stretched away forever until it met the blue arch of the sky. Tattered crows with frost dusting their wings flapped over the canyon, raucously cawing Kilcoyn to full wakefulness, and the horses stomped and blew columns of smoke from their noses, rested and seemingly eager for a trail to anywhere so long as it was out of this harsh country.

Kilcoyn rose and built up the fire. He filled the coffeepot from the stream, threw in a handful of the tea he'd bought at Pettyman's store and set the pot on the coals to boil.

He turned and looked down at O'Neil, who was just rolling out of his blankets. "Boiling us up tea," Kilcoyn said. "You like tea?"

O'Neil nodded. "That's what we drink in the old country. I never tasted coffee in my life until I arrived in Dodge. Our British overlords drank coffee, but it was too expensive for most Irish people."

"I like tea my ownself, and it makes a change sometimes," Kilcoyn said. "And it will do us good before we take to the trail."

"We going after them, John?"

The marshal nodded. "Yes, we are, but I figure all we'll have to do is head for Dodge and Ivers will find us."

"Then you really think this man Ivers is behind the kidnapping of Angela and the others?"

"I'm sure of it. Ivers wants the money all right. I don't know if he intends to trade Angela and Doc and Bat for the ten thousand dollars, or if he'll just try to take it. I'd say about now he's considering both options."

O'Neil smiled. "John, if we all get through this alive, for heaven's sake tell Angela to stay home for a while."

Despite the worry nagging at him, Kilcoyn laughed. "I'll try, but she's not the kind of gal to stay on the farm."

Before they left, Kilcoyn turned out the dead outlaws' horses, then he found Doc Wilson's deringer, and he and O'Neil saddled up and took to the trail.

Depending on what way Ivers decided to jump, they could be riding into an ambush somewhere along the Cimarron, or they'd meet the gunman and have a war talk. Either way, they were two against six and that didn't stack up to be the best kind of odds.

And there was yet another worrisome thing on Kilcoyn's mind—Frank Ivers was a fast gun, but the man had also made a career of being a sure-thing killer from a distance. There were some who claimed Ivers could shoot a man off a horse at a distance of a mile . . . and that was not a reassuring thought.

The sun rose in the sky, sparkling on the snow, as Kilcoyn and O'Neil headed through the gently rolling hill country along the Cimarron. They rode around the spot where Delagrange and his troopers had been killed. The bodies were covered in mounds of snow, as though nature herself had wanted to bury them after her fashion, but the guidon had been knocked over by the force of the blizzard. Kilcoyn dismounted and stuck the flag back into the frozen ground.

He turned and saw that O'Neil had brought a rosary from his pocket, the beads clicking through his fingers as his white lips moved in prayer. Not a praying man himself, Kilcoyn was grateful. He had not wanted to turn his back on the place a second time and simply walk away without saying something to mark the passing of brave men.

He knew he didn't have the words, but in any event, he could not have improved on what O'Neil was already saying.

After O'Neil's prayers were finished and the man had crossed himself, they mounted up and headed for the ruined cabin were they'd stashed the young man's equipment.

When the two riders reached the cabin they found that O'Neil's mule had returned and was searching for the scant graze along the riverbank.

"John, can we stay for a while and load up my camera and the rest of my stuff?" O'Neil asked. "I don't want to leave it here."

Kilcoyn nodded. "Go ahead. I'll help you get it up on the mule."

There was no hurry. Ivers was unlikely to harm Angela and the others until he'd made a play for the money, either with talk or bullets. The gunman would meet Kilcoyn at a time and place of his own choosing—and there was nothing the marshal could do to change that or bring the event closer.

The mule seemed glad to see them and made little fuss while Kilcoyn and O'Neil loaded his gear onto its back. They stayed long enough at the cabin to boil coffee and fry some salt pork they'd brought from the canyon, then took to the trail again.

They camped that night among some sheltering cottonwoods on the Cimarron, and were in the saddle again at first light.

So far, the snow was holding off, and the wind had dropped, though the morning was bitter cold and smelled hard, raw of winter. A small herd of buffalo passed at a distance, heading south, frost on the humps of the great shaggy bulls, the vaporizing breaths of the animals hanging over them in a steaming gray cloud. From horizon to horizon the lemon-colored sky was cloudless, brightening in the east to pale pink where the sun would very soon begin its climb.

Kilcoyn and O'Neil had been an hour on the trail when they spotted the rider.

The man was sitting his horse on top of a rise, brass field glasses to his eyes. He lowered the glasses and leaned forward in the saddle, intently peering at Kilcoyn. Then, his mind made up, he swung his horse around and galloped fast to the north.

"One of Ivers' men?" O'Neil asked, his eyes following the fleeing rider.

"Looks like," Kilcoyn allowed. "The Pawnee heard me tell Lieutenant Delagrange that I was carrying ransom money to Jake Pride. Ivers took a chance and gambled that I'd survive, or maybe the Pawnee convinced him that my medicine was good and I was a hard man to kill. However it happened, now he knows for sure I'm still alive and what I have in my saddlebags."

The marshal slid his Winchester from the scabbard under his knee. "Shuck your Henry, Barry. From now on we ride real careful."

O'Neil grinned. "Hell, I've been riding real careful since we left the canyon."

Kilcoyn nodded. "That makes two of us. Expecting a bushwhacker's bullet at any second isn't calculated to relax a man, is it?"

But after another hour passed, it wasn't Ivers who showed up, it was T. J. Pettyman riding a good-looking sorrel, and he was alone.

The man was wearing a fur coat and hat, and the only weapon Kilcoyn could see was a rifle in a scabbard behind his right leg.

When Pettyman got within hailing distance, he reined up and put both hands on the saddle horn and waited until Kilcoyn and O'Neil stopped in front of him.

Kilcoyn got right to the point. "Was that your man who was spying on us?"

Pettyman shrugged. "A necessary precaution. I wanted to know when you were coming back in this direction."

"Why?" Kilcoyn asked, his eyes searching Pettyman's face, knowing the man was not to be trusted.

Pettyman ignored that question and answered another that was on the marshal's mind. "Frank Ivers and some others stopped by the settlement yesterday morning. Had friends of yours with him."

Kilcoyn was stunned. "Did he have a woman with him?"

Pettyman smiled. "You mean Angela Wilson?"

"You know Angela?" the marshal asked, surprised.

Pettyman shook his head and smiled. "What do you think? You think I've never been in Dodge before? Everybody with the slightest claim to manhood knows about Doc Wilson's pretty daughter."

"Was Angela all right?"

"As right as a body can be with guns pointed at her the whole time. Same with Doc Wilson and Bat Masterson. Frank is real careful with ol' Bat. He knows he's a dangerous man with a gun."

"Why the hell didn't you stop Ivers?" Kilcoyn asked, his eyes drilling hard into Pettyman.

"Marshal, I own the settlement, or most of it anyway, but I'm not the law. I don't believe I could have rounded up some vigilantes and gone after Ivers. Everybody knows Frank is lightning-fast with the iron, and when it came down to it there would be shooting and dead men all over the street. Let's just say I'd have gotten mighty few volunteers. If any." He paused. "Another thing, men on the dodge know they can come and go at T. J. Pettyman's and no questions asked. If I went after a guest like Frank Ivers, my reputation would be ruined and I'd soon be out of business."

Despite his growing irritation, Kilcoyn could understand Pettyman's problems. The man was right.

He wasn't the law, and hard and tough though the buffalo hunters and trappers at the settlement were, they couldn't stack up to Frank Ivers in a gunfight. Besides, what Ivers did was none of their affair. And if put to it, they would choose to let the man be.

"When did Ivers leave, and which way was he headed?" Kilcoyn asked.

"Left early this morning and rode east. Had Miss Angela in a surrey with her father and Bat Masterson."

"Doc and Bat seem all right to you?"

"Right as rain. Of course, how long they'll stay that way is anybody's guess." Pettyman's shrewd eyes searched the marshal's face. "Frank, now, he wants the ten thousand dollars you're carrying, or so he says."

Exasperated, Kilcoyn snapped, "Hell, it seems everybody in the territory wants that money. How did Ivers know I was still alive?"

Pettyman smiled. "I don't have a sure answer for that, but I'd say the Pawnee told him. I reckon after your friends were taken, the Indian faded back and watched Black Mesa. Believe me, Marshal, he would see you, but you wouldn't see him. Seems to me Frank had it covered both ways. If you lived, he figured he could trade Angela Wilson and the others for the money. But if you were dead, he'd just take it from whoever had it. As for the ten thousand, even split six ways, it's enough to keep a man in whiskey and women for a long time."

"Why are you here, Pettyman?" O'Neil asked, snatching the question from Kilcoyn's lips.

Pettyman ignored O'Neil and addressed his answer to the marshal. "Somebody wants to see you. He thinks he can help."

"I need all the help I can get," Kilcoyn said. "Who is he? A lawman?"

After a moment's pause for effect, Pettyman said, his voice low like he was speaking in church, "He's no lawman. He's Tyler Pickett."

Kilcoyn was taken aback. He held for a while, then said, "Tyler Pickett is dead."

Pettyman shook his head. "He's alive as you or me; at least he was when he sent for me yesterday, shortly after Ivers and his crowd rode in. Mr. Pickett asked me to bring you to him, and what Mr. Pickett asks, Mr. Pickett gets."

"Who in God's name is Mr. Pickett?" O'Neil asked.

Kilcoyn turned to the young man and answered, his breath smoking in the cold, "Tyler Pickett was a bounty hunter, the best of the breed. He operated out of Pecos Plains country in the New Mexico Territory and they say he captured two hundred outlaws, most dead, a few alive. He was good with a rifle, but with the revolver he was a legend, maybe the best man with a Colt who ever lived or will ever live, come to that."

"What happened to him? Why is he here?" O'Neil asked.

Pettyman took up the story. "About ten years ago

Tyler Picket was hired to clear nesters out of the northern San Luis Valley up in Colorado. One time he saw two nesters carrying rifles near their cabin and he drew down on them. When the smoke cleared there were two dead men on the ground, only they weren't men. The day was cold and Pickett had gunned two young girls wearing heavy coats belonging to their pa. One was fourteen, the other twelve. After that, Pickett dropped from sight, then he turned up near my settlement with an old black couple in tow and built himself a cabin. That was nine years ago, and he's been there ever since. He doesn't welcome strangers, keeps folks at a distance with a Sharps ranged for a hundred yards, and most around here don't know who he is anyhow."

"And you never told anyone until now?" O'Neil asked.

Pettyman shrugged. "Like I told you, why a man drifts into this part of the country is his business. I knew who he was, but kept it to myself."

"What kind of help is he offering me?" Kilcoyn asked. "I'm fresh out of nesters."

A slight smile touched Pettyman's lips. "That I don't know. Best ask him your ownself. By the way, he's got more money than God, but you'd never know it by the way he lives."

Kilcoyn sat his saddle in silence and thought it through. He was sure that Ivers was waiting on the trail ahead of them. Did Pickett know the gunman? And did Ivers give him his offer and tell him to pass it along? Anything was possible. It would take a couple of hours out of Kilcoyn's day to talk to Pickett, but it might be worth the ride. As for Ivers, well, he could wait.

"I'll talk to him, Pettyman," Kilcoyn said. "How do I get to his place?"

"I'll take you there," the man answered. "Tyler Picket knows me and he won't shoot."

"You sure about that?" Kilcoyn asked.

"Hell, no," T. J. Pettyman said.

18

A Living Legend

Pettyman leading the way, the three riders crossed the Cimarron, thin sheet ice already forming in the shallows. On the banks, the branches of the willows and cottonwoods were heavy with snow, and among them crows quarreled, now and then knocking down lacy veils of white.

"A place called Sand Arroyo lies about fifty miles to the north of us," Pettyman said to Kilcoyn. "I've been told that Pickett rides up that way sometimes when he wants to be alone with his memories. But I'm sure he'll be to home since he's expecting you."

After an hour's ride through flat, open country, snow stretching away on all sides of them, Pettyman pointed ahead of him. "See the cabin, Marshal?"

Kilcoyn's eyes scanned the distance and made out a small cabin, and an even smaller one connected to it by a dogtrot. Behind the cabins were a barn and corral. Only when they rode closer did the marshal see the barred iron gate and the barbwire fence that surrounded the entire place.

"We'll stop at the gate and let Mr. Pickett get a good look at us," Pettyman said. "He's not a trusting man."

A hand-painted notice was wired to the gate and its warning was plain:

IF YOU WERE NOT INVITED
KEEP OUT!
THIS GATE IS COVERED
BY A SHARPS BIG 50
AT ALL TIMES

"Friendly sort of lad, isn't he?" O'Neil said.

Pettyman nodded. "Like I said, Mr. Pickett is not a trusting man."

He stood in the stirrups, put a hand to his mouth and yelled, "Hello the house."

The door opened and a man's voice called out, "What do you want?"

"It's me. T. J. Pettyman."

"Hell," the man in the cabin hollered, "since I spoke to you yesterday you still haven't been hung?"

"Give it time, Mr. Pickett," Pettyman yelled, taking no visible offense. "Give it time."

Kilcoyn heard a chuckle, then the man said, "Pettyman, you skedaddle. But send those other two fellers on ahead, and tell them to ride slow with their hands away from their guns."

"I heard him," Kilcoyn said. He rode to the gate, leaned down and slid open the steel bolt. He rode through and O'Neil followed.

"Good luck." Pettyman grinned. He waved to Kilcoyn, swung his horse around and cantered away.

"Close the gate behind you, damn it," Pickett yelled. "Were you born in a barn?"

Kilcoyn did as he was told, then he and O'Neil rode to the cabin. The young man made to step out of the saddle, but Kilcoyn stopped him. "It's customary to wait until you're invited," he said.

After a few moments the door to the cabin swung open and an elderly black man walked onto the narrow porch and said, "Mr. Pickett said for you two gennelmen to please step down and come into the house."

Kilcoyn and O'Neil swung out of the saddle and followed the old man inside.

The cabin was spare and neat, brass pots gleaming over the cherry red stove, the pine floor scrubbed to an all-over white. A man who looked to be in his midfifties rose from a wooden chair by the stove when Kilcoyn and O'Neil entered.

He stuck out his hand to Kilcoyn. "I'm Tyler Pickett."

"Heard of you," Kilcoyn said, shaking the man's hand. "I'm United States Marshal John Kilcoyn."

Pickett nodded, smiling. "Heard of you too." He extended his hand to O'Neil. "And you are?"

"Barry O'Neil. I'm a photographer."

"And Irish, and just off the boat if your speech is any guide." He studied O'Neil intently for a few moments. "Had my picture made a few times. Never liked a single one of them."

Pickett was of medium height, with observant brown eyes and a neatly trimmed mustache and goatee. He was slender and trim and moved gracefully, and his deeply tanned skin gave him the look of an old-time Spanish conquistador.

Despite his age, Pickett seemed confident and ready for anything, and his body was hard and muscular, without apparent stiffness.

An old black woman, plump and smiling, had walked into the cabin from another room and Pickett waved a hand in her direction. "This is Bessie. She cooks and cleans for me, and does both very well. Her husband you've already met. His name is Elijah Rowe and he can do just about anything he turns his hand to. Best danged blacksmith who ever lived, I'll tell you that."

Pickett looked at Kilcoyn from the toes of his scuffed, down-at-heel boots to the top of his head. "For such a big, strong feller you look a mite peaked," he said. "When did you boys last have a decent meal?"

"Been a spell," Kilcoyn allowed. "I reckon I'm missing quite a few."

Pickett turned to the woman. "Bessie, you think you can fix these boys up with some grub?"

"I can surely do that, Mr. Pickett," Bessie said, grinning. "Dinner's just about ready anyhow."

"Shuck those coats and come sit at the table," Pickett said. "I think you'll discover that Bessie is a wonderful cook."

Kilcoyn took off his mackinaw and hung it on a peg behind the door. He adjusted his cartridge belt and holster but made no move to remove it, something that Pickett saw and approved.

"Careful man, aren't you, Marshal Kilcoyn?"

Kilcoyn nodded. "Live longer that way."

He sat at the scrubbed pine table, O'Neil beside him, found room for his long legs, then said, "Pettyman said you wanted to help us. What kind of help are you offering?"

Pickett made a face. "Pettyman gets nothing right. Notice that thick neck of his? Now that's a neck that was born for a rope." The man held for a moment or two, then said, "Marshal, I want only to help myself. Now, if in doing that I help you, then that's just fine."

"Lay your cards on the table, Pickett," Kilcoyn said. "What do you want from me?"

"Tell me about this man Frank Ivers, Marshal. He has kidnapped some friends of yours, I believe."

Kilcoyn nodded. "Yes, he has. I'm carrying ten thousand dollars that belongs to the citizens of Dodge City. Ivers wants it."

"So tell me about him," Pickett said. "How good is he?"

"He's good, or so I've heard. Very fast with the Colt on the draw and shoot."

Pickett nodded. "I've met men with that kind of reputation before. Most of them turned out to be much less than I expected. Come now, how good is he really? Better than Clay Allison?"

"Faster, they say."

"And John Wesley?"

"Faster on the draw than Hardin and shoots just as well."

"Hickok?"

"I'm told Hickok backed down from Ivers in Abilene a few years back." Kilcoyn looked at Pickett, trying to gauge the man's motives. "Pickett, let me sum it all up for you—Frank Ivers is real good with a gun. Maybe the best around."

Pickett's hand slammed on the table, and out of the corner of his eye Kilcoyn saw O'Neil jump in surprise. "This is intolerable," the man said. "Now I've begun hearing that people are saying Frank Ivers is better than Tyler Pickett ever was."

"Do you care?" Kilcoyn smiled. "After all, you came here to be forgotten."

"Yes, I wanted to be forgotten, live in a place where no one knew me. But I didn't want my reputation to be forgotten. Long after I'm gone, I want the history books to say I was the best who ever lived."

"And now the only way you can do that is to kill Frank Ivers," O'Neil said.

"Your perception does you credit, young man,"

Pickett said. His eyes lifted to Bessie as she stepped to the table. "Ah, here is Bessie with food. We'll eat and then talk more."

The old woman laid a huge platter of buffalo and beefsteaks on the table, along with mashed potatoes, boiled onions and pinto beans. Moving plates and silverware around, she also made room for a domed apple pie, steam rising straight as a string from a hole in the middle of its golden crust, and a pot of coffee.

"Dig in," Pickett said. "Don't let the food get cold."

Kilcoyn and O'Neil ate heartily, as did Pickett, and after he'd refused a third piece of pie, Kilcoyn eased back in his chair and smiled at Bessie. "A grand meal, Mrs. Rowe, and we surely do appreciate it."

Bessie gave a little curtsy. "You're most welcome. I like to see young men eat."

"Told you she was a good cook," Pickett said, mopping gravy off his plate with a piece of bread. He popped the bread into his mouth, then said, "Now back to business. I propose to ride with you, Marshal. When we meet up with this Ivers, let me reckon with him."

Kilcoyn shook his head. "You're free to ride with us, Pickett, but I aim to try and release my friends without gunplay. I don't want bullets flying around when I meet Ivers. Other people might get hurt."

"You mean Angela Wilson in particular?" Pickett smiled. He waved away the amazed question on Kilcoyn's tongue. "I know things, Marshal. I have spies everywhere."

"Yes, Angela in particular," Kilcoyn admitted, realizing that to say otherwise would be an untruth.

Pickett nodded and went on. "Then let me set your mind at rest. What will happen will occur only between Ivers and myself. Trust me, Marshal, I don't waste lead. There will be no flying bullets, as you fear. I will gun Ivers, bid you good day and be on my way."

The marshal shook his head in wonderment. "Years ago, I heard about gunfighter pride, and later I saw it in action a few times. But, Pickett, I have to say, when it comes to pride, you take the biscuit."

"False pride is a vice, Marshal, and I have none of that. Pride in oneself is a virtue and that's why I wish to leave a legacy behind me. Generations from now, men will talk about Allison, Hickok and Hardin and a dozen others, and when the talking is done and they sum it all up, they'll say: 'But the best of them all was Tyler Pickett.' "

Without waiting for Kilcoyn's comment, Pickett turned to the old black man who had just entered the room and said: "Elijah, I will be riding out today."

The man called Elijah beamed. "After near ten years, Mr. Pickett?"

Pickett nodded. "It is high time."

Elijah stepped through a door off the main room of the cabin and returned a couple of minutes later with a flat, brown paper parcel. He opened the strings and showed Pickett what lay within. The man nodded his satisfaction and said, "And the dragon box too, Elijah, if you please."

Pickett rose from the table, picked up the parcel and gave Kilcoyn a slight bow. "Excuse me, Marshal. I must go into my bedroom, but I'll be back directly."

After Pickett left, Elijah stepped to a gun rack on the wall, opened a drawer and removed a rectangular ebony box decorated with a silver Chinese dragon, and this he laid on the table.

The railroad clock on the wall ticked away several minutes. Then Pickett reappeared. Gone were the worn shirt and pants he'd been wearing, replaced by a black broadcloth suit and an immaculately white frilled shirt and four-in-hand tie under a brocaded vest. He had highly polished, elastic-sided boots on his feet and a low-crowned hat with a flat brim completed his attire.

Elijah walked into the other room, returned and stepped behind Pickett, settling a heavy cloak of black wool over his shoulders, closing it at the neck with a clasp of thick, engraved silver.

Without a word, Pickett lifted the lid of the box on the table and removed a short-barreled Colt. In contrast to his sartorial finery, the man's revolver was a plain working gun, blue, with a short barrel and black rubber grip plates. Pickett opened the loading gate, thumbed back the hammer to half cock and removed cartridges from the box. He inspected each round carefully, then filled one chamber, rotated the cylinder, missing the next, then loaded the remaining four. He cycled the Colt, the hammer coming to rest on the empty chamber.

Pickett dropped the gun into the right pocket of his frock coat. "My horse, Elijah," he said.

Elijah Rowe nodded, then grinned. "You look mighty fine, Mr. Pickett, mighty fine. Just like in the old days."

"Thank you, Elijah. I must confess, I'm starting to feel like I did in the old days." Pickett looked at Kilcoyn and smiled. "Ready when you are, Marshal."

Kilcoyn and O'Neil rose to their feet, and the big marshal hesitated a moment, a scowl on his face as he chose his words carefully before he said, "Frank Ivers shucks a gun real fast from the leather. You sure you want to carry the Colt in your pocket?"

"Good heavens, Marshal, where else would I carry it?" Pickett asked, surprised. "Oh, I see what you mean. Why not a cartridge belt and holster? Well, I tried that once in my younger days, but found it most uncomfortable. Pained my kidneys after a while."

Kilcoyn gave a slight shake of his head. "Pickett, I guess you know what you're doing."

"I should hope so, Marshal. I did it for a long number of years."

After a few minutes, Elijah Rowe stepped into the cabin, accompanied by a gust of icy wind and a few stray flakes of snow. "Your hoss is saddled, Mr. Pickett."

Pickett nodded, then said: "Elijah, you know where my money box is kept. Give me a week, and if I don't come back, then you'll know I'm dead."

Bessie covered her face with her hands and wailed, "Oh, don't say that, Mr. Pickett. I can't bear to hear you say that. Look at me, I'm all a-tremble."

Pickett ignored the woman's outburst and said, "Elijah, now listen carefully and understand. There are five double eagles in the money box and a paper. That paper is my will. I know you can't read, so take the money and the will to Pettyman. Give him the hundred dollars and ask him to read what I've written, then tell him to get in touch with my lawyer in Denver. The lawyer's name is Wilson G. Battles and he takes care of my money.

"All of it, little as it is, will go to you and Bessie for putting up with me for so long."

Pickett placed his hand on the old man's shoulder. "Pettyman is a whiskey-peddler, a pimp and a rogue, but he won't try to cheat you. My lawyer won't let him. He also knows that if he did, I'd come back and haunt him." Pickett looked intently into Rowe's eyes. "Do you understand what I'm saying to you, Elijah?"

The old man nodded, his eyes stained red with tears. "You come back to us, Mr. Pickett. You hear me? You come right on back to us now."

"I'll sure try, Elijah. I'd hate to be sitting in hell, pining for Bessie's cooking."

"You're going up, Mr. Pickett, up to the glory of the Lord," Bessie said. "You ain't going down.

What's in your past is done and you've surely grieved for it. The good Lord knows that."

"I hope he does." Pickett smiled. "He and I have never exactly been on speaking terms."

"Mr. Pickett, before we go . . ."

It was O'Neil's voice and Pickett turned to him.

"I want to make your picture," O'Neil said. "For posterity's sake."

Pickett's eyes moved to Kilcoyn. "Do we have time, Marshal? For posterity's sake?"

"I guess we do." Kilcoyn smiled. "Since it's for the history books."

Kilcoyn's smile was slight and forced, because suddenly a real bad feeling was nagging at him.

But who was the goose flying for now?

19

The Return of Bat Masterson

It took an hour before O'Neil was finished with Pickett, posing the man standing, sitting on a chair and sitting his horse against the backdrop of the cabin.

"You made a real handsome subject, Mr. Pickett," O'Neil said after he packed away his camera. "It was an honor to make your picture."

Pickett seemed to take the compliment in stride, as no more than his due, acknowledging O'Neil's flattery with a smile and slight inclination of his head. Once again Kilcoyn saw gunfighter pride in action and he understood it no better than he had before.

The three riders left the cabin and headed east, Pickett riding a tall black gelding with four white stockings and a blaze face. Above them the sky was still cloudless and blue, the sun bright but shining without warmth. The air seemed to be formed of ice crystals that entered the lungs like broken glass and made the chest hurt.

Kilcoyn and the others met up with the Cimarron again in flat country and swung with it to the northeast, the land around them covered in snow, broken up here and there by mesquite and prickly pear, scorched brown by cold.

Another, larger herd of buffalo passed them, heading south like the last one, toward the sheltering canyons and steep-sided arroyos of the Sangre de Cristo.

O'Neil wanted to photograph the great shaggies, but decided they'd be long gone before he could set up for a shot.

"Maybe you could shoot one, John, and pose with it," he suggested, watching helplessly as the herd plodded past.

Kilcoyn shook his head. "There will be none of them left soon enough," he said. "I don't aim to make it happen any faster."

An hour later they spotted a lone horseman loping toward them, but as the rider got closer, it became obvious to Kilcoyn that the man was astride a tall horse with a familiar gait. Judging by the rider's erect posture, English coat and white sombrero, it could only be Bat Masterson.

That notion was confirmed when Masterson rode closer and threw up a hand in greeting. "Figured you'd stay to the Cimarron, John," he yelled from a distance. "That is, if you were still alive. And I see Barry is with you. Glad he made it."

Kilcoyn spurred his horse, rode alongside Masterson and slapped the sheriff on the back. "Good to see you again, Bat." He grinned. "How are Angela and Doc and how did you escape?"

Masterson shook his head. "I didn't escape, John. I have a message from Frank Ivers. As to Miss Angela and her father, they were doing fine the last I saw them, though that Hank Poteet says he's had just about enough of Doc hollering at him and calling him stupid all the time."

"Sound likes Alan Wilson." Kilcoyn smiled. He saw the sheriff's eyes move to Pickett. "This is Mr. Tyler Pickett. He's riding with us."

Masterson was stunned. "You mean Tyler Pickett the bounty hunter? The man they say was the best of the best with a gun? But . . . but I thought you were dead."

"Not likely," Pickett said, smiling, pleased that Masterson had remembered. "Since I'm right here."

Kilcoyn saw the question on the sheriff's face. "Later. Now tell me what Ivers said."

"I will, John. But that can wait a moment. First off, tell me what happened to you after we left the canyon. Is Jake Pride dead?"

"The snow killed him, Bat," Kilcoyn said. "Not me."

Using as few words as possible, Kilcoyn told the sheriff about Pride's death and how he met up with O'Neil at the canyon, and their subsequent visit to Pickett's cabin.

"And you still have the money?" Masterson asked.

Kilcoyn slapped his saddlebags. "Right here."

"That's good, John, because Frank wants that ten thousand real bad. He wants it bad enough that he was willing to go up against Jake and take it from him if you were killed."

"What does Ivers say?"

With the back of his hand, Masterson rubbed an icicle that was hanging over his mouth off his mustache and said, "Frank says you're to leave the money on the west bank of Crooked Creek, at the big bend. He says you'll see a granite rock with Indian pictures." The sheriff's stud was acting up and it took him a few moments to settle the horse. "Have you ever been there, John?"

Kilcoyn shook his head.

"I have," Bat said. "Doc Holliday took me out there one time. Doc is real interested in stuff like that. He reckoned the pictures were drawn long before the Cheyenne got here, by Indians who vanished centuries ago." The sheriff smiled. "Doc was always gallivanting off somewhere to look at Indian ruins up on cliffs or out on the plains. He'd come back with bits of broken clay pots and stone arrowheads and such." Masterson shook his head. "I never could quite understand why he set such store by stuff that somebody else had thrown away."

The sheriff let his horse nose around in the snow for a few moments, then yanked up its head. "Frank said one other thing, John. He says after you leave the money at the rock you've got to fog it back to Dodge. He says he won't let Angela and her father go until you do."

Pickett had been listening to Masterson. Now he said, disappointment clouding his eyes, "Then it seems I won't get my chance to meet Ivers after all."

"I wouldn't bet on it," Kilcoyn said. "A man like Frank Ivers says one thing and means another."

"Do you think it could be a trap, John?" O'Neil asked.

The marshal shrugged. "I don't think so. Ivers has nothing to gain from killing us. But he may have something else in mind. I wonder . . ."

"Wonder what?" O'Neil prompted.

"Just a passing thought," Kilcoyn said. "Probably means nothing, but it's possible Ivers may try to up the ante by keeping Angela and her father and demanding more money."

"What do we do if that happens?" Masterson asked.

"I don't know. But in the meantime we'll do as Ivers said and ride to Crooked Creek. If he shows with Angela and Doc, we'll take it from there."

They camped that night on the Cimarron, and next morning crossed a shallow, iced-over branch running off the river before reaching Crooked Creek a few minutes after noon. As Kilcoyn had expected, they'd seen no sign of Ivers and his outlaws, or even encountered tracks.

So far, the snow was still holding off, and the sky remained blue, free of cloud, though it was growing even colder, a freeze so numbing that Kilcoyn rode with his gun hand in the pocket of his mackinaw. A few of the tall cottonwoods along the creek had already split from the cold, and the frost-covered willows were bare and dropping branches.

Kilcoyn led the way to the southeast and an hour later he rode up on the bend of the creek, less than forty miles from Dodge.

The snow around the granite rock was free of tracks, and there was nothing to indicate that Ivers, or anyone else, had been there. Kilcoyn reined up and looked around him at the flat, empty landscape. Nothing moved in that snowy wasteland, and even the birds seem to have deserted the place.

The ancient pictographs on the rock were fading, a hunting scene that showed running buffalo and humans on foot armed with bows, done in colors taken from the earth, muted tones of brown, green, black, red and yellow.

Masterson rode alongside Kilcoyn and asked, "Well, what do we do now, John?"

"Give me time to think, Bat," the marshal said. "I believe maybe I have a plan, but whether it will work or not depends on Frank Ivers."

Kilcoyn studied the lay of the land around the creek. The granite rock, vaguely coffin-shaped and as tall as a man on a horse, stood thirty feet back from the bend. The bend itself was covered in cottonwood and willow, the thick brush at their roots buried under snow. If a man hid among the trees, he'd have a view of the rock and an open field of fire.

The question was—could Kilcoyn stay concealed without freezing to death while he waited for Ivers?

Then it came to him.

A far-seeing man, he could climb to the top of the glyph rock and have a view of the country for many miles around. When he spotted Ivers and his riders approaching in the distance, he'd have plenty of time to climb down and take up a position among the trees.

Against a fast gunman like Ivers, surprise would be the one thing that could stack all the chips on his side of the table, and he might be able to avoid gunplay altogether.

Now he had a proposition for Pickett.

Kilcoyn rode beside the man. "There's a Pawnee with Ivers, but we didn't see any sign of him on the trail, so I'm betting that Ivers doesn't know you're with us."

Pickett nodded, his eyes puzzled. "Seems likely enough."

"But if the Pawnee is on the scout, looking for us to head for Dodge, he'll expect to see me. And that's where you come in, Pickett."

The man was wary and it showed. "And your idea is?"

"That you wear my hat and mackinaw and ride my dun. From a distance even the Pawnee will be fooled."

"And what will you do, Marshal?"

Kilcoyn nodded toward the trees. "Hole up in there until Ivers gets here, and then try my darndest to save Angela and her pa."

"How many of them are there?" Pickett asked.

"How many, Bat?" Kilcoyn asked without taking his eyes from Pickett.

"Six, John, including Ivers," the deputy said. "One of them is the Injun and another is Poteet, and he's maybe the worst of the bunch, good with a gun and pizen mean. He says he aims to shot Doc Wilson afore long. Says Doc talks too much."

"One man against six, Marshal?" Pickett asked. "I don't think even you can cope with those odds."

Kilcoyn shrugged. "I've got it to do. It's my job, why they pay me the money."

"Your dedication to duty does you credit, sir," Pickett said. "But I say again that even you can't buck odds like that. I'll stay with you. I don't want to lose my chance to meet Ivers."

"You don't understand," Kilcoyn said. "I guarantee Ivers will have that Pawnee out, and the Indian expects to see me ride away from here."

"And ride away you will, Marshal," Pickett said. "I'll handle that little problem. I've done it before."

20

Gunfight at Picture Rock

Kilcoyn and the others made camp by the creek that night. Masterson and O'Neil built a small fire at the base of the rock on the side away from the ancient drawings, at Kilcoyn's insistence. Bessie had packed food for Pickett, and they ate well on thick bacon sandwiches and wedges of pie.

They dozed as best they could, huddled around the fire, and Pickett, older than any of them and unused to the trail, was beginning to show signs of exhaustion.

He made light of it, joking that a man as old as the Brazos River misses the comforts of home, but there was no denying the lines of strain gathered around his eyes and the gray pallor under his tanned skin.

Kilcoyn was worried. When Ivers and his men showed up, would Pickett be able to hold his own in a fight if it came to gunplay? The man was a legendary shootist and manhunter, but even legends grow old and stiff in the joints, and the present passes them by.

As he shivered in the icy, keening wind, Kilcoyn glanced over at the sleeping Pickett and wished only for tomorrow.

The dawn brought a few flurries of snow that swirled and chased each other around the standing rock. Gray clouds covered the sky and the rising wind blew from the north, cold and pitiless, adding to the bleak gloom of the morning.

Kilcoyn rose to his feet, wrapped himself in his blanket, walked down to the creek and filled the coffeepot after using its weight to crack through a thin sheet of ice.

Masterson was on his feet and he was building up the fire with damp wood when Kilcoyn returned.

The marshal nodded to Masterson, then said, "Bat, I'd like you and O'Neil to move out this morning. Head in the direction of Dodge unless you're close enough to hear shooting. Then fog it back here. In any case, give me today and tomorrow, then come looking for me. How does that set with you?"

"Just fine, John," Masterson answered, "but Pickett said you'd be with us."

"In spirit, maybe." Kilcoyn smiled as he kneeled and placed the pot on the fire. "Though Pickett seems to think I can be in two places at once."

"And you can," the old gunfighter said from

where he was hunched over in his blankets. "Marshal, you'll be a wooden lawman on a dun horse."

"I don't get your drift," Kilcoyn said.

"I'll show you. That is, just as soon as I work up the courage to get out from under my blankets and work the frost out of my bones."

Pickett rose stiffly to his feet, groaning from the effort. He huddled in his cloak, stood and watched Kilcoyn throw a handful of coffee into the pot. "While the coffee is making, O'Neil, will you help me gather some wood? Maybe even cut some?"

"Sure thing," O'Neil said.

"Then I'll show you what we need," Pickett said.

The coffee was boiling when Pickett and O'Neill returned, their arms full of willow branches and long blades of the tough bunchgrass that grew along the creek bank.

Pickett stepped beside the fire and rubbed his hands, grinning. "Coffee first, then we'll make us a new Deputy United States Marshal John Kilcoyn."

Kilcoyn drank from his steaming cup, stepped back and admired Pickett's handiwork. "Well, it doesn't look like me, but I guess it could fool somebody at a distance."

"It's not finished yet," Pickett said, smiling. "I need your hat and coat."

Reluctantly, Kilcoyn shrugged out of his coat, took off his hat and handed them to Pickett. Helped by

Masterson and O'Neil, Pickett draped the coat around the vaguely man-shaped willow framework roped to the saddle of Kilcoyn's dun, then shoved the marshal's hat on top of its head.

"It works, I think," Pickett said. "I'm betting it will even hoodwink the Pawnee."

"Let's hope so," Kilcoyn said, shivering. He picked up his blanket and draped it around his shoulders. "I'm sure going to miss that coat."

"Well, John, I guess it's time Barry and me were moving out," Masterson said. He smiled. "And we'll take you with us."

"What about Mr. Pickett's black?" O'Neil asked.

"Take that too, and try to keep it hidden," Kilcoyn answered. "But I guess if the Pawnee is on the scout, he'll be counting men, not horses."

Masterson and O'Neil left thirty minutes later, the sheriff leading Kilcoyn's dun, with its swaying burden, and Pickett's black, keeping the big horse between his stud and the pack mule.

The marshal and Pickett watched the two men leave until they were swallowed up by distance and the gray morning. Kilcoyn had to admit that the wooden marshal looked all right, and might even fool the Pawnee's keen eyes. If it didn't . . . then they wouldn't have to search too far to find a whole heap of trouble. Frank Ivers would come a-shooting.

After Masterson and O'Neil were out of sight, Kilcoyn climbed to the top of the rock, helped by Pickett, who pushed on his rump when the going got difficult. The marshal's perch was precarious, the rock slick with ice and frost. His blanket did little to protect him from the cold and wind.

Pickett kept the fire small, barely enough to keep the coffee hot, and he piled up snow next to the coals, ready to douse the smoky flames when Ivers and his men showed.

The dreary morning wearied on until noon. Snow flurries tossed in the bucking wind and the cottonwoods flung their arms around, creaking and groaning like tuckered-out old men. Around Kilcoyn the silent country stretched away flat and white until it met the clouds at the horizon, where earth and sky became one. He looked out on a wild, uncaring and unforgiving wilderness, yet he was neither detached from it nor afraid of it. A man of his time and place, John Kilcoyn was close kin to all he saw, a relative to the snow and the wind and the raw, endless and beautiful land.

Another hour passed and nothing moved in the distance.

Then, after the passage of more time, when the hands of the watch in his vest pocket showed two, Kilcoyn saw riders emerge from the under the veil of the low cloud, five dark exclamation points of danger against the white backdrop of the snow.

"They're coming!" Kilcoyn called out to Pickett, and the man instantly killed the fire. The big marshal jumped down from the rock and said to Pickett,

"Now we get down among the trees, and it's not going to be pleasant."

"Cold, I imagine," Pickett said, smiling. He pretended sympathy. "Dear, dear, and you with no coat."

Kilcoyn nodded, his smile matching that of the other man. "It's the only coat I own, too. I sure hope Bat Masterson takes care of it."

Both men worked their way into the underbrush at the base of the trees, dislodged snow showering over them. There was nothing to be done about their footprints surrounding the rock, but then Ivers had told Kilcoyn to leave the money here and he would expect to see tracks.

Through a gap in the brush the marshal watched the five riders get closer.

Five riders!

Where was the surrey carrying Angela and her father? And was Ivers among the men now heading toward the bend in the creek?

Kilcoyn had no time to ponder those questions because the riders reined up a couple of hundred yards from where he and Pickett were hidden, wary and alert for any sign of danger.

The Pawnee, easily spotted in his black turban, rode forward from the rest, his rifle held upright, the butt resting on his thigh. He stopped about fifty yards from the rock, sitting tense and ready in the saddle as his eyes scanned the creek.

Kilcoyn swore bitterly under his breath. Damn that Indian! Did he suspect something was wrong?

A few minutes ticked past as the Pawnee studied the rock and the bend of the creek, then the man rode to his right and Kilcoyn could no longer see him. Moments later hooves crunched on the snow and the Pawnee appeared just yards away from Kilcoyn, studying the ground around the rock.

He was looking for the saddlebags, now miles away on the marshal's horse.

Kilcoyn's numb fingers flexed on the handle of his Colt and beside him he felt Pickett tense. The Indian rode around the rock, his eyes fixed on the ground. Finally he raised his rifle over his head and yelled for the others to join him.

Kilcoyn felt a surge of relief. The Pawnee had been so intent on looking for the saddlebags his eyes hadn't once strayed to the underbrush among the cottonwoods.

As the others drew closer, the Pawnee spat into the snow, then said, "Money no here."

Hank Poteet swore viciously and turned to Caleb Early. "This is a fine howdy-do. What the hell happened?"

Early shrugged. "Maybe Kilcoyn is dead."

"Kilcoyn is not dead," the Pawnee said. "I told you I saw him leave the canyon at Black Mesa, and I saw him riding east of here this morning with two others."

"Hell, why didn't you kill him and take the money while you had the chance?" Poteet asked.

The Pawnee flashed a rare smile. "Some things are easier said than done, and John Kilcoyn does not kill easily, I think."

"Then let's get after them," Poteet said, gathering the reins of his horse. "Hell, I got big plans for my share of the money."

"Now, Pickett!" Kilcoyn yelled.

The two men burst from the underbrush and Kilcoyn hollered, "You men are under arrest!"

"You go to hell!" Poteet cried, his hand streaking for the Colt in his waistband.

Beside Kilcoyn, Pickett drew from his coat pocket and fired. His bullet hit Poteet square between the eyes and the man fell backward off his horse. A shot cut past Kilcoyn's head as Pickett fired again and again, working his gun faster and surer than Kilcoyn had ever seen it done. Two outlaws immediately went down to Pickett's bullets, before they'd even cleared leather.

The Pawnee yipped a war cry and kicked his horse toward Kilcoyn, holding his Winchester straight out in front of him. Kilcoyn fired and the Indian reeled in the saddle, triggering the rifle into the air. He fell off his horse and thudded, sprawled on his face, into the snow.

A gun blasted and Pickett went down on one knee, hit hard, sudden blood splashing bright scarlet on his white shirt. Kilcoyn saw Caleb Early steady his prancing horse for another shot, his thumb on the hammer of his Colt. The marshal fired at the man and missed, but Pickett, shooting from his kneeling position, hit Early in the chest. The man screamed and Pickett put a second bullet into Early's head before he hit the ground.

Greasy gray gunsmoke drifted around the standing rock as Kilcoyn cocked his revolver, his darting eyes searching for another target. There was none. Five men were down, and all but the Pawnee had fallen to Pickett's deadly fire. Kilcoyn heard Pickett groan, and the man slumped to his right and fell to the ground on his side. Gently the big marshal eased Pickett onto his back, and the old gunfighter smiled. "Which one was Ivers?" he asked.

Pickett was very close to death, and Kilcoyn told him what he wanted to hear. "The first man you shot, the one drawing from the waistband, that was Frank Ivers."

Pickett nodded. "Figured it was him. He had sand, but I showed him, didn't I? Cut his suspenders for him."

"You sure did," Kilcoyn said. "Tyler Pickett, I'd say you're the best there is with a gun, or ever will be."

"Then I guess I really am one for the history books," Pickett whispered, his smile widening. Then his eyes closed and he was gone.

Kilcoyn crossed the dead man's hands across his chest, placed Pickett's Colt in his cold hands, then closed his cloak around him.

He rose and looked around at the dead outlaws. All of them had been hard, tough men, good with the iron, but they'd never in their lives encountered someone like Tyler Pickett. They'd come up against a legend, and learned too late that such men become legends for a reason and that their reputation is hard-won.

The Pawnee's horse was standing near the glyph rock, its reins trailing. Kilcoyn gathered them, picked up his blanket and stepped into the saddle. He wrapped the blanket around himself and looked out at the distance stretching away between him and Dodge, at the reckless wind spurring the flurrying snow. Where, in all that wilderness, were Angela and Doc?

And where was Frank Ivers?

21

Return to Dodge

John Kilcoyn rode into Dodge as the day died around him. A gray pall of wood smoke from stoves hung over the town at rooftop level and the oil lamps were being lit along Front Street, their reflectors casting shifting yellow pools of light on the snow. Every window Kilcoyn passed was brocaded thickly with frost except for the Sideboard Restaurant's, where the panes were steamed up and the tang of coffee and frying steaks drifting from the door set the marshal's stomach to grumbling, nudging him to remember his growing hunger.

Huddled in his blanket and numb from head to toe, Kilcoyn rode past the Alamo Saloon, open for business as the tinkling piano confirmed, but somehow the place looked dim and bleak now that the raucous Texas cowboys were gone.

A sad kind of weariness tugging at him, the marshal unsaddled the Pawnee's horse at the livery stable and rubbed down the wiry little paint with a piece of sacking. At first the pony tried to buck and kick, but after a while it settled down, enjoying the man's attention. Kilcoyn gave the horse a bucket of oats, then forked some hay into the stall. He realized he was being extravagant with the oats, but since he'd ridden the horse on city business, Mayor Kelley would get the bill.

Kilcoyn's dun stood in another stall. He grabbed a handful of oats, stepped over and fed them to the big horse. Like the paint, the dun seemed to enjoy being the center of attention, and he whinnied softly and rubbed his forehead against the marshal's blanketed shoulder.

The wind tore at Kilcoyn and drove icy snow into his face as he stomped quickly along the boardwalk, his spurs clanking. A drummer in a flapping greatcoat stepped out of the Alamo, then stopped in the doorway to let the marshal pass. Kilcoyn felt the man's puzzled eyes follow him all the way to the sheriff's office.

When Kilcoyn stepped inside he was surprised to see Masterson and O'Neil already there. Masterson was sitting in his chair, his feet on the desk, and the young Irishman, who looked to be stone-cold sober, was standing at the stove, open hands extended to the heat.

Masterson jumped to his feet, stammering as his crowding questions got tangled up on his tongue.

"Wha—wha . . . happened, John?" he asked finally. "Where's Angela and her father?"

Kilcoyn shook his head. "They didn't show at the creek. Neither did Ivers."

"But . . . but . . ."

"Let me get some coffee first, Bat," Kilcoyn said. "I swear my jaws are frozen shut."

O'Neil poured coffee for Kilcoyn and passed the cup to the marshal. Kilcoyn drank it gratefully. Masterson, as intent as a hawk, watched until he gauged that the coffee was half gone. Then he said, "Now will you tell us what happened?"

"Or what didn't happen," Kilcoyn said.

Briefly he told Masterson and O'Neil about the fight at the creek and the death of Tyler Pickett. "There were six men dead on the ground when the smoke cleared and it was all over, but Frank Ivers wasn't one of them," he concluded.

"But where are Angela and Doc Wilson?" Masterson asked again, his face troubled.

Exasperation niggled at Kilcoyn. "Bat, if I knew that, would I be standing here drinking coffee and talking to you and Barry?"

Kilcoyn saw a sudden wounded look in the sheriff's eyes, and he said, "Sorry, Bat, that was uncalled for on my part. I guess I'm riled up some."

"I understand, John," the sheriff said. "And I take no offense. We're all feeling a mite on edge."

O'Neil asked, "Well, where do we go from here?"

Kilcoyn drained his coffee. "First I'll talk to Mayor Kelley and tell him what's happened. I guess he'll still want to pay the money when we hear from Ivers."

"The mayor planned to ride with us tomorrow when we headed back to the creek to find you, John," Masterson said. "He says he's worried as a frog in a frying pan about Miss Angela and Doc Wilson."

"Well, I'll go tell him the bad news," Kilcoyn said. He stepped to the door and took down his mackinaw and hat. "They don't seem to be any the worse for wear," he said, looking them over.

Masterson nodded. "We took right good care of them, and so did the wooden marshal."

Mayor Kelley and his wife lived in a white-painted, rambling house near the railroad tracks that marked the Deadline, the border separating the rowdy portion of Dodge City from the genteel. Across the tracks was Kansas, a place of ivy-covered churches and the lace-curtain homes of the respectable citizens who congregated in the street to hear sober and profitable conversation on the weather, the availability of land and the raising of crops. On Mayor Kelley's side of town was Texas, where everything was "full-up," a den of saloons, dance halls and brothels where the talk was of ranching, water and cattle prices.

Kelley, though he could afford it, had turned his back on the genteel and embraced the wild side of town. It had also been pointed out to him, on several occasions, that his kind would not exactly be welcomed with open arms across the tracks and that it might be just as well if he continued to stay away.

Kilcoyn rapped the Kelley's brass knocker. The door was answered by the mayor himself, dressed in black pants, a striped collarless shirt and bedroom slippers.

"John!" the man exclaimed, his face alight. "You have good news?"

The big marshal shook his head. "I have news, but all of it's bad."

Kelley's face fell. "Then you'd better come inside."

The mayor led the way to his parlor, where cheery logs burned in the fireplace and the room was well lit by lamps, warm and welcoming. Kelley waved Kilcoyn into a chair. "Bat Masterson filled me in on some of what happened. May all the blessed saints in heaven preserve us, but you've been through the mill." Kelley stepped to a trolley of crystal decanters. He held one of them up for Kilcoyn to see. "Good Irish whiskey. Would you care for a snort?"

The marshal was not much of a drinker, but the whiskey would do him good. He nodded. "Don't mind if I do."

Kelley poured three fingers of whiskey into a glass and handed it to Kilcoyn. "Now tell me what happened after Masterson and my nephew left the creek—how was the lad, by the way?"

Deciding to answer the easiest question first, Kilcoyn said, "Barry did well. He stood his ground and played the man's part. Did he tell you about Jenny Early?"

Puzzled, Kelley shook his head.

"Then you'd better hear that from Barry his ownself," Kilcoyn said.

"He played the man's part, you say?" Kelley said, for the moment forgetting about Angela and her father; deciding, at least for the time being, that blood was thicker than water. "Barry stood his ground like a true son of Erin?"

"I reckon so. He was a boy when he left Dodge, Mayor. Now I believe he's a man, and a fine one too."

Pride showed in Kelley's eyes. "That's good to hear, especially coming from you, John. I was beginning to despair of that boy."

"Man," the marshal said.

"Yes, indeed, man." Kelley sat back in his chair. "Now, tell me what happened at the creek."

As he had for Masterson, Kilcoyn described the events at the bend of Crooked Creek, sidetracking to tell the story of Tyler Pickett, a man the mayor probably never heard of and would care little about. When he was finished he summed it up. "The bottom line is, I don't know where Angela and Doc are. Frank Ivers must have them hidden somewhere."

Kelley sat in silence for a few moments, absorbing what the marshal had told him. Finally, his mind made up, he said, "John, we'll organize a posse and leave at first light tomorrow morning. We'll search in all directions, north, east, south and west, until we find Angela and Doc Wilson, and bring this outlaw, Frank Ivers, to justice."

A slight, tired smile touched Kilcoyn's lips. "You don't want to pay him, Mayor?"

Kelley shook his head. "No, I don't. We tried to appease a criminal the first time and it didn't work. All that happened is that we ended up right back where we started."

"I sure can't argue with that," Kilcoyn said.

The door swung open and Kelley's wife, a plump, motherly woman with cheeks that looked like red apples, stepped inside. "Marshal Kilcoyn, you look half dead from exhaustion, and I declare you're as thin as a bed slat. You need some good food in you, not whiskey."

"Rose," Kelley said, "don't fuss now. John is feeling just fine."

"And that he isn't, James Kelley." Rose put her hand on Kilcoyn's shoulder. "I'll be bringing you a nice bowl of Irish stew, made from fresh lamb I just bought from Ted Erbson, the butcher." She nodded to her husband. "It's himself's favorite."

She began to walk away, but stopped in her tracks and turned. "Oh, I forgot to ask, how is Miss Wilson, the poor thing, and Doctor Wilson?"

Before Kilcoyn could answer, Kelley told his wife what had happened. Rose, looking stricken, pulled a chair from under the parlor table and sat down heavily. "James, look at me," she said. "I'm so upset, I'm shaking like a leaf."

"We're riding out at sunup tomorrow, my dear," Kelley said, his voice soothing. "Don't worry, we'll find Angela and Doc."

"Oh, I hope so," Rose said, her bottom lip quivering. "I swear I won't draw an easy breath until you do."

"Maybe you should get the marshal something to eat, my dear," Kelley suggested. "It will take your mind off things, my love."

Rose nodded. "Yes, yes, I'll do that, though I'm trembling so much I don't quite know how I'll manage."

After the woman left, Kelley said, "Tell Masterson and Barry that we need them to ride on a posse tomorrow. And then have them comb the saloons and round up as many likely lads as they can find. Later I'll head across the tracks meself and rustle up volunteers."

Rose soon appeared with a tray of food, and fussed like a mother hen over Kilcoyn until he'd eaten more than he wanted. Afterward he headed back to his office and told Masterson and O'Neil about the posse.

The two men left to recruit volunteers and Kilcoyn, an aching weariness in him, sat in his chair and put his feet on the desk. He closed his eyes, the cozy warmth of the stove and Rose Kelley's food making him drowsy. Soon he was asleep.

The clock on the wall showed seven when the office door swung open, letting in a blast of ice-cold air that woke Kilcoyn immediately.

He lifted his eyes and saw a man standing over him, scowling.

It was Doc Wilson.

22

A Fruitless Search

"**A** fine thing. I'm captured by a bloodthirsty out-law and all you do is sit there and sleep," Doc grumbled.

Kilcoyn sprang to his feet, grinning. "Doc, it's great to see you! Is Angela—"

"No, John, Angela isn't here. That miserable, hair-trigger whelp Frank Ivers still has her."

"Alan, I don't understand. How did you escape?"

"Escape, hell: Ivers let me go. He told me to get in the surrey and head for Dodge. Said he didn't want an extra mouth to feed, that Angela was all he needed."

"Where were you when he let you go?"

"South of here, at an abandoned buffalo hunter's dugout on Rattlesnake Creek."

"When was that?"

"Early this morning. I've been driving through this damn blizzard all day."

"Then Ivers might still be there."

The physician shook his graying head. "I doubt it, John. Like all his breed, he moves around a lot."

Kilcoyn hesitated, fearing the answer to the question he had to ask. "Doc, how is Angela?"

"Holding up, last I saw her. John, as you well know, my daughter is a very beautiful girl. Men have come at her just about all her adult life, wearing different faces, saying different things. She's learned how to handle them."

"Including Ivers?"

"That I don't know. He wants ten thousand dollars for her and seems pretty intent on getting it. If he doesn't . . . well, I don't know what will happen." Doc took an empty cup from off the stove, an odd expression on his face that Kilcoyn couldn't read, and filled the cup with coffee. He turned to the marshal. "I'm completely used up, John. Got any whiskey lying around?"

Kilcoyn shook his head. "Then this will have to do, at least for now," Doc said. He sipped his coffee, his eyes tangled up with different emotions.

"Alan, there's something you're not telling me," Kilcoyn said. "What is it?"

The man hesitated for a few moments, blowing steam from his cup, then asked, "Ever hear of a belly-crawling lowlife who calls himself Jess Tracy?"

"Can't say as I have," Kilcoyn answered.

"Well, that doesn't surprise me. Ivers picked him up at T. J. Pettyman's stockade. He was a buffalo skinner for a spell, and he's a filthy animal—smells like the business end of a polecat. Ivers told me Tracy has killed three or four men, and that number again of women. Does most of his killing with a knife."

"Tracy is riding with Ivers?"

"Yes. And Ivers has promised Angela to the man if he doesn't get the ransom money."

Anger slid into Kilcoyn like a hot iron. "Doc," he said, "I'm going to find Frank Ivers and I plan to kill him. I don't care if I find him armed or unarmed, singing in the church choir or kneeling by his bed saying his prayers. I'm not going to call him out, I'm just gonna put a bullet in him."

Doc looked into the marshal's eyes and saw a hard coldness in them that made the cup in his hand tremble.

"Sometimes, John," he said, "I see something in you that scares me. It's not evil scary or even plain, ordinary bad scary; it's different, like I'm looking into the face of an avenging angel standing with a fiery sword at the gates of hell. Right now I'd rather be anybody else in the world—the poorest leper in the streets of Calcutta or a starving, legless beggar in China—than Frank Ivers."

Kilcoyn allowed a small smile to touch his lips. "I sure hope he knows that," he said.

"He may know it soon," Doc said. He stepped closer to Kilcoyn, and he suddenly looked old. "John, bring my daughter back to me. She's all I've got in the world. She's my life and, since her mother died, my only reason for existing."

Thirty mounted men assembled outside the Alamo Saloon in the raw chill of the predawn morning, their breaths smoking in the icy air.

Mayor Kelley grandly ordered a stirrup cup for everyone, promising that the brandy would be supplied at city expense, and bartenders from several other drinking establishments hurried to serve the riders.

With the exceptions of Masterson and O'Neil, the members of the posse were indeed acting like they were off on a foxhunt, Kilcoyn decided. What they were not keeping in mind was that Frank Ivers was a mighty dangerous fox, and cornering him on Rattlesnake Creek would mean men dead on the ground.

Kilcoyn and Masterson riding beside him, Kelley led the posse down Front Street, crossed the bridge across the frozen Arkansas River, and swung to the southeast toward the creek.

"We'll get him, John, don't worry about that," the mayor said as they rode into the snow-covered plains. "He won't escape us."

Kilcoyn nodded, but secretly he was worried. Thirty men meant a lot of flying lead, and Angela would be right in the middle of it.

Following a map drawn by Doc Wilson, the posse

reached the dugout on the creek just before noon, but the place was deserted, its wooden door hanging askew on one hinge.

Kilcoyn dismounted and walked into the cabin, little more than a hole dug in a shallow rise, with a dirt floor and sod walls and roof. A roughly made bunk stood in one corner. An equally crude table and bench were placed near the door. The marshal looked around, but saw nothing that could serve as a clue to the whereabouts of Ivers.

Disappointed, he stepped outside again and his eyes lifted to Kelley, who was sitting his buckskin a few yards away. "Nothing," he said. "They've gone."

"Then we'll spread out and look for them," the mayor said. "They can't have gotten far."

The posse split up into several different groups of riders, Kilcoyn at the head of one of them, Masterson and Kelley leading others.

Kilcoyn and his eight men recrossed the Arkansas, then swung west across Saw Log Creek. The country they were riding through was mostly flat, but here and there snow had drifted to a height of five or six feet in the hollows, and most of the shallow streams running off the creek were frozen solid. Ten miles northwest of the Saw Log, as the weather worsened and snow began to fall, Kilcoyn looped his riders due south for a distance, then turned east again toward Dodge.

They had seen nothing.

The rest of the posse, dispirited and blue with cold,

were already going their separate ways when Kilcoyn and his men rode into town, darkness falling
around them. After a few minutes only Mayor Kelley
was left. He and Kilcoyn stood outside the sheriff's
office, their worry about Angela lying unspoken between them.

Kilcoyn's thoughts went out to Angela. She was a
brave, enduring woman and she'd be holding up,
but like all men who lived by the gun, Frank Ivers
could be sudden and unpredictable, and looming
over all was the sinister, malignant shadow of the
feral Jess Tracy.

Kelley, his face gray with fatigue, broke the silence.
"Well, John, I have to be going," he said. "Mrs. Kelley, good woman that she is, will be worrying about
me." The mayor's eyes sought the marshal's in the
gloom. "I told the lads that we'll be riding out again
tomorrow. If need be, we'll search all the way to the
Texas border until we find her."

It was not a boast, nor an idle promise, but it was
just as empty and both men knew it. Around them
spread a vast wilderness of endless, snowy plains
and vistas that stretched away forever. In all that
lost, lonely land, looking for one woman was nigh
on a hopeless task.

Such were John Kilcoyn's thoughts, but aloud he
said, "Best you go home and get some rest, Mayor.
I'll see you at first light in the morning."

Kelly nodded, then, hesitantly, as though he was
half-ashamed to say it, said, "John, the missus and

me will say a rosary tonight for Angela. I know you're not a religious man, but it might help."

"Mayor," Kilcoyn said, smiling, "I'd say right about now we need all the help we can get. Get to praying."

Kilcoyn decided to spend the night at Masterson's office, forgoing the comforts of a room at the Dodge House. He poured himself a cup of coffee, then stepped to the window and glanced outside.

It was not yet six, but darkness had already come to the town. Deep shadows angled across the alleys that the lamps along Front Street did little to dispel, and through the frost-laced windows of the Long Branch and the Alamo, Kilcoyn could make out the dim blue glow of the gas lamps on the walls. Out on the plains, the coyotes were yipping, and from somewhere closer an agitated dog barked until a man's voice yelled the animal into silence.

The office door opened and a shivering Masterson stepped inside, the collar of his box coat pulled up around his ears. "It's getting colder, John," the sheriff said. "I swear my teeth are chattering like they were in a jar on the dresser."

"Get yourself some coffee and set a spell," Kilcoyn said. "Nothing much going to be happening until tomorrow morning." He looked at Masterson, a question on his face. "Where's your shadow?"

The sheriff seemed puzzled for a moment, then

realization dawned on him. "Oh, you mean Barry." Masterson poured himself coffee. "He's down the street talking to Sad Sam Nelson."

"What does Barry want with an undertaker?" Kilcoyn asked. "Is he fixing to cash in his chips?"

"No, nothing like that. He wants to head back to the Black Mesa country and bring Jenny's body back to be buried in Dodge. Says he wants his wife close, not lying in foreign soil."

"Bat, I only pretended to marry them," Kilcoyn said. "You know I didn't have the authority to make them man and wife."

"Doesn't make any difference to Barry. As far as he's concerned, he and Jenny were hitched, all legal as you please. He says he's going to write the name, Jenny O'Neil, on the poor little gal's headstone."

"That's love I guess," Kilcoyn said. "Amazing how a man can be so changed by love you don't even recognize him as the same person."

"Changed Barry all right," Masterson allowed. "He isn't drinking and shooting at the moon anymore, I can tell you that. He seems wiser and much older." Masterson sat on the corner of the desk and his eyes slanted to Kilcoyn. "Think we'll find Angela, John?"

The big marshal shook his head. "I don't know, Bat. But I sure hope we do, and soon."

A silence stretched between the two men, each trying to find words of comfort or hope that would not come. The quiet was finally broken by a loud thud on the door, followed by the sound of pounding hooves on the snow.

"What the hell!" Masterson yelled.

He stepped to the door and opened it wide, then looked down at the object lying at his feet. It was a rolled-up scrap of paper tied to a rock. Masterson picked up the rock, brought it inside and slid off the paper. He then spread the note out on the desk, flattening it with his palms. It was from Frank Ivers.

BE AT HORSE THIEF CANYON AT FIRST LIGHT. COME UNARMED AND ALONE. IF YOU WANT THE WOMAN ALIVE BRING MONEY.

After he was sure Kilcoyn had read the note, Masterson said, "You can't do that, John. I mean, ride out to the canyon without a gun."

"Seems like I don't have much choice," Kilcoyn said. Suddenly he remembered that he had shoved Angela's deringer into his saddlebags. He crossed the room and picked up the saddlebags, and Masterson asked, "The money still in there?"

Kilcoyn nodded. "And this." He showed the little gun to the sheriff. "I'll stop off on the way to the livery stable and get cartridges for it from Will Norman, the gunsmith."

"You giving Ivers the money and have it done?" Masterson asked, his voice hopeful.

Kilcoyn shook his head. "Not a chance. I'm all through being pushed this way and that by badmen. One way or another, it all ends tomorrow morning."

Masterson had horror all balled up in his eyes. "But, John, you can't go up against Frank Ivers with just a stingy gun; he'll drop you for sure. And another thing: I've been in a shooting scrape at Horse Thief Canyon before. Remember the Raster brothers? Took me and another eight men six days to root those bank robbers out of there. I know what the place is like. Frank Ivers can set up there in the rocks with a rifle and blow you right out of the saddle."

Kilcoyn smiled. "Bat, you've got me dead before I've even left Dodge."

After shrugging into his mackinaw and settling his hat on his head, the marshal took the wrapped bundles of money from the saddlebags and threw them in a desk drawer. "Bat, if things go bad up at the canyon, take this money to Mayor Kelley. He'll make sure it gets back to the right folks. And one other thing; don't tell him I've gone. I don't want an armed posse charging out there."

"At least let me come with you," Masterson said. "I can hang way back, so Frank doesn't see me, and come a-running when the shooting starts."

"I can't take that chance, Bat," Kilcoyn said. "I'd surely love to have you with me, but you might be

265

seen, and it's going to be dangerous enough for Angela as it is."

"You have a plan, John?" Masterson asked, his face hopeful.

"Not at the moment," the marshal answered, a smile touching his lips. "But it's a long ride out to the canyon, so I'll study on things and maybe I'll come up with one by and by."

He picked up the deringer, dropped it into his pocket and grabbed the saddlebags.

"You carrying the gun there?" Masterson asked. "In your pocket?"

"Where else would I carry it?" Kilcoyn asked in turn, smiling, remembering another man who had said those very words.

"You'll be right slow on the draw." The sheriff shook his head. "John, I'm real boogered. I don't have a good feeling about this whole thing."

"That," Kilcoyn said, "makes two of us."

Will Norman's gun store was closed when Kilcoyn got there, but he hammered on the door, and from deep within he heard the gunsmith yell, "Go away, I'm closed! Come back tomorrow."

"Will, it's John Kilcoyn," the marshal called out. "Open up, it's official business and mighty important."

After a few moments, a bolt was slammed back and the door opened a crack, and Norman's bald head appeared, something blue and gleaming held at his waist. "Oh, it is you, John," the gunsmith said. "A man can't be too careful with all that's been happening. Step inside."

The marshal told Norman what he needed and the man nodded. "Come into the store."

Norman led the way and lighted an oil lamp above the counter, revealing stacked rifles and shotguns in racks, and a variety of Colt and Smith & Wesson revolvers in long glass cases, glinting with an oily sheen.

He found the box of shells Kilcoyn needed and passed it over the counter, then watched in silence as the marshal loaded both barrels of the deringer.

"Not carrying your belt gun, Marshal?" he asked.

"No, Will, I guess not," Kilcoyn answered, his eyes guarded.

"Then you've got your reasons and they're none of my business," the gunsmith said. "But just hold on a second."

Norman bent, opened a drawer under the counter and placed a beautiful little gun on the counter, nickel-plated with yellowed ivory grips. "This is a Colt Pocket Navy, a percussion revolver converted to fire five .38 cartridges. Cowboy who owned it and sold it to me had the barrel cut down to three and a half inches, but she hits right to the point of aim." A slight smile touched Norman's lips. "If a man was trying to hide the fact that he was carrying a gun, he could shove this piece in his back pocket and nobody would be any the wiser. That's what a man could do. Maybe he could."

Kilcoyn nodded. "Thanks, Will. I appreciate it."

"Think nothing of it, Marshal. I'm always willing to help the law." Norman reached behind him, found a box of .38 shells and loaded the little Colt.

"How much do I owe you, Will?" Kilcoyn asked, shoving the gun into the back pocket of his pants.

"Nothing." The gunsmith hesitated a heartbeat and added, "Just bring Miss Angela back."

23

A Wolf on the Plains

The dun was still tired after the long trail from Crooked Creek, standing head down in his stall. Kilcoyn threw his saddle on the tough, enduring paint mustang and left the livery stable at a trot. He rode directly north into the dark plains and the flat, long-riding country. The night was bitter cold, but the clouds had parted and a bright horned moon touched the fallen snow with a luminous light.

The marshal crossed frozen Duck Creek and lifted the paint into a steady, distance-eating lope. The prairie rolling away from him on all sides was level, cut through by dozens of small streams running off the creeks. Here and there yucca had managed to rise above the fallen snow, casting tattered blue shadows.

A few miles ahead of Kilcoyn lay the Saw Log, a meandering creek with stands of cottonwood and willow growing on both banks. After clearing the creek another nine miles or so would bring him to Horse Thief Canyon.

Kilcoyn was well aware of the danger he faced.

As he'd considered earlier, there was always the possibility that Frank Ivers wanted more money. If that was the case he could shoot Kilcoyn, believing he carried the ten thousand dollars. Once the money was in his possession he could demand more for Angela's safety.

It would be a desperate play on Ivers' part, taking the chance that Mayor Kelley and the citizens of Dodge would pay up rather than risk Angela's life by coming after him.

But Kilcoyn didn't really think this was a likely course of action. Murdering a United States marshal was no small thing, and the man must know that the law would not rest until he was hunted down and hanged.

The more he thought about it, the more certain he felt that the gunman had decided to take the money and run.

If that was the case, it would all end soon in a showdown at the canyon, about a heartbeat after Ivers looked into Kilcoyn's empty saddlebags. The big question in the marshal's mind was, could he find some way to match Ivers' flashing speed with a gun?

He'd be betting his life that the answer was yes . . . but he reminded himself that he'd always been an unlucky gambler and that's why he was not a betting man. That gloomy thought did little to comfort Kilcoyn as he slowed the paint to a walk and his eyes searched ahead into the moon-splashed darkness for the creek.

Around him the coyotes were calling, and once he heard a hunting wolf pack in the far distance, their howls echoing for miles across the uninterrupted flat.

As he rode closer to the creek, Kilcoyn saw the tall cottonwoods first, slender, snow-covered limbs turned to silver by the moonlight. He rode closer, then followed the bank, looking for a break where he could cross. Sheet ice had formed along both banks, leaving only a narrow channel in the middle of the creek where the water still ran, making a small sound in the silence.

Kilcoyn forded the creek at the narrowest point he could find, the paint's hooves crunching through thin ice. The horse clambered up the opposite bank and the marshal swung due north again at a walk, the cottonwoods falling behind him.

He heard the gunshot at the same instant the paint shuddered and suddenly went down on its front knees, its nose pecking into the snow. Kilcoyn was thrown over the mustang's head and he hit the ground hard, then rolled, scrambling clear of the falling horse.

The paint lay on its side, white arcs of fear and pain showing in its black eyes. Its legs kicked, pounding again and again into the snow; then it shuddered and lay still.

Kilcoyn got up on one knee and looked around him. He saw a man emerge from the trees along the creek, a rifle slanted across his huge body.

"Stay right where you are or I'll kill you," the man yelled as Kilcoyn rose to his feet.

The rifleman stepped closer until Kilcoyn could see him clearly in the moonlight. The man stood well over six feet and was dressed in a ragged buffalo skin coat, a shapeless black hat shading his eyes. Tangled strands of long hair fell over his shoulders, the same color as the red beard that hung over his chest. Even at a distance Kilcoyn smelled the feral stench of the man, and felt the aura of pure malice that surrounded him.

"Is your name Kilcoyn?" the man asked. "I don't want to be killing the wrong feller."

"Yes, I'm Deputy United States Marshal John Kilcoyn," the big lawman said, allowing himself his full title in the hope it would give the bushwhacker pause.

The man seemed less than impressed. "Did you bring the money?" he asked.

"It's in the saddlebags on the horse you killed," Kilcoyn said. "But that money is for Frank Ivers."

"The hell with Ivers," the man said. "My name is Jess Tracy and I want the money for my ownself." Tracy's eyes slid over Kilcoyn. "You packing a gun?"

Kilcoyn shook his head. He slowly unbuttoned his mackinaw and pulled it apart, showing that he was not wearing a gunbelt. "The note Ivers sent me said to come unarmed," he said, hoping that would be enough for Tracy. The man didn't seem overly bright.

To Kilcoyn's relief Tracy nodded, smiling, showing badly rotted teeth. "You done good, lawman. But you shoulda heeled yourself on account of how I aim to gun you pretty damn quick."

Desperately Kilcoyn played for time as his hand slid into the pocket of his coat and closed on the deringer, hunching his shoulders as though against the cold. "Tracy, Frank Ivers is going to be real unhappy at you taking his money," he said.

"Yeah, well I'm taking it and be damned to him. I asked him for my woman tonight, to have a little fun like. But he wouldn't give her to me, said he wanted to keep her. So I lit out and laid for you here—been holed up since sundown. But I knowed you'd come on account you want the woman your ownself. Well, now I don't give a damn about Miss High and Mighty Angela Wilson. With ten thousand dollars Jess Tracy can buy all the women he wants."

Tracy swung the rifle level with Kilcoyn's belly. "So long, lawman."

Kilcoyn dived to his left, drawing the deringer as he hit the ground rolling, then came up on one knee. Taken by surprise, Tracy hesitated a split second before swinging his Winchester in the big marshal's direction. Lying on his left side, Kilcoyn fired at the same time the rifle came level. The .41 caliber slug tore into Tracy's throat and the man's finger jerked on the trigger, his bullet kicking up snow in front of the marshal's face. Kilcoyn thumbed back the hammer of the little gun and fired the second barrel. Hit in the chest, Tracy dropped his rifle and crashed face-down onto the ground, then rolled, bent over, on his side.

Kilcoyn rose to his feet and walked over to the fallen man. Tracy was still breathing and the marshal pushed him onto his back with his boot. The outlaw's eyes lifted to Kilcoyn and, after a struggle, he managed to croak from his mangled throat, "Bad things . . . always . . . happen to me."

"Yeah," Kilcoyn said, "that's real sad, and just when you thought you were about to get rich too."

But he was talking to a dead man. Tracy's eyes were wide open, but he was seeing nothing.

Kilcoyn slipped the deringer back into his pocket, stepped over Tracy's body and walked to the paint. He stripped off his saddle and went in search of the bushwhacker's horse. He found the animal hidden among a stand of cottonwood and willow, a small, hammer-headed mustang with a swayback and a mean eye.

Quickly the marshal switched saddles and led the horse out of the trees. He stepped into the saddle and swung the mustang to the north.

He didn't look back at Jess Tracy lying sprawled and still in the soft, indifferent moonlight.

24

Horse Thief Canyon

Kilcoyn did not push the mustang as he rode north. He planned to reach the canyon just before first light, having no desire to spend hours waiting out in the darkness and intense cold of the windswept plains.

The long night had just begun to shade into a gray dawn when Kilcoyn caught sight of Sentinel Rock, a tall spire of weathered sandstone that marked the entrance to Horse Thief Canyon, red cedar and a few stunted wild oaks growing around its base.

Reining in the mustang, the marshal sat his saddle in the uncertain light and studied the layout of the place for a few minutes. The rocky walls were steep, roughly cut, shaped by slow-turning centuries of snow, rain and wind. Here and there large sections of cliff had been broken away by water seepage and its seasonal freezing and thawing, leaving raw scars.

Grama and buffalo grass grew on top of the rusty

brown walls. Within the canyon, shadows angled dark and mysterious, the only sounds Kilcoyn's breathing and the jangle of the mustang's bit as he tossed his head, anxious to be on the move again and find a place out of the wind and cold.

Kilcoyn kicked the little horse forward, alert and ready, his restless eyes scanning the canyon and the land around him. He saw no sign of life, nothing to indicate that Frank Ivers was even here.

He walked the horse into the cedar break to the right of the canyon mouth and swung out of the saddle. There was grass growing among the trees, most of it clear of snow, and the mustang immediately began to graze, its reins trailing. Kilcoyn lifted the saddlebags and draped them across his left shoulder, then stepped from the cedars and made his way to the canyon entrance.

The morning was slowly brightening, but the sky was clouding again, and the wind was picking up, blowing from the north, sharp and tangy with the promise of more snow. Deep within the canyon, the midnight blue shadows had not yet been washed away by the morning light and remained dark and brooding, heavy with unseen menace.

There was no need for caution. Kilcoyn had come here to meet Ivers, and the man could even now be hidden somewhere, watching his every move.

The marshal stopped at the entrance to the canyon and threw back his head. "Ivers," he yelled, "I brought the money."

The following silence mocked him, the echoes of his own voice bouncing among the high walls before they faded away into nothingness.

Stepping slowly, Kilcoyn walked deeper into the canyon, steep rock parapets rising sheer on either side of him. There were many small pools scattered around the canyon floor, all of them glinting with the sheen of ice. The prints of deer and coyotes were everywhere. Once, not long before, buffalo had watered here, but now the great animals were all but gone; the deer had moved in to take their place.

After he'd walked a hundred yards, Kilcoyn stopped and called out again. "Frank Ivers, can you hear me?"

Ringing echoes repeated the question, time after time demanding an answer, but again, the marshal's only reply was a sullen silence.

Where was the man? Had Ivers brought him here on a wild goose chase? At that thought Kilcoyn's lips moved in a brief smile. That damned goose was flying again; he had no doubt about that.

Two hundred yards into the canyon, the marshal found a cave, a shallow opening in the rock to his left, about four feet above the floor. Was that where Ivers was holed up?

Kilcoyn looked into the cave, his eyes trying to penetrate the gloom. "Ivers, are you in there?" he asked.

"No, Marshal, I'm right behind you."

Kilcoyn turned, keeping it slow. Ivers might be a

nervous man. The gunman had stepped out of a shadow cast by a ledge of rock. He held Angela in his left arm. The muzzle of his gun was pointed at the woman's temple.

"Good, I see you brought the money," Ivers said, his eyes lifting to the saddlebags on Kilcoyn's shoulder.

"Ten thousand, just like you asked for, Frank," the marshal said.

The gunman nodded, his mouth with its crowded teeth stretching into a thin smile. "Only thing is, everything's changed," he said. "See, I've decided to keep the woman for a spell."

Kilcoyn looked at Angela. She was white-lipped and there were dark shadows under her eyes. "Angela, are you all right?" he asked.

The woman nodded, but before she could speak Ivers said, "Sure she's all right. Her and me, we're taking the money and heading for Mexico." He squeezed Angela hard against his side. "Gonna live it up. Ain't that right, li'l darlin'?"

"That's not the deal, Frank," Kilcoyn said. "The deal was that you'd let Angela go."

"I told you, the deal's off," Ivers snarled. He motioned to Kilcoyn. "Now shuck the iron you're carrying and throw it on the ground. Do it now or I'll forget all about Mexico and scatter this gal's brains."

"You told me to come unarmed, Frank," Kilcoyn said.

"Yeah, like I thought you really would. Now shuck

the iron. Wherever it's hid, use just two fingers of your left hand."

Trying to look as sheepish as possible, Kilcoyn did a credible job of acting as he reached around to his pocket and produced the deringer.

Ivers nodded. "Thought so. Now throw the stinger away."

Kilcoyn did as he was told, tossing the gun into the shadows of the canyon.

"Open your coat. Let me see your waist," Ivers said.

As he'd done for Tracy, Kilcoyn undid his buttons and opened the mackinaw wide.

Ivers seemed satisfied, and that was confirmed for Kilcoyn when the gunman said, "How did you kill Tracy? Use that stingy gun on him?"

"He didn't expect it," Kilcoyn said. "He was trying to take off with your money."

"I would have caught up to him," the gunman said. "Tracy was nothing. He was trash." Ivers' smile grew wider. "But he actually did me a great service. After I kill you, and take my money and my woman, your body will be found lying right alongside Tracy. He'll be blamed for your murder, leaving me and Angela here to whoop it up south of the border."

Angela moved then. She desperately tried to wrench out of Ivers' arm, her back arching. "You low-life scum, I'd die before I'd go anywhere with you!" she screamed.

Smiling, Ivers let the woman go, and Angela spun

away from him. The man's gun came level with her heaving breast. "That," he said, his voice a low, menacing hiss, "can be arranged right now."

Kilcoyn reached behind him and drew the Navy, knowing at that moment he was slow, way slow. Ivers was surprised, but he reacted instantly. As time telescoped to a single split second, the gunman swung on Kilcoyn and fired. The big marshal, standing tall, grim and as immovable as an oak, took the hit without flinching. He triggered the Navy and his slug slammed into Ivers just above the gunman's belt buckle. A small man, Ivers reeled from the shocking impact of a belly wound, his face ashen. He leveled his Colt, fired. The bullet cut the air beside Kilcoyn's head and slammed into the soft sandstone of the canyon wall. Walking in on Ivers, Kilcoyn's gun hammered, flaring in the darkness of the canyon. Ivers was hit again, the bullet smashing the middle button of his mackinaw before crashing into his chest. A second shattered Ivers' knee and another ripped into his stomach.

Ivers screamed in fury, his gun suddenly too heavy for him. He triggered round after round into the dirt at his feet, then stood on his toes and fell forward on his face.

Blood staining his coat just above the right pocket, Kilcoyn held the Navy ready and stepped to Ivers. As he'd done with Tracy, the marshal rolled the man on his back with his boot.

Ivers' eyes were open and scared, and he was

barely clinging to life. The ground around him was stained scarlet as he rapidly bled out, his mouth opening and closing as he desperately gasped for breath.

Kilcoyn looked down at Ivers. The gunman was dying hard and in great pain, but the marshal's eyes were cold and uncompromising. "Ivers, ever hear of a feller called Tyler Pickett?" he asked.

Ivers' fixed, unbelieving stare told the marshal that the man could hear, but he was unable to speak, a thin line of blood trickling from the corner of his mouth and over his ear.

"Well," Kilcoyn said, "if he'd ever braced you, Ivers, you wouldn't even have come close. Tyler Pickett was good with a gun, the best there was or ever will be."

Ivers' shocked eyes opened wider and the man tried to talk, making a low, gurgling sound in his throat, but speech had fled from him. Everything had fled from him. He was dead.

Angela ran to the big marshal. "John, you've been hurt."

She threw open Kilcoyn's coat and looked in horror at the blood welling up from the wound in his side. "You're hurt bad, John. I've got to get you back to Dodge and my father."

A distant clamor of honking sounded in the canyon, and Kilcoyn looked up and caught a glimpse of a V of Canada geese angling across the backdrop of the gray sky.

He smiled, "Look Angela, the geese are up there where they belong. They're not flying over my grave any longer."

A frown of worry wrinkled the girl's forehead. "That's it, John, you're starting to talk crazy. I'm taking you home right now."

"You're taking me home, Angela?" Kilcoyn asked.

The girl nodded. "Yes, I'm taking us both home. Home where we belong."

After he took his lips from Angela's, John Kilcoyn smiled. "I like that sound of that . . . home where we belong."